"Steven Ramirez has created a well-imagined fictional universe and populated it with characters with real warmth and humor in *The Blood She Wore*, a well-constructed supernatural mystery that will entertain fans of the genre."

IndieReader

"Sarah and Carter are gifted with psychic and paranormal powers, and the demonic energy that is corrupting their town has particular plans for them. By putting faith in God and trust in their friends, these protectors of Dos Santos find strength while facing the fight of their lives against an army of the dead."

*Forward* Clarion Reviews

# THE BLOOD
# SHE WORE

Books by Steven Ramirez

## Sarah Greene Mysteries

*The Girl in the Mirror*

*House of the Shrieking Woman*

*The Blood She Wore*

## Tell Me When I'm Dead

*Tell Me When I'm Dead*

*Dead Is All You Get*

*Even The Dead Will Bleed*

## Other Books

*Chainsaw Honeymoon*

*Come As You Are: A Short Novel and Nine Stories*

Glass Highway
Los Angeles, CA
stevenramirez.com

Publisher's Note: This is a work of fiction. Names, characters, places, and incidents are a product of the author's imagination. Locales and public names are sometimes used for atmospheric purposes. Any resemblance to actual people, living or dead, or to businesses, companies, events, institutions, or locales is completely coincidental.

The Blood She Wore / Sarah Greene Mysteries Book Three / Steven Ramirez.—1st ed.
ISBN-13: 978-1-949108-09-5
Library of Congress Control Number: 2020912244

Edited by Shannon A. Thompson
Cover design by Damonza

# THE BLOOD
# SHE WORE

A Sarah Greene Supernatural Mystery

STEVEN RAMIREZ

Glass Highway
LOS ANGELES, CALIFORNIA

*For Shirley, who taught me terror.*

Glancing at one another, they tried to smile, tried to look courageous under the slow coming of the unreal cold and then, through the noise of the wind, the knocking on the doors downstairs. Without a word Theodora took up the quilt from the foot of the doctor's bed and folded it around Eleanor and herself, and they moved close together, slowly in order not to make a sound. Eleanor, clinging to Theodora, deadly cold in spite of Theodora's arms around her, thought, It knows my name, it knows my name this time.

Shirley Jackson, *The Haunting of Hill House*

# THE BLOOD
# SHE WORE

## One

The Englishman knelt next to the fresh grave and removed one of his black leather gloves. He ran his fingers over the soft, sandy loam when he heard what sounded like someone sighing. The voice was distant and hurt, and it spoke of suddenness and loss.

Adjusting his onyx-and-silver ring, he stood facing the ground and, whispering an ancient Hebrew prayer, raised his right hand, commanding whatever it was lurking just below the surface to rise up and face him.

The earth trembled as small rocks and dirt juddered away...

Fingers burst through the ground, becoming a hand, then an arm...

A man, pale and frightened, and wearing a crumpled business suit covered in blood, glanced around furtively, unsure where he was.

Translucent in the cold moonlight—his throat slashed —he stared at his rescuer. He opened his mouth to speak when dark pieces of earth tumbled out. Taking the ghost's hand, the Englishman pressed one of its fingers to the ring.

Instantly, the specter was swallowed up in a blindingly bright light.

And then, it was gone.

Looking down at the undisturbed grave, the Englishman put on his glove. He returned to his nondescript beige rental car and drove away from the abandoned oil field. Once he was at a safe distance, he would call the local police and let them know where to find the body of the businessman whose car had been stolen and who, so far, no one had missed.

He had been tracking Laurel Diamanté since arriving at LAX on a nonstop flight from London. The information he'd been given indicated she was heading north. He guessed that she and Ana Robles would stop soon to rest for the night, having fled Dos Santos like frightened birds ahead of a firestorm.

When he reached Lost Hills, he exited the freeway and checked Google Maps, where he found two well-known motel chains. He guessed Laurel would want to remain anonymous and would probably stay at one of these. No one fitting the women's description had checked into the Days Inn.

Driving on, he found the late-model white Lincoln Navigator—the vehicle Laurel had killed to get—parked in front of a row of rooms at Motel 6. Sitting in his vehicle in the lonely parking lot, sipping hot tea from a to-go cup, he waited. And prayed.

It was nearly 3 a.m. A chilly wind sent debris spinning across the asphalt. He thought he saw something move near a corner of the building. The figure became clearer. It was a featureless man, hulking, his clothes and hair the color of night. Someone else joined him. Soon, there were ten—maybe more.

A rap on the passenger-side window got the Englishman's attention. He turned to find a woman vaguely in her fifties, with unruly hair and missing teeth in a mouth full of rot. She grinned ghoulishly at him. Soon, the vehicle was surrounded.

Calmly, he placed his tea in the cupholder and showed the woman the depiction of the old man with the staff that was etched on his ring—Abramo Levy, the first Guardian. Her eyes widened. Screaming, she tumbled backward.

Instantly, the Englishman was out of the car and, slamming another demoniac's head with the door, made a wide sweeping motion with his right hand. A burning blast of white light sent all of them flying backward, arms windmilling.

They lay on the ground, cowering and in pain. He brushed the straight blond hair from his eyes and picked his way through them, his hand still raised. They clutched their heads—eyes spinning in their sockets. Wailing like banshees, they sounded like mortally wounded animals. Their pathetic voices mixed with the sound of the howling wind.

Turning in a circle, he swept his hand over the parking lot as a brilliant blue light shone all around him.

Then, he was alone.

Rubbing his ring finger, the Englishman returned to his vehicle to wait for morning.

***

It was five-thirty and still dark when the door to Laurel Diamanté's room opened, causing the Englishman to open his eyes. Two women emerged, the first older and of average height, and the second quite small.

Raising her hand, Laurel said something to her companion. They stopped. The older woman keenly scanned the parking lot. Apparently sensing nothing, she proceeded toward her car, with Ana meekly following.

He could have easily ended the affair here, but he was curious to know where they were going. So, he waited for them to drive off. Starting his engine, he followed.

An hour later in Coalinga, Laurel pulled off the I-5 and drove to a Denny's. The Englishman decided to wait next door in the parking lot of an auto repair shop. He parked facing the restaurant's entrance. The women must have eaten quickly, because after only forty-five minutes, they exited Denny's and drove off toward the freeway.

In another ninety minutes, he had reached Los Banos. Keeping a safe distance, he observed Laurel getting off the freeway and continuing east until she reached the 165. The women headed north toward the Great Valley Grasslands State Park.

Somewhere along the way, Laurel took a side road that led into a densely wooded area. There were fewer cars up this way, and the Englishman had to ensure he wouldn't be seen. So, he slowed, allowing a truck pulling a tractor trailer to pass him. On Bear Creek, Laurel turned off onto a dusty dirt road that led to a remote farmhouse.

Rather than drive, the Englishman parked out of sight under the redwoods and walked in. The air had warmed, though he still felt a late morning chill. When the house was in sight, he veered off to the side and squatted in the bunch grass, brushing the dust from his bespoke black wool suit.

Several vehicles were parked in front, including Laurel's. The wind shifted, carrying the voices of a man and woman. They were arguing. Careful to maintain his cover, the Englishman moved closer.

Just then, the front door banged open, and an angry-looking man who stood well over six feet emerged, dressed in a flannel shirt, ski vest, blue jeans, and dusty work boots. Wearing a scowl, he appeared ready to strangle anyone who got between him and the barn.

The Englishman listened for the sounds of other voices but heard nothing. There was no telling how many were inside. He jogged toward the house and pressed himself against the dirty white clapboard.

A woman was speaking Spanish with an American accent. He guessed it was Laurel. Now, he heard another female, pleading softly. From what he could make out, Laurel was telling Ana that she was leaving and that the girl needed to remain there with the man. It was evident she didn't want to.

He could enter now while the other one was occupied in the barn. But he couldn't be sure the man wouldn't return before the Englishman could get Ana safely away. So, he loped across the dirt yard and waited at the entrance to the barn.

The sound of an idling vehicle echoed inside. He guessed Laurel had asked her associate for another car. As he moved toward the door, a meaty hand grabbed his shoulder from behind. It was the huge, angry man. The Englishman saw him clearly now. His face was unwashed, and his breath smelled of tooth decay and coffee. His eyes were black as oil.

The demoniac raised a hand and struck the Englishman hard across the face, sending him to the ground with a bloody nose. He looked around to get his bearings, then scrambled to his feet. The creature came toward him fast but stopped when he saw the ring as the Englishman held up his hand.

As dark blood gushed from his nose and ears, the demoniac wailed. Becoming a blur, his head whipped back and forth in the throes of some overpowering invisible force.

Steadily, the Englishman moved closer, his hand still out in front of him. A searing light burst forth from his palm. The demoniac's face caught fire, the skin and bone falling inward and leaving a smoldering crater of foul, cooked meat as the blue flames consumed everything from the neck up.

The man fell to his knees, still alive. He couldn't even whimper because he no longer had a mouth. His arms waving helplessly, he stuttered and gasped. Wiping the blood from his nose, the Englishman stood over the writhing creature and spoke three words.

*"T'h tzrch lmvt."*

The demoniac stopped moving. The Englishman wiped his shoes on the dead man's jeans and, turning to leave, found Laurel standing in the doorway, her mouth open and a look of terror in her eyes. As soon as he raised his hand, she ran toward the house. Continuing to pray in Hebrew, he marched after her, easily closing the distance between them with each stride.

When he entered the house, he saw the vacant front room. Though he knew they wouldn't be there, he checked the kitchen. He proceeded down a dimly lit hallway toward the bedrooms. There were three. He opened the first door.

Empty.

Then, the second.

Also empty.

At the third door, he hesitated.

Slowly, he gripped the doorknob and turned it. When

the door swung open, the smell of carrion and sulfur assaulted him. Ana sat alone on the bed, her hands folded in her lap. She was shivering. He entered the room and saw too late Laurel lurking in a corner, her hand outstretched, holding something black.

Shrieking like a death messenger, she flew toward him, clutching her Warlock knife. With a powerful backhand to the head, he batted her away. She rolled onto the floor with a grunt.

Ignoring the pain from his arm, which she'd managed to slice open, he marched up to her, grabbed her face with both hands, and yanked her to her feet like a broken marionette. In her eyes, he saw hundreds of tortured souls crying out to him. This time, he pronounced the fatal words in English.

"You shall die," he said.

A chorus of wailing voices left Laurel's body in an ascending column of yellow smoke as she collapsed on the floor in a heap. When he saw Ana's face, he knew what was looking back at him was not her. Confident she wouldn't try to escape, he went in search of a bandage for his badly bleeding arm. Then, he returned to the barn to find some rope.

He tied Ana up in a chair and began the Jewish exorcism. Though the demon inside her was crafty, it was not powerful. The Englishman saw it in Ana's eyes—an enormous creature with long, stringy dark hair and red eyes. He addressed it, demanding its name.

It took only two hours for the thing to give it up and depart its host. He concluded the ritual by praying a psalm in Hebrew. Then, he untied the diminutive Guatemalan woman.

He handed her a silver flask and encouraged her to drink. When she swallowed the holy water, he observed no adverse reaction. Ana Robles was finally free of the dark spirit that had plagued her since she was fifteen.

It was well past noon when they left the farm. The Englishman had rolled up the windows of the beige rental car to keep out the acrid smoke as the house, the barn, and every vehicle burned in an all-consuming holy fire.

# Two

Sarah Greene's eyes fluttered open, and she realized she was dressed, lying on top of the duvet. The dream had been a bad one. With a heaviness in her chest, she turned, hoping to find Joe. But all she saw was Gary, curled up in a ball next to her. What time was it? She reached over and picked up her Apple watch from the nightstand. Seven-thirty.

"Alyssa," she said, groaning. "I need you."

Clumsily pressing the wrinkles from her clothes, she wandered into the kitchen, where she found her ex-husband. He was sitting at the counter, drinking coffee and looking at his phone. When he heard her come in, Joe looked up.

"Hey," he said.

"Morning."

Sarah grabbed a cup and poured coffee for herself. She took a seat next to him, unsure what to do or say. After he had told her about the accident with the girl all those years ago, he seemed to shut down. It was as if everything in his life had come undone, and he was finished. She remembered trying to kiss him. He'd withdrawn so much into himself, she was unable to get through. And so, feeling lonesome, she fell asleep next to him.

She reached out her hands and took his. "Do you want to talk about it?"

"No." He stood and rinsed out his cup in the sink. "I have to meet Manny. I'll see you tonight."

"Joe?" He was about to leave the room, then stopped. "You're a good man—a good human being. And I love you."

"I'll see you," he said.

Sarah listened as the front door opened and closed. Gary trotted in and sat in front of her, his eyes squishy. She picked him up and set him on her lap. He began to purr. She wished she could see her therapist, but the woman was out of the country on vacation.

Drinking coffee, Sarah thought about their weekend away. It had been wonderful. Or had it? She tried recalling how Joe had acted in Half Moon Bay. Honestly, she'd had no inkling that something this bad was bothering him. *Was he acting?* Had their trip been his way of telling her good-bye? *Stop being dramatic. He's hurting, that's all.* Her thoughts drifted back to the nightmare.


Sarah stood before a huge, rambling mansion surrounded by pine trees. A terrible place filled with rage, it glowed a ghastly yellow in the moonlight. She had never seen this house before and wondered if it really existed.

As she stood there in the darkness, a girl screamed. Time sped up.

An invisible force pulled Sarah through the walls and into the house. She found herself at the base of a staircase.

An imposing woman stood on the landing. She wore a

black beaded flapper gown. And in her hair, there was a silver filigree comb. Dismissively, she looked past Sarah at someone else and laughed.

"You know better than to come up here," she said.

Somewhere, the girl screamed again. Bored, the woman glanced over her shoulder.

She began descending the stairs. As she did, she kicked something. It was a wooden spool of scarlet thread. Tumbling down, it unraveled and eventually stopped at Sarah's feet.

When she had reached the bottom of the stairs, the woman stood still, looking at Sarah this time. Sarah felt her neck, searching for her St. Michael medal. But it was gone.

"God won't help you," the woman said.

Her voice cut through Sarah's brain like a hacksaw. Then, the woman's eyes became a liquid black.

Though disturbing, the nightmare hadn't turned Sarah into a gibbering mess. She had almost died at Devil's Bluff, and so much had happened since. But she had *survived*. What she felt now wasn't fear—it was anger. Fury at the rampant evil that had put so many people in danger and had led to an innocent young woman's death.

"God won't help me?" she said, her tone mocking and defiant. "Just watch."

As if in response, something outside made a loud thud, alerting the cat. He maowed nervously as Sarah set him on the floor. She went to the front door and listened. Then, she squinted through the peephole. The street was empty except for her dark green trash cans on the sidewalk.

Across the way, her neighbor, a heavyset old woman wearing a faded housecoat, kicked a plastic recycling box toward the curb. Sarah opened the door. The first thing she saw was the bright red smear across the door. She covered her mouth.

A dead, gray animal, mutilated beyond recognition, lay on her mat. A cat? The eyes and tongue had been cut out, and it was gutted. The blood covering its fur looked fresh. She gazed toward the street. The old woman was nowhere in sight.

She felt something brush up against her leg. Gary. Shooing him back, she closed the door. She stood there with her arms crossed and thought of calling Joe. No, this was something *she* needed to deal with.

"So, this is how we're playing?" she said.

Gathering cleaning supplies, a garbage bag, and a hose, Sarah made a mental note to replace the ruined welcome mat.

---

Carter Wittgenstein was late. She pulled her white MINI Cooper into the lot behind The Cracked Pot and parked next to the catering van. One of the other servers—Sherrie —had texted her last minute, asking if Carter could cover her breakfast shift; her kid was sick.

After the dream she'd had the previous night, the last thing the girl wanted was to serve food to a bunch of chatty customers. But Sherrie had always been nice to her. The single mother was the one who had trained Carter when she first started. So, she agreed.

Hurrying in through the back, she realized she wouldn't have time to fix her makeup. The line cooks grinned when they saw her pass by. One of them said something to the others.

*"Escapó de Isla de las Muñecas."*

Ignoring their laughter, she continued into the bathroom to wash her hands. Taking a quick look in the mirror, she brushed back her short black hair, pasted on a plastic smile, and returned to the kitchen. She marched up to the wise-cracking line cook and pointed a finger at him.

"If you're not careful, Hector, I'll send *you* to the Island of the Dolls. And by the way, they *hate* short men."

Satisfied, she walked away. The line cook looked sheepishly at the others while they jeered him.

Carter entered the restaurant area. Another server, loaded down with plates, nodded toward the counter where Tim Whatley sat, brooding. The last time she had seen him, he had a moustache. Now, he was clean shaven.

Poor Tim. Carter knew how he felt, having witnessed something unexplainable. All of it, in fact, had made no sense. Not to a cop who had been trained to look at facts and evidence. Though he hadn't told her what he'd seen that night at the women's shelter, she was certain it was bad.

"Have you decided?" she said.

"No. I still don't know if what I saw was real."

Carter stifled a laugh. "I mean, about breakfast."

"Oh. Um, bacon and eggs over easy."

"Toast?"

"I guess."

She felt sorry for him. Tim was around her age. When she had first met him, he seemed confident. And happy. Now, he was sullen and resistant to making eye contact. She hoped he wasn't suffering from depression—a condition she was all too familiar with.

"I'll make sure you get extra bacon," she said, and walked away to put in his order.

He thought again about that awful night. Looking up at the ceiling and finding Ana Robles on her hands and knees, naked, her head twisted all the way around so she could see him better. And her tongue, impossibly long and snake-like. *Take me now, cop*, she had said.

In a few minutes, Carter returned with Tim's food, warning him about the hot plate.

"Can I ask you a question?" He leaned forward and spoke softly. "These things I saw. Is this what it's like for you and Sarah?"

Carter didn't know what to say. For most of her life, she had been keenly aware of the paranormal. At some point, she'd accepted that this was how she and others like her—and Sarah—saw the world. It was hard for her to imagine what it felt like *not* seeing the things that were always lurking in the shadows and in dark dreams.

The leering face of the demoniac she had killed materialized in front of her eyes, reminding her of her nightmare. To dispel it, she looked toward the windows and focused on the normal traffic outside. When her eyes met Tim's again, she saw that he was desperate for an answer.

"It's different for us," she said. "We see things all the time. What's weird is, now other people are starting to see them."

"Is something bad happening in Dos Santos?"

She wanted to tell him everything. About The Darkness and the Guardian sworn to defeat it. Something *was* coming—something final. And she was scared. But she couldn't risk it. In his current state, the truth could send the young cop over the edge.

"I don't know," she said. "I wish Harlan was around."
*Shit, did I say that out loud?*

"What do you mean?"

"It's just that he's been really nice to me and… Forget it. I'm being stupid."

Behind her, the call bell rang. "Sorry, I need to get back to work."

He grabbed her hand. "Is it true you were the one who killed that creepy dude? It was self-defense, right?"

"I…" Her chest ached. "I didn't do anything."

She left him and, hurrying through the kitchen, ran out the back door and stood in the parking lot. It was hard to catch her breath. So many times, she'd found herself out here, smoking.

Desperate for a cigarette, she remembered when Sarah had followed her, a stranger asking about The Darkness. And Carter pretending she didn't know what the loopy lady was talking about. The dream came back to her full on.

Carter stood in the street again at night. The demoniac with the yellow-spiked hair laughed in that irritating high voice.

She grabbed the back of his neck and pulled him close. His skin felt damp and greasy.

Filled with a rage she had no idea was in her, she pressed the St. Benedict medal to his forehead until his head burst into a cold blue fire. She watched as he fell to his knees on the wet asphalt.

At that moment, she told herself she destroyed him only because she knew he would've killed Sarah and her.

Taking a calming breath, Carter knew what she would do now. Like the other horrible thing that happened when she was thirteen, she would push the events of that night way down deep. And she would lock them up there forever— where they could scream all they wanted. *She* was in control. And she would get on with her life.

Pulling the small hand truck behind her, Mary Mallery entered Harlan's private hospital room and found him dozing. It was still early. The staff had already delivered meals to the patients. On the overbed table, she found a pot of coffee, a glass of concentrated orange juice, and a covered plate of something that smelled appalling.

Mary removed everything, starting with the coffee pot, and left the unwanted breakfast on the floor outside. Then, she unzipped the black nylon food delivery bag and pulled out a Hydro Flask and a glass. She poured out Harlan's smoothie. When she looked at her employer, she found him smiling at her.

"They do provide meals here, you know," he said.

"Not the right kind."

She handed him the smoothie. He sat up and took a sip.

"It's good, as always. But it won't save me."

"Be quiet," she said. "I've decided. You're to think nothing but positive thoughts from now on."

"You're right." He glanced at the table. "Is that coffee I smell?"

"Finish your breakfast."

"Yes, dear."

"I'm serious, Harlan. You have to fight this."

He looked into her eyes. "I will. I am. Have you made the arrangements we discussed?"

"He's arriving this evening."

"And the girl?"

"It's my understanding he's bringing her. I've already prepared her room."

"Excellent. Have you notified Sarah and Carter yet?"

"I wasn't sure when they'd be releasing you."

"I want them there. Tonight."

"Okay, but are you sure—?"

"What about Charlie? How's he doing?"

"He's worried about you."

"He's a good man, Mary. Who seems to have a schoolboy crush on you."

The housekeeper laughed, putting her hand out as if warding off the thought. "I'm too old. And, like you, I'm set in my ways."

"Like I said, he's a good man. Catholic, too."

"Stop playing matchmaker, or you won't get any of that coffee."

She waited as he finished the smoothie and handed the glass back to her. There was a slight tremor in his hand. When had that started? Her heart was breaking, and it was all she could do not to weep openly. But tears were not what Harlan Covington needed; he needed prayer. And someone strong to look after him.

"Sarah and Carter have been asking about you," she said. "They were wondering if they could visit."

"Not here. Wait until I'm discharged."

"You seem pretty confident it will happen today."

"It has to. I can't spend another night here. Too much left to do."

Mary sighed. "I'll speak to the charge nurse. Oh, they told me someone's coming in a little while to drain your lung. I forget what they call the procedure."

"Thoracentesis."

"They said they could show me how to do it at home. Harlan." He looked at her with a defeated expression. "I'll pour your coffee."

She removed a stainless steel coffee pot from the nylon bag and thought of Sister Helen at the convent. The nun was in her nineties when she died. Mary had been there only a year. She remembered seeing the old woman's face, gray; her skin like paper.

That was days before the kind, elderly nun closed her eyes for the last time. Harlan looked like that now. And Mary was sure he didn't have much longer. But how could she tell him? Perhaps he already knew.

Once again, she wondered what she would do after her employer was gone. In the convent, she had been instructed to live in the present and not worry about the future. *God is in the now*, Mother Superior had told her often.

Handing Harlan a cup and saucer, she smiled brightly and remarked at what a beautiful day it was outside.

## Three

Lou Fiore adjusted his large frame on the too-small kneeler and clasped his hands in front of him. Confessionals didn't look the way they portrayed them in the movies, dark and cloying. Though the light inside was dim, you could see everything around you. If you wanted darkness, you had to close your eyes.

"Bless me, Father, for I have sinned," he said to the shadow behind the screen. "It's been... I haven't— I mean, I don't remember the last time—"

"It's okay, Lou," Fr. Brian Donnelly said, his tone reassuring.

"These are my sins. I thought about a woman in a way that was...not proper."

"Are you having relations with her?"

"What? No. It's just— I think about her a lot. I've been divorced a long time, and—"

"I see."

The police chief felt awkward and wished he had put this off. He heard the priest shift in his chair.

"If you really care for this woman, you must try always

to see her as God's creation and not as an object of desire."

"I think I might be in love with her. Wait, no. It's too soon. Christ, I don't know. Sorry."

"This is Rachel we're talking about? How does she feel about you?"

"I wish to hell I knew. Oh, jeez. Sorry, *sorry*."

"Perhaps the two of you should come see me. Is there anything else?"

The police chief went through a litany of venial sins he'd committed over the years, including fixing his own parking ticket one time. But they were things that amounted to little in the big picture. Why *had* he come? To ask forgiveness for impure thoughts? He cleared his throat and went on.

"I… I failed to protect someone." Lou's voice broke. "It wasn't my fault."

Before he could change his mind, he told Fr. Brian about how he had arrested Laurel Diamanté and placed her in a holding cell, only to find her gone. As a result, two police officers died, and the woman he was supposed to protect—Ana Robles—was now considered a missing person.

"You did not sin, Lou," the priest said. "But it's good you unburdened yourself."

"So many things have happened recently that are— Father, they're not natural. I think… No, never mind."

"What is it?"

"I think I might be losing my faith."

"Listen to me, my son."

Fr. Brian's voice was stern now and reminded Lou of his father. He winced as he recalled that speeches like this were usually followed by the belt.

"There is evil in the world," the priest said. "Great evil,

much of which is of our own making. But the Prince of Lies tempts us to celebrate it.

"He tells us that evil is just another word for knowledge and, with that knowledge, we are free to do whatever we like. And many believe him.

"But his greatest triumph is to take a single soul away from God. To make him believe there is no hope. To make him despair.

"Lou, I'm afraid you're being tested. You must pray for strength. And speak to Sarah about your doubts. She can be a good friend to you."

When it was all over, Lou slid into a pew and said the prayers of his penance. He thought about Fr. Brian's advice. Sarah *was* a dear friend, someone who had been through so much herself—much more than Lou. How was it possible she could keep *her* faith?

Outside the church, the police chief stood next to his vehicle and gazed at the zinc-colored sky as clouds moved in. The wind chilled him, and he wondered again about what the priest had said about being tested. A flock of crows flew past, cawing. *Evil of our own making.*

Lou climbed into the SUV and started the engine when he felt his phone vibrate. Before putting on his seatbelt, he pulled the device from his pocket and read the text. It was from Rachel Zamora.

She had sent him another *Angie Tribeca* meme. This one was captioned I WAS YOUNG AND STUPID, and featured a shirtless mayor whose torso was filled with inappropriate tattoos.

A raucous burst of laughter shook the vehicle. Lou began texting *I love y*, then stopped himself. Backing out the letters, he retyped *Thx. I really needed that.* He put on his seatbelt and pulled out of the church parking lot, feeling lighter than he had in weeks.

Sauntering into the police station, Lou greeted everyone he passed. He ignored the stares of confusion and continued toward his office, where he found Tim laying several papers on his desk.

"Oh, hey, Chief," the officer said.

"You okay? You look— What's that?"

The kid stiffened as he reached for the papers. One of them was a form, which he handed gingerly to his superior. Lou recognized the film permit application. The only other one he'd ever approved had been for Bad Blonde Productions, the creators of the TV reality show *Dubious*.

"Looks like they're at it again," Tim said.

He gave Lou a certificate of insurance and a check for twenty-five hundred dollars, meant as a deposit. Lou's eyes moved down the page. There were two signatures—Donnie Fisk and Debbie Fisk—and the name of their company.

"Why would they come back here?"

Helpfully, Tim pointed out the filming locations. "Seems they've been doing their research."

Lou let loose a string of expletives that could be heard across the bull pen, causing some to pop up their heads over the dividers. His eyes averted, Tim exited the office.

At Greene Realty, Rachel sat at her desk, reviewing the texts she and Lou had sent each other over the past few days. She had started it, sending him funny photos she'd come across in her news feed. Gradually, she fine-tuned her selections to include mainly cop-related humor. She found Lou to be open to playing along, and that made her feel connected to someone other than her family. But that last exchange.

After sending over the *Angie Tribeca* meme, she suffered through that annoying animated ellipsis as Lou began to respond, then stopped. What he ended up texting seemed perfunctory, and she worried that he'd meant to say something else.

Now, she heard voices outside. Sarah had just walked in with a blonde woman who looked to be in her forties. Rachel's sister had been showing her client townhomes in the area, and from the gist of their conversation, Sarah had once again hit it out of the park. The woman said goodbye and left. Rachel got up and left her office.

"I assume you made the sale," she said.

"Oh, yeah. She loved the place. She had to run off to a meeting but said she'd be back tomorrow to sign the papers."

"But what about—?"

Grinning, Sarah waved a personal check in her sister's face. "Gotcha covered."

"Nice. Hey, want to have lunch?"

Sarah glanced at her watch. "Sure. Can I meet you over at The Cracked Pot? Just need to send an email."

"Okay, see you over there."

Grabbing her purse, Rachel walked out the front door and over to the restaurant next door. It wasn't crowded, and she made her way to a booth by the window. When she was seated, Carter walked over and set down a glass of water.

"By yourself today?"

"No, Sarah's joining me." Rachel looked out. "Oh, she's coming now."

"I'll be right back."

Sarah joined her sister. Carter returned with two menus and another glass of water.

"I don't know why I keep bringing you guys menus. You always know what you want."

"Doesn't every woman?" Sarah said. Rachel and Carter rolled their eyes. "So, Carter, is your latest story blowing up the internet? What's it called again? 'House of the Shrieking Woman'?"

Carter beamed. "Actually, it is. So far, it's gotten almost ten thousand hits."

"Wow," Rachel said. "That's like twice the last one."

"People do seem to love the supernatural. What are you having?"

Sarah watched her sister as she gave the menu a perfunctory glance and handed it back. She thought about mentioning the dead animal she had found outside her door but decided against it. Rachel would only worry.

"Cobb salad," Rachel said. "Light dressing."

Sarah never liked ordering the same thing as someone else, unless it was Joe. *Oh, what the hell.*

"Same," she said.

When Carter had left, Sarah leaned in conspiratorially. "So, how's everything going with the randy police chief?"

"Why don't you ask him yourself?"

Sarah looked up and found Lou heading for their table.

"Mind if I join you?" he said. "I'm not staying."

Before Sarah could answer, Rachel had slid all the way over to the window. Lou sat down and caught a passing server by the shirtsleeve.

"Triple espresso, please. To go."

The server nodded, an annoyed look on her face.

"We were just talking about you," Sarah said, side-eyeing her sister.

"Nothing bad, I hope."

"How's it going with you two?"

"Great," Rachel and Lou said at the same time.

"Uh-huh." Sarah turned to the cop. "What's so important that you needed to interrupt a very private girls-only lunch?"

Lou took Rachel's hand and kissed it. He continued to hold it as he answered Sarah's question.

"You're not going to like it." He cleared his throat. "Our friends Donnie and Debbie Fisk are back."

Sarah's face went slack. "In Dos Santos? Why?"

"They want to film another show at the cemetery. This time, the mausoleum where John Dos Santos is buried."

Sarah thought about the last time she had seen The Darkness hovering in the cemetery. Had its source been that cursed crypt all along?

"There's more," Lou said. "They also plan to shoot at his mansion."

Sarah nearly did a spit-take and set down her water glass. "His *mansion*? You mean, that house of horrors is still standing?"

"The city purchased the land decades ago but never did anything with it. I took a ride up there earlier. It's in a remote area of the forest that's been fenced off to keep out intruders."

"But how do they even know it exists?"

"I guess those two are better at research than we gave them credit for."

"What do they hope to find?" Rachel said.

"I don't know. But they're planning a two-part episode. I've already signed the permit."

"Why would you do that?" Sarah said.

"Because they're following the rules."

As he said this, his eye twitched. Sarah rubbed her temples.

"Everything okay over here?" Carter said, carrying two salads. Then, to Lou, "Oh, hey. Want a menu?"

"No, I was just leaving." He kissed Rachel on the cheek and climbed out of the booth.

"What about your espresso?"

"I'll pick it up at the bar. Nice seeing you again, Carter."

"Yeah, same."

Carter looked from Rachel to Sarah. "Do I want to know what's going on?"

"I'll fill you in later," Sarah said.

Wearing a sullen expression, she left her salad untouched. Her watch vibrated. She dug out her phone and answered.

"Hello? Oh, Mary. Yes, just a minute."

Sarah walked outside and continued the phone conversation. Afterward, instead of returning to her table, she walked over to the counter and found Carter placing an inviting slice of lemon meringue pie on a plate.

"Carter? That looks good. I just heard from Mary. Harlan's back home, and he wants us to come to the house for dinner. Can you make it?"

Out of the corner of her eye, Carter noticed her manager looking at her, his annoying moustache twitching like a cutworm in heat.

"What time?"

"Eight."

"Okay. Can you pick me up, though?"

"Sure. See you then."

Sarah returned to her table and sat. Her sister had already started. Sarah said a quick blessing and dug in.

"Sorry, Rache," she said.

"So, what's up?"

"Just something I need to take care of."

"Mary… Isn't that Harlan Covington's housekeeper?"

Sarah arched her eyebrows. "Lou seems to be getting pretty affectionate. And in public, no less."

"He's been very attentive lately. After everything that's happened, I'm amazed he has the time."

"I'm not."

"What do you mean?"

"Any idiot can see that man is crazy about you. How do you feel about him?"

Rachel looked out the window, twirling strands of her hair, the way she did when she was a little girl.

"I really like him," she said. "In fact, I might even… No. I am not jinxing this. Are you crying?"

Embarrassed, Sarah brushed away a tear. "I'm okay. I've been praying for you, you know. That you'd find someone."

"Let's not get ahead of ourselves. I mean, we've only had a few dates."

"Rachel, I see how you guys are with each other. Has he said anything?"

"No. And that's what worries me. What if it's only me who feels this way? That would be horrible."

"It's not—I'm sure it's not. You know how slow men are. And chicken. They're terrified of making a commitment."

"I don't know…"

Sarah reached across the table and took her sister's hand. "But when it's right, it's right."

"How can you be so sure? Have you added seeing the future to your list of paranormal talents?"

"No. But I have faith. And you should, too. Why don't you have dinner with him tonight? My treat."

"Really?"

"You deserve to be happy. Okay, it's settled. I'm making a reservation. And you'd both better be there."

Covering her face with her hand, Rachel shook her head. Then, splaying her fingers, she peeked through.

"You do realize that if this thing happens," she said, "you're going to have a cop for a brother-in-law."

"And I'll also never pay another parking ticket again."

"Always the pragmatist."

## Four

L ou took a sip of his Barolo and looked across the table at Rachel. His only conscious thought at this moment was, *don't blow this*. The white cashmere sweater she wore showed off every curve, and he struggled not to see her as an object of desire, as Fr. Brian had advised.

"What are you staring at?" she said, blushing.

"You. I can't believe how lovely you are." *Where did that come from?* He reached over and took her hand. "I guess I'm feeling pretty lucky."

"You are seriously embarrassing me right now."

"Can't a man give a woman a compliment?" *A compliment sure, but for God's sake, don't scare her off.*

"Yes. It's just that, I never saw myself that way," she said. "It was always Sarah who was the pretty one. The one people wanted to be with."

"I'll admit, your sister's cute. But to me, you are the most beautiful woman in the world." *Holy crap—abort!*

"My gosh. I never thought cops could be so romantic."

"Well, I am Italian."

She squeezed his hand. "You do know Sarah insisted we have dinner together, right? I think she was hoping… It's nothing."

"No, what?"

A server appeared to tell them about the specials. After he left, Rachel took her time looking at the menu, wondering why she'd even agreed to this stupid date. Things had been going smoothly so far. Why jinx it now?

When her sister booked the reservation at Mollie's in Santa Barbara, she'd made sure to get their best table—the one next to the front window. Pedestrians passed outside in the twilight. One of them reminded Rachel of Paul, her late husband. Was this a sign? She knew in her heart he would want her to be happy. And he'd want Katy to have a father again. Still.

She laid down the menu. "I love you. There, I said it."

"I… Rachel—"

"It's okay, you don't have to say it back. I just wanted you to know how I felt. We can get this to go, if you want."

For the longest time, Lou sat there, unable to speak. Suddenly, his clothes were two sizes too small, and he felt as if his head were in a vise as his brain bellowed at him. *WHAT ARE YOU WAITING FOR?*

The server had returned to take their orders. Lou concentrated on the menu.

"I suck," he said.

Rachel looked up. "What?"

Lou turned to the server with a defeated smile. "I said I'll have the duck."

Sarah pulled her black Ford Galaxie into Harlan Covington's lighted driveway. One of the cars parked there was a Land Rover.

"Nice wheels," she said.

She and Carter got out. Sarah's friend stopped and took a deep breath.

"Is it my imagination, or does the air smell better in Montecito?"

Sarah smiled knowingly. "I think it might be the fact that you quit smoking." She squeezed Carter's arm. "I'm very proud of you."

"Well, I'm not out of the woods yet." The girl held up her arm. "Still wearing the stupid patch."

"All in good time, my friend."

At the front door, Sarah listened to the music coming from inside. She looked at her friend quizzically.

"It's a Beethoven string quartet," Carter said. "I forget which one."

Sarah rang the bell. A minute later, Harlan's maid opened the door.

"Hi, Elsa."

She led the guests to the living room, where the music was louder. Sarah took in the room. Harlan sat on a floral sofa, a cup of coffee next to him. Charlie Beeks, the private investigator, and Mary Mallery were standing with another man Sarah didn't recognize.

He was tall and blond, and wore an expensive black suit. When the women entered, the man acknowledged them. Sarah walked forward to introduce herself, then realized she was alone.

Carter stood staring at the stranger, her eyes huge. He was the man she had dreamt about, and he was dressed exactly the same. In the dream, they'd been standing outside her apartment building. He spoke the same words

Harlan had said to her that night at the women's shelter. *You have an extraordinary gift. Can you see now why they fear you?*

Her chest tightening, she turned to Harlan, who watched her intently.

"Carter?" Sarah said, side-eyeing the man.

"Sorry."

She joined them. Sarah put a protective arm around her.

"And this charming young woman is my friend, Carter Wittgenstein."

"Ah yes. Carter. I had the pleasure of reading about your latest adventure."

His accent was English, just as she remembered. As he took her hand, she felt she might swoon. He seemed dangerous—no, *powerful.* And the way he was looking at her, it was as if he already knew everything about her. His nails were manicured. But it was the onyx-and-silver ring on his right hand that caught her attention. It was identical to the one Harlan wore. *He's a Guardian!*

"And you are?" Carter said.

"Alistair Goolsby. I'm a friend of Harlan's, just in from London."

"Oh?"

"When I learned he was ill, I came straight away." He turned toward the attorney. "Excuse me a moment."

The Englishman took a seat next to Harlan and said something Carter couldn't hear. Like a pair of conspirators, they looked at her.

"Sarah, he's a—"

But before Carter could tell her friend, Elsa moved between them to get to Mary. The maid whispered something to the housekeeper, who nodded.

"Dinner is served," Mary said. Then, to Sarah and Carter, "I've always wanted to say that."

The others made their way to the dining room, with Mary out ahead of them. The Englishman helped Harlan to his feet, and with Charlie trailing, they headed for the other room, leaving Sarah and Carter alone.

"Sarah, didn't you notice the ring? He's a Guardian."

"But I thought they weren't supposed to communicate with each other."

"Do you think it's because Harlan is so ill?"

"Don't worry. We're not leaving until we get some answers."

In the dining room, Sarah marveled at how the table was laid. A beautiful Irish linen tablecloth covered it. Crystal water glasses and stemware had been set out, along with elegant china and silverware. Two floral arrangements featuring white roses and tulips adorned the table. And there were place cards.

She circled the table, looking for her name. Her breath caught as she picked up a card. ANA ROBLES. She was about to say something to Carter when Mary entered with Ana, who was holding her arm. Sarah quickly replaced the card and moved out of the way.

The girl wore a simple black dress and flats. Her hair shone, held back by pretty silver barrettes. She looked radiant. Mary helped the petite girl to her seat. Sarah turned to Carter, who seemed equally dumbfounded.

Harlan was already seated at the head of the table. Sarah found her card to his right. Charlie was on his left. Mary sat between the investigator and Ana, and the Englishman was seated between Sarah and Carter.

When she looked over at her friend, Sarah caught Carter looking at her pleadingly. Why was she afraid? Elsa and another server appeared and began placing bowls of soup in front of the guests.

"Well, I think we're almost ready to begin," Harlan said.

When Elsa had set down the last bowl, he led his guests in a blessing. Afterward, he stood and raised his glass of water.

"Thank you all for coming," he said. "I want to thank Alistair for bringing this dear girl back to us, safe and sound. Everyone here has played a part, though. And you, too, have my deepest appreciation. Thank you all."

Embarrassed, Ana looked at her hands. When everyone had taken a drink, Harlan sat.

Sarah wanted to ask him about Ana, but everyone else was engaged in lighter conversation. All except Alistair and Carter. Focusing all his attention on her, he seemed to be interrogating her, much the way Harlan had done at another dinner.

Sarah was about to say something to Charlie when he got up and, excusing himself, left the room, holding his phone. She decided to try Harlan.

"How are you feeling?" she said.

"As well as can be expected. Mary has advised me to remain positive."

"That's good advice." She squirmed in her seat.

"Sarah, I know you have questions. This dinner is meant to be a celebration." He nodded toward Ana. "A small victory. I promise you, Alistair and I will explain everything."

"So, it's true. He's a Guardian?" She felt herself tearing up. "Please don't say he came here to replace you."

He patted her hand. "I seem to recall you feeling differently about me the first time we met."

"I was being stupid."

"No. Just cautious."

She looked at Ana, who had hardly spoken. "I'm so happy she's here. Is she…?"

"She's fine."

"But how did Alistair find her?"

"Later. I promise."

The young Guatemalan woman smiled shyly, her expression so unlike what Sarah had seen before. When Charlie returned, he seemed more serious than usual.

---

After dinner, Sarah and Carter followed the others to the library. Mary had said goodnight and taken Ana upstairs. Nervous, Carter stayed close to her friend. So far, she'd said nothing about her conversation with the Englishman.

"Does anyone want coffee?" Charlie said, getting himself a cup.

Sarah raised an index finger. "I'll take one, thanks."

The fireplace was lit. The two Chesterfield chairs had been turned to face the room. Harlan sat in one, and Charlie in the other. Alistair had chosen to sit behind Harlan's desk. The attorney looked intently at Sarah and Carter. His breathing sounded labored, and Sarah wondered if their evening together had been too much for him.

"I realize you have questions," Harlan said. "We'll do our best to explain what has happened so far. After that, feel free to ask anything you want.

"But first, I want to thank you both for being at the shelter. And Carter, I want to thank you especially for coming to the rescue of an old man."

The girl gaped at him. "I don't even know what I did."

"You did a great thing. Always remember that." He turned to the investigator. "Charlie?"

Sarah took her friend's hand and squeezed it. Then, in a whisper, "You saved us."

"Okay," Charlie said. "As you know, despite our best efforts, Laurel Diamanté abducted Ana Robles from the women's shelter. In the process, she murdered two police officers.

"Alistair was able to track her down to a house in Los Banos. There, he freed Ana and brought her here."

Sarah observed the Englishman. He seemed not to be paying much attention. *A little false modesty to go with that suit?*

"What happened to Laurel?" she said, still looking at Alistair.

Charlie hesitated. Then, "She's no longer in the picture."

An unwanted memory erupted in Sarah's mind. A flock of angry ravens at Devil's Bluff, sending a man over the cliff to his death. Had that been Laurel's fate? Or something worse?

"Anyway," Charlie said, "the plan is for Ana to return to Guatemala. I'm taking her there myself. We've already been in touch with her mother."

Harlan coughed, then cleared his throat. "The women's shelter will reopen. And new residents will move in very soon."

Carter glanced at Sarah. "And you're sure there's nothing residual there?"

The Englishman stood and joined the others. Even leaning against the desk, his tall frame seemed to dominate the room.

"There'll be no further disturbances at the women's shelter," he said.

Sarah raised her hand. "You wouldn't mind if Carter and I went over there? We'd like to see for ourselves."

He smiled at her like an Eton prefect sizing up a new

boy. "I don't see a problem." Then, to Carter, "And to answer the question that's on *your* mind: Ana has completely recovered."

"She was possessed, though, right?"

The Englishman glanced at Harlan. "Yes."

Charlie cleared his throat and spoke to Sarah. "Earlier this evening, I got a call from my friend in the Seattle PD, Det. Martens. They've confirmed that the body you and Carter found in Mt. Rainier National Park is that of Grace Zielinski."

Sarah's heart ached. In one of her visions, she had seen Grace die, her head bashed in by that madwoman Laurel Diamanté.

"And what about those other bodies?" Carter said. "There were so many."

Charlie looked at his shoes. "Twenty. They're still working on identifying them against missing persons databases."

Sarah glanced at Carter. "I'd like to know why Lou Fiore wasn't invited. Shouldn't we be keeping him in the loop?"

"Everything I've told you tonight is in my report. I plan to send a copy to the police chief."

Harlan struggled to get to his feet. Charlie tried helping, but the lawyer waved him off.

"Now, I said earlier that tonight we are celebrating a small victory. Mainly, that we've gotten Ana back and stopped a dangerous killer. But we have more pressing problems now."

Alistair straightened up and, smoothing the wrinkles in his pants, addressed the room like a peer of the realm.

"Right. Demoniacs have been appearing regularly in Dos Santos. Sarah, you and Carter encountered them on the street that night, outside the women's shelter."

"One of them left a present at my front door this morning. I found a mutilated animal."

"Ew," Carter said. Then, to Alistair, "But where do these crazies come from?"

"We don't know. But I'm fairly confident they're outsiders. Harlan and I are concerned that their activities have increased as a prelude."

"A prelude to what?" Sarah said.

"It's not clear. But it's our feeling—Harlan's and mine —that this entity you call The Darkness is behind it all. And, I'm afraid, it's become stronger."

Though she wasn't sure yet how it connected, Sarah decided to tell the others about her dream of the house next to the forest.

"When that horrible woman came down the stairs, she said, 'You know better than to come up here.' But she wasn't speaking to me."

"And you've never been to that house before?" Alistair said.

"No. But I felt drawn to it."

"The Darkness has been after Sarah since this thing started," Carter said. "How do we stop it?"

The Englishman deferred to Harlan, who answered her. "Alistair and I are working on that."

"What does that mean?"

The Englishman stood in front of Carter. "It means, when we have more information, we'll let you know. Yes?"

The girl felt a hotness at the back of her neck. She was about to say something when Sarah touched her arm. Sarah turned to Harlan.

"There's something else," she said.

She told everyone what she'd learned about Donnie and Debbie Fisk coming back to Dos Santos.

"I don't understand what business they have poking around John Dos Santos's mausoleum," Harlan said.

"It gets better. They've located his mansion. Wow, I wonder if that's the house I dreamed about. Anyway, they plan on shooting there, too."

Harlan turned to Alistair. "This changes everything."

"Indeed."

The Englishman looked at Carter evenly, his eyes betraying nothing. She shifted uncomfortably, unable to meet his gaze.

"Tell me about that night," he said.

"What?"

"I want to know what you did to that demoniac."

Carter's hands were like ice, and her legs ached. "I don't wanna talk about that."

Then, she got up and quickly left the room.

## Five

On the trip back to Dos Santos, Sarah had the feeling her friend was still seething. She decided to test her theory.

"So, what do you think of Alistair Goolsby?" Carter glared at her. "I see."

"He's just so...*frustrating*," Carter said.

"Well, he's English."

"I mean, did you hear the way he dismissed us? Like we're just a couple of—"

"Skirts?"

"Exactly."

"I know. But at the risk of incurring your wrath, I have to say, he does have a point—let me talk.

"The Darkness is bigger than anything you or I have ever had to face. And those guys are *Guardians*. We aren't. Maybe they're trying to—"

"Protect us? Isn't that a little medieval? And what's with there being no women Guardians, anyway?"

"You have a point."

"And as long as we're dissecting the evening's festivities,

there's something else that's bothering me. When did you become so reasonable?"

"You mean, *professional?*"

"Oh what, and I'm not?"

Sarah pulled over and parked on a residential street. "Carter, let's not fight."

"I'm not fighting, I'm just…confused. It wasn't that long ago you would've let these guys know what's up."

"I guess I've had a lot of time to think about my limitations."

"Meaning?"

"It's one thing to have this natural ability. But you have to know its limits. When I saw what you did to that demoniac, I was humbled."

Carter drew her legs up and made herself into a ball. "Not that again."

"I'm pretty sure I don't possess that kind of power. But you do."

The girl pulled at her hair, twirling it around her finger. "But I don't even know what I did."

"I don't think it matters. You've changed. What I mean is, you've grown."

Carter thought again about how in her dream, the Englishman had appeared to her. She *had* changed. She looked at her St. Benedict bracelet.

Why had Harlan given it to her? And why had it felt so natural putting it on? It was almost as if the bracelet represented the missing puzzle piece in her life—the thing she never realized she'd been searching for but could never find. Her own inner strength.

But that newfound power had resulted in a man's death. Sure, he was a demoniac. She had to remind herself that if she hadn't taken action, then she, along with Sarah and Harlan, would most likely be dead. *Is it true you were the one who killed that creepy dude?*

"Can I ask you something?" Carter said. "Aren't you terrified of The Darkness? It seems hell-bent on hurting you."

Sarah didn't answer. When she stopped to think about all that had happened since nearly perishing at Devil's Bluff, she realized she'd been afraid almost every waking moment. But somehow, she had found the strength to go on.

"Maybe if you left town for a while. What if that dead animal you found had been Gary?"

Sarah shuddered. "Please don't say that. Besides, leaving doesn't solve anything. The Darkness would be here when I got back."

"Harlan and Alistair might be able to destroy it by then."

"No, I'm not running away from this. What if it comes after Joe? Or my family? I may not have your powers, but when the time comes, I will face it with whatever strength I have."

"I just hope I'm there when you do."

"So do I," Sarah said, and threw the car into first.

Sarah exited off the 154 and descended toward the familiar stop sign at the bottom of the ramp. The area was poorly lit, and she didn't see them right away.

"Sarah!"

She looked at where Carter was pointing. A group of shabbily dressed men and women were gathered in a circle. They stood stock still, staring at something. Sarah turned at the intersection and drove past them.

Warily, Carter observed the seedy, dangerous-looking group. One of them turned to face her, a scowl on her face, her eyes black. Carter saw what looked like a naked limb inside the circle—someone's leg. It spasmed violently, then stopped moving.

"I'm calling 911," she said, and got out her phone.

"What is it?"

"I think there might be a body."

———

Sarah pulled into her garage and, using the remote, closed the door immediately. They had left before the cops arrived, neither of them wanting to get involved. She would call Lou in the morning to follow up.

Exhausted, she wanted nothing more than deep, dreamless sleep. Tomorrow, she and Carter would visit the women's shelter. Though she was confident things were as Alistair had said, she wanted to see for herself.

She walked into the house through the kitchen. It was dark. In the distance, she heard the television. Not bothering to switch on the light, she dropped her purse on the counter and went into the living room, where she found Joe watching TV, with Gary purring next to him.

"Hey," he said. "How was dinner?"

"Good."

She didn't want to talk about the body Carter had seen. Joe was keyed up enough already. She picked up the cat and set him on the floor. Then, she snuggled next to her ex-husband. When she saw him continuing to stare at the screen, she picked up the remote and switched off the television.

"I was watching that."

"I need you to pay attention." She took his face in her hands. "I don't want you to leave me."

"Sarah, what makes you think—"

"Just listen. Do you remember when they were looking

for that murderous woman? And you tried leaving the house to be with me? And you couldn't?"

"There were those weird people outside."

"Don't you see, Joe? That's how I feel now. It's like you're slipping away, and I can't find a way to get to you."

"Sarah, I'm not going anywhere."

"Sure?"

"Promise." He took her hands in his and kissed them. "I hadn't thought about Leah Talman for a long time. But then, strange things started happening. It was like someone was toying with me."

Sarah recalled having read about the stages of demonic possession. The first was infestation, the presence of demonic activity. Usually, it was tied to a haunted place or a cursed object. But she had no such objects, and the house had been blessed when she moved in.

"And then, when those demoniacs—or whatever they were—showed up," he said, "I felt like... Like it was a punishment."

"Joe, those people have nothing to do with you. It's this town. I can't go into any details, but there's this evil, right? And it's growing."

"Well, that explains the dead animal. Why didn't you call me the minute you found it?"

"Because I didn't want you to worry. These past weeks, you haven't been yourself, and— I'm sorry, I shouldn't have said that."

"No, you're right. I haven't. Are *you* in danger?"

"We're all in danger. And I need you to be the Joe you used to be. The one who..."

"What?"

"I was going to say, the one who wasn't afraid. But that's not fair. Of course, you were afraid. Anyone would be. Maybe we can be strong together."

He thought of that night and the strangers surrounding the house. With those expressionless faces and lifeless eyes. And he recalled the total, undeniable feeling of helplessness.

"Sarah, I'll get past this. I promise."

"I need you, Joe." She held him. "I'll always need you."

When they kissed, he felt all the fear and frustration he had been keeping inside evaporate, like steam from a kettle. Yes, he'd done a horrible thing all those years ago. But it wasn't his fault. He made a promise to himself. He would find a way to be happy again.

---

Several police cruisers and an SUV were parked next to a fire truck, their headlights and spotlights directed at an area in the soft, damp ground. Police chatter played over the radios, disturbing the nighttime quiet. No need for barrier tape; the place was deserted.

EMTs stood ready next to the ambulance, their breath luminous against the black cold. They, along with the other police officers and firefighters, waited as Lou Fiore examined the body, holding a penlight in his gloved hand.

*Male. Caucasian. Fourteen–fifteen years of age. Eyes and tongue missing. Deep, long incised injury on the front side of the neck, starting at the left ear and deepening with severance at the left carotid artery. Cut ends on the right with a tail abrasion. No defensive wounds present on either hand.*

The police chief stood and stretched his back. It was almost ten-thirty. He studied the pool of darkening blood seeping into the earth around the victim's head. Though years of homicide work had prepared him for this, it was never easy.

He surmised that the kid had been drugged first, then

brought here. The ME would be able to confirm. Judging from the footprints, there were perhaps a dozen others involved. They'd all stood in a circle like witnesses as the victim bled out. The thought sickened him.

The sound of another vehicle made Lou look away. Thank God—Forensic Science Unit. Dos Santos was small and couldn't afford their own forensics team. So, they relied on the Santa Barbara PD. Until recently, he'd never had a need for their services.

Careful to avoid the other footprints, he walked over to the van as a civilian technician named Tiffany Gersh climbed out. Lou knew her from the old days when he was in SBPD Homicide.

The last time he'd seen her, she and her partner had come out to investigate the deaths of the two police officers at the women's shelter. She was in her mid-forties. Divorced, with a teenaged son. He liked her because she was no-nonsense and cultivated a bawdy sense of humor.

"It's good to see you, Tiffany. I—"

"You can put it back in your pants, Lou. So, what do we got?"

After getting her up to speed, he tilted his head toward the body. "All yours. Don't hesitate to call me at any hour. I mean it."

"You mean, like a booty call? I always knew you were hot for me."

Laughing, he made his way back to the SUV. He tried imagining how the crime had played out. This wasn't a run-of-the-mill murder. It was a ritual sacrifice. Once again, his faith was being tested.

He decided he would meet with that private investigator, Charlie Beeks. A former homicide detective himself, he'd probably seen enough horrors of his own to last a lifetime. Maybe Charlie could help.

Lou started the vehicle and pulled out. Carter had been the one to call 911. He would have to interview her. And Sarah, of course. Remembering Fr. Brian's advice, he planned to tell Sarah about his feelings of doubt. He hoped that after what she had gone through, she could appreciate his spiritual agony. And when those things were done, he would go back to attending Mass every Sunday.

---

It was after two, and Sarah lay in bed, unable to sleep. Next to her, Joe snored. But that wasn't what had kept her awake. *Infestation.* She couldn't stop thinking about it. But here in this house? Why else would Joe have been haunted by a distant memory to the point of distraction?

*The blue bouncing ball.*

Joe told her he had seen it in her driveway as the demoniacs surrounded the house that night. She recalled the sketchy woman on the street who'd been watching her as she left for work. And then, she panicked. Could one of those things have gotten into her house and planted something?

She climbed out of bed, almost knocking over the lamp on the nightstand. The cat was nowhere in sight. Using the light from her phone, she entered the hall. She would have to search the entire house, starting with the kitchen. Remembering that Joe had to be up early for work, she made her way back to her bedroom and closed the door.

The important thing was to be organized. She began by searching the floor, peering under the cabinets and under the butcher block table and chairs to see if anything was hidden there. Next, the double oven. Opening the top door, she remembered she had used these recently. Anything left inside would have burned up.

She checked the dishwasher, but again, she would have easily detected a foreign object. Then, she looked inside the refrigerator, examining every item in every drawer, including the freezer. Grunting, she rolled the heavy unit forward and peeked behind it. Nothing but a few dust bunnies. She'd vacuum those later.

Now came the tedious part. Methodically, she went through every cabinet, taking out items, examining each one, and returning them before starting on the next. It was after three now. Gary wandered in from somewhere and watched her curiously, his head tilted. *The trash!* As she went through it, she remembered it had been taken out many times.

When she was satisfied the kitchen was clear, Sarah moved to the living room. Taking her time, she crawled on her hands and knees across the floor, checking under and behind things to make sure nothing lay hidden. She tore apart the sofa and squeezed the cushions to see if something might have been inserted. Then, she moved to the bookcases.

Gary was playing with one of his toys. She walked over to take a closer look. The cat had a red-and-white sisal ball between his paws and batted it back and forth. Sarah tried remembering when she might have bought it. She couldn't.

She returned to the basket of cat toys she had checked earlier and dumped them on the carpet. There were seven in total. Three she'd picked up when she first moved in. One was a gift from Rachel. Joe had contributed another. Katy had bought one for Gary's birthday. And the seventh was the newest—a recent gift from Carter.

*Seven toys.*

With growing fear, she turned around and stared at the sisal ball. Bored, the cat had abandoned it and was trotting away toward the kitchen. She glanced at her phone. Four-thirty. Joe would be up soon.

A hand touched Sarah's shoulder, and she snapped awake. Looking around, she realized she was in the kitchen, sitting at the table. Her eyes focusing, she saw Joe, dressed for work. Lying on the table in front of her was the sisal ball inside a sealed plastic freezer bag. As he reached for it, she grabbed his hand.

"Don't touch it."

"Why?"

"It's cursed."

"What? Where did it come from?"

"Someone must have broken in and left it. I've been up all night, tearing the house apart."

"What made you look for it?"

She touched his hand. "You. Joe, a cursed object is the only logical explanation for what you've been going through."

He sank into a chair next to her and took her hand. "I can't believe it. Did *you* touch it?"

"No. I used salad tongs to put it in the bag. I threw those out."

"What are you going to do with it?"

"I've read that one way to get rid of something like this is to burn it. But I don't trust that advice. I might release whatever's inside."

"Just what we need—*more* evil."

"Don't worry. It'll be gone by the time you get home tonight."

He stared at the cat toy warily. It looked normal. "What about Gary? Did he play with it?"

On cue, the cat trotted over, complaining bitterly. His

head was drenched and his ears were flat. Joe looked at Sarah.

"I might have gotten overly zealous with the holy water," she said. "He'll be fine."

Joe got up. "I have to go."

"No time for coffee?"

"I'll grab something on the way." He knelt in front of her and kissed her. "Promise me you'll be careful with that thing."

"I promise. Have a good day, okay?"

After Joe had gone, Sarah struggled to her feet to make coffee. She would take the cursed thing to Harlan. He would know how to dispose of it in the proper manner. She would arrange for a Mass to be said in her home. And she would change all the locks and install an alarm system.

She held her St. Michael medal in her fingers and rubbed it.

"You won't win," she said. "Not while I'm alive."

## Six

It was early when Sarah pulled up to Harlan's house. And cold. She hurried to the front door, the heels of her black booties tick-ticking against the brick. Mary answered almost immediately and, after exchanging a greeting, let Sarah through.

"How's Harlan feeling?" Sarah said.

"He's resting at the moment. Would you like coffee?"

"No, nothing." Sarah touched Mary's hand. "You should rest, too, you know."

"I wish I could. Can you see yourself to the library?"

The housekeeper walked across the polished floor and continued up the carpeted stairs. Halfway up, she disappeared into the light streaming from the tall windows. The library door was open slightly. Unsure, Sarah approached.

"Hello?"

Inside, Alistair Goolsby, dressed impeccably, perused a small black book. At first, Sarah thought it might be the journal Charlie had found in Guatemala—the cursed thing that had transported Sarah to an abominable place of evil in the jungle.

"Alistair?" she said.

"I've been reading his housekeeper's diary." He didn't look up. "Seems John Dos Santos was a real piece of work."

He laid the book on the desk and walked over to shake hands. His were warm.

"Nice to see you again, Sarah."

"You, too."

She had expected to meet with Harlan and, although the Englishman was also a Guardian, she found herself feeling—

"Disappointed?" he said, gesturing toward the Chesterfield chairs.

"Sorry, what?"

"You look a bit disappointed."

"No, I… Do you want to see it?"

"Yes. But first, I'd like to hear how you discovered it."

She recounted her activities the previous night, beginning with her suspicion concerning Joe and ending with dousing her cat with holy water.

"And did the object affect you as well?"

"No. At least, I don't think so. I'm convinced it was meant for Joe."

He rose and, towering over her, said, "Right. Well, let's have a look at the thing."

Outside, Sarah unlocked her truck and stepped away as if the interior were radioactive. The Englishman peered inside, where he found the plastic bag with the red-and-white sisal ball. He reached in and picked up the bag. Sarah looked on in astonishment as he unzipped it and removed the ball.

Unafraid, he observed the toy and, further surprising Sarah, sniffed it. He set it on the ground and, taking out a stainless steel folding knife from his jacket pocket, methodically sliced the ball in two.

Her curiosity getting the better of her, Sarah crouched to get a closer look. The inside was hollowed out. Something dark reddish was nestled inside one of the halves, wrapped in what appeared to be human hair. It was dry and fleshy.

"What is it?" she said.

"The heart of a small animal. Maybe a cat." Setting the knife aside, he straightened up. "You might want to stand back."

He raised his right hand—the one with the onyx-and-silver ring. Whispering something she couldn't understand, he directed it at the things on the ground. The two halves of the ball began to vibrate, emitting a low, menacing drone that sounded like an enormous, faraway horn.

The objects twirled insanely, becoming a blur. She expected them to burst into flame at any moment. Instead, they spun into nothingness, along with the bag.

"But how…"

Alistair removed a flask from the inside pocket of his jacket. For a second, Sarah thought he might need a drink. He unscrewed the cap and sprinkled holy water on the ground and inside the trunk of her car. As a final step, he drenched his knife.

"You won't have any more trouble from that," he said, and returned to the house.

---

Gillian Davies exited the 154 and continued down the narrow asphalt road to the intersection. Traffic had been horrendous coming from Burbank. She needed coffee. Bad. And she had to pee.

Something caught her eye at the stop sign. A dark, brownish patch in the dirt surrounded by crows pecking at it. Not leaving the intersection, she found herself staring. A dog emerged from the brush, scaring away the birds, and trotted toward the stain.

The animal looked sickly, its ribs visible in the early-morning light. The mangy fur was a patchwork of sores and old scars. When the dog met Gillian's gaze, it bared its yellow teeth.

Behind her, a car horn blasted. Checking the rearview mirror, she completed her turn. She would be in Dos Santos in minutes. Driving toward town, she couldn't get the image of the dog out of her head. There was something malevolent about it. Something in the eyes.

When she reached Dos Santos Boulevard, Gillian saw The Cracked Pot up ahead. She found a parking space on the street and maneuvered in the SUV.

Inside, it was busy. Making her way toward the restrooms, she nearly bumped into a server with a choppy bob and an anime tattoo on her neck. The dark-haired girl seemed to recognize her. Gillian kept going.

On her way out, she stopped at the coffee bar. That same girl was now behind the counter, making a cappuccino.

"Can I get a grande drip to go?" Gillian said.

"Sure. Give me one…sec."

"Excuse me. But have we met?"

"Not officially. I saw you at the cemetery when you guys were here last time. I'm Carter."

"Gillian. You and that other woman…"

"Sarah."

"She was the one trying to get a read on that headstone. I remember it didn't work. Didn't you guys come to our offices?"

"Yeah." Carter handed the woman her coffee. "We weren't very welcome."

Gillian let out a laugh. "Donnie and Debbie. They can be a handful sometimes."

"So, what do you do for them?"

"I'm the Unit Production Manager. UPM for short. What I really am is a jack-of-all-trades. Or is it jill?"

Carter laughed. "And you guys are shooting here again?"

"Yeah. I'm headed over to the cemetery now to check out the mausoleum."

The server looked concerned. "Be careful, okay?"

"Sure. What do I owe you?"

"Don't worry about it. It's on me."

"Thank you. Maybe I'll see you around."

Gillian walked out, recalling what the girl had said. *Be careful, okay?* But it was the way she'd said it—like she knew a secret.

Carter sprinted out the rear door of the restaurant, across the alley, and over to Greene Realty. In the old days, she would have been winded running that short distance. But now, she breathed normally.

Sarah's car sat in the small parking lot. Carter opened the door and went inside, and marching up the hall, found her friend at her desk, squinting at her computer screen. Waving, she knocked on the door frame and walked in.

"Well, this is unexpected," Sarah said.

Carter pointed at the monitor. "Sure you don't need glasses?"

"Never. So, what's up?"

"I'm on my break." Carter sank into a chair. "I just saw that woman Gillian from *Dubious*. She's headed over to the cemetery. I guess the shoot is really happening. Hey, did Lou contact you about last night?"

"Yeah. You?"

"He stopped by the restaurant and took my statement."

"So, what's the concern with Gillian?"

"I feel like someone should be with her when she, you know, wakes up the dead."

"Right. And that someone…"

"I'm sorry. I don't get off work until three. We've got a new manager now, and he's a dick."

Sarah considered the stack of files on her desk. "I guess I'll head over there now."

She grabbed her phone and slung her purse strap over her shoulder. Then, she pointed a warning finger at Carter.

"You owe me."

"I really appreciate it. I just have this feeling, you know? Ever since we saw that body last night."

"*You* saw. I never got a good look at it."

"Anyway, this couldn't be worse timing. After what Harlan and Alistair said, the last thing we need is a ghost-hunting camera crew."

Before walking out with her friend, Sarah poked her head into Rachel's office.

"Rache, I'm going out for a bit."

"What about all those contracts?"

"I'll take care of everything today, I promise."

"Okay." Her sister looked troubled. "See you soon, I guess."

Carter accompanied Sarah to her car. "I need to get back. Will you text me and let me know what's going on?"

"Sure. I have to say, you're being awfully proactive about this."

"Like I said, I have this feeling. Hey, we're still getting together later, right?"

"Yes. Meet me there when you get off work. I'll tell you all about the cursed object I found in my house last night."

Carter blanched. "Are you kidding me?"

Sarah looked past her at a man with a moustache standing outside the kitchen.

"Is that him?" she said.

Carter turned to look. "Shit."

Sarah watched her friend appraisingly as she jogged back to the restaurant. Her form was good—she was turning into a strong runner. Sarah thought about how to level up their training program to get ready for the Wicked Wine Run in March. Then, she remembered the cemetery. *If I'm still around in March.*

———

Sarah pulled up to the gates of Resurrection Cemetery and parked along the road. Up ahead, she saw an SUV and assumed it belonged to Gillian. The last time she was here, The Darkness had made a dramatic appearance, taking on an almost human form. And then, she remembered the phantasmal burning bird she'd held in her hands.

Nervous, she pulled her leather jacket closed against the cold and hurried onto the grounds. A sharp breeze followed as she made her way over the wet fallen leaves.

The mausoleum stood at the rear of the cemetery. The building was large and imposing, architected in the Spanish style, with stark white walls and a red tile roof that had seen better days. The heavy door was made of dark mahogany. It was slightly ajar.

Sarah approached the structure when she felt a chill, as if an invisible hand had deposited itself on her back, warning her away. Is this where The Darkness dwelled? The beginnings of a headache erupted at the base of her skull.

When she heard a cry, she pushed the heavy door the rest of the way open. Inside, it was dank and musty. Weak bands of late-morning light poured through high windows graced with decorative ironwork. She waited for her eyes to adjust.

"Hello?" she said.

Stepping closer, she found the woman from *Dubious* on one knee.

"Gillian?"

"Sarah, is that you?"

Sarah helped the other woman to her feet. "What happened?"

"I tripped. Careful. This tile floor is uneven in places. What are you doing here?"

"Mission of mercy. Carter let me know you were here."

"I see. Word gets around fast."

"We already knew you were coming. The police chief told us you guys are filming here."

"Mm." Gillian gazed around her and, using her phone, took pictures. "I'm scouting the location. Looking for the best angles to shoot."

"Do you mind if I stick around?"

"No. I'm glad I'm not alone. Even after all the episodes we've done, these places still creep me out."

Out of the corner of her eye, Sarah saw something move. When she looked again, it was gone.

"What do you know about John Dos Santos?"

"Not much," Gillian said. "Donnie and Debbie were the ones who did the research. I do know he was the town's founder and that there were some weird activity at his house."

"Putting it mildly."

"Why? What do *you* know about him?"

"Not much more," Sarah said. "Look, can I be honest? There's been some very strange occurrences recently, some resulting in people's deaths."

"I read about that poor girl killing herself at the women's shelter."

"Carter's friend," Sarah said. "There's more. We think there's something supernatural at work."

An ear-splitting scraping noise echoed off the walls, making Sarah cover her ears. When she looked up again, Gillian was staring at something. Sarah's eyes followed her gaze. An iron door off the main room was now open.

"You first," Gillian said, snapping a quick photo of the door.

Wishing she were anywhere but here, Sarah crept toward the door and, using the light from her phone, peeked inside. The pain in her head was more intense now, making her dizzy.

"Are you okay?"

"It's just a headache," Sarah said.

A sarcophagus stood in the center, dominating the room. A single beam of light fell on it, its origin a small, high window. With trepidation, Sarah approached the tomb. She was unaware of whether Gillian was following her.

The closer she came, the more her vision blurred. Eager, whispering voices played in her head. Struggling to focus, she stared at the writing on the lid.

JOHN DOS SANTOS. WAR VETERAN. 1894–1925.

"Should we open it?" Gillian said, her muted voice directly behind Sarah.

"I don't think we could by ourselves."

Though Sarah was curious, she couldn't bring herself to touch the smooth stone. When Gillian put her hand out, Sarah pulled it away.

"Maybe we should go," she said.

Behind them, the iron door slammed shut. A high-pitched keening screamed inside Sarah's head, weakening her legs. Something was attacking her.

Gillian shrank back. "What's going on?"

Ignoring the pain, Sarah used the light on her phone to examine every corner. The light beam passed over a cluster of shadows. A man with flaming red eyes and black slicked-back hair stood staring at her. She looked at Gillian. But when she turned back, the image was gone. And the noise in her head with it.

Together, the women forced the heavy iron door open and squeezed through. They hurried across the main room to the exit. As they were about to leave the building, a man blocked their way.

"What are ya doin' in here?"

All the tension in Sarah's body released as soon as she realized the man was a groundskeeper.

"Oh my gosh, you scared me."

"Sorry," Gillian said to him, recovering herself. "I'm from the television show *Dubious*. We have a permit to shoot here."

Sarah couldn't wait to get out into the warmth of the day and moved past him. Outside, the cemetery worker looked to be in his sixties. His face and neck were leathery from being in the sun.

"Thought you might be one o' them crazies been hangin' around here."

"What do you mean?" Sarah said.

"Someone's been cuttin' up animals. Leavin' the bodies on the graves. Cats and squirrels mostly. Found a raccoon the other day." He squinted at Gillian. "You said you got a permit?"

"In my car. Do you want to see it?"

"Naw. Think I heard somethin' about it. I suppose you're gonna shoot here at night?"

"Yes."

He scratched his chin, taking in the grounds. When he faced them again, his small eyes were deadly serious.

"That's a bad idea."

He ambled away, got into his golf cart, and drove off toward a stand of tanbark trees.

## Seven

At The Cracked Pot, Carter placed the mug of hot tea in front of Gillian. With jittery hands, the woman tried picking it up and dropped it.

"Shit," she said.

"I'll get you more tea."

Carter took the cup. She signaled a passing busboy, who quickly mopped up the hot liquid. Gillian looked across the table at Sarah, who calmly sipped her coffee.

"I feel like an idiot."

"Why?" Sarah said.

"I can't understand what got into me. Thing is, I could feel something malevolent in there. I mean, am I crazy?"

Carter returned with more tea. "So, I guess you made it to the cemetery."

"Does it show?"

"It's all over your face."

"Great." Gillian let out a sigh. "The crew is headed over there now. And we're supposed to shoot tonight. I've got a bad feeling about this."

Sarah looked at Carter. "I think you and I should be there tonight."

"Agreed. Did you guys want anything to eat?"

Gillian stared glumly at her tea. "Not me."

"I'm good," Sarah said.

As Carter returned to the kitchen, Sarah noticed the manager stalking her friend. He didn't look happy.

"Thanks for volunteering," Gillian said.

"What do you think Donnie and Debbie will say?"

"I'll give them a heads-up. They'll be cool once they realize they don't have to pay you."

With both hands, Gillian raised her mug to her lips and took a sip. In her mind, she heard the iron door slamming shut and winced.

"Sarah, what exactly did happen in there?"

"I don't know. But whatever it was, I could feel it—in my head."

"I thought you were going to pass out."

"There was this intense pain—something I've never experienced before."

"All I felt was the cold," Gillian said. "It was like a meat locker. The only other time I've experienced something that intense was at a house in Connecticut."

Then, she laughed. "It used to be a funeral home. Donnie insisted the house was just drafty."

Sarah toyed with her cup. "Are you sure you guys know what you're up against?"

"I think so. Anyway, Donnie and Debbie are pretty excited."

"This isn't going to be like those other episodes you've done. They won't be able to explain away the phenomena this time."

"You mean, this is some serious paranormal shit?"

"Yeah. Maybe even demonic."

Gillian drummed her fingers on her mug and looked off somewhere. "Do you think we're in danger?"

"Not to be an alarmist, but yes, I do."

"Well, anyway, we have a security team."

"That's good. Where are you staying?"

"The Ramada on Calle Real." She looked at her watch. "I'd better get over there and check in."

The women slid out of the booth. Before Sarah could open her purse, Gillian laid down a twenty.

"I'm charging this to the production," she said.

"Thanks. See you tonight."

Sarah walked over to the coffee bar to say goodbye to Carter. Her friend was scowling.

"Everything okay?"

Carter glanced around, then spoke in a low voice. "I am so done with that guy."

"The manager?"

"He said I needed to be 'less talkie and more workie.'"

"How rude. See you later?"

"You bet."

Sarah walked away, smiling to herself at the whoosh of the steam wand as Carter cranked it up to eleven.

---

In a quiet neighborhood near the forest, Elizabeth Chernov pulled her Volvo V90 into the driveway and parked in front of the garage. Her four-year-old daughter, Mia, sat safely strapped in her car seat, singing her heart out to Selena Gomez.

"Okay, missy, let's get you inside and ready for lunch."

"Yay!"

The woman opened the door and unfastened the

straps. Making a motor noise, she lifted the giggling munchkin out and placed her on the ground.

"I want to see the puppies," the little girl said.

"Okay. Race ya to the front door. One... two... three... *Go*."

Elizabeth deliberately held back as her daughter ran full tilt, her tiny backpack bouncing up and down.

"Oh, I can't believe you beat me again."

"That's because you're old, Mommy."

Dramatically, the thirty-year-old grabbed her lower back. "Tell me about it."

Inside, Mia dropped her backpack in the middle of the foyer and ran into the den. She approached the sliding glass door leading to the backyard and looked out.

"Hang on, let me unlock the door," her mother said.

"Mommy, I know how."

"Excuse me. Make sure to wash your hands after."

"Okay."

Elizabeth had been to the salon and regarded herself in the mirror by the door. She smoothed her cardigan and picked up the backpack. In the kitchen, she flicked on the small television and washed her hands in the sink.

Outside, her daughter screamed. Panic made everything visible swim in front of her eyes. She tore into the den and continued toward the glass door, which was open.

"Mia?" she said.

As she looked up at the tall trees, a feeling of dread overcame her. She made her way across the redwood deck and to the side of the house, where her husband had built a shelter for their golden retriever and her litter.

Rounding the corner, she found her daughter frozen, her little balled fists pressed against her mouth.

"Honey, what—"

When she saw all the blood, Elizabeth approached the

trembling child and, as gently as she could, turned her away. Crouching, she pressed Mia's head against her and held her tight.

"It was the devil," her daughter said. "I seen him before, Mommy."

---

Tim Whatley stood facing the tiny redwood shelter, his arms hanging at his sides like lead weights. The body of the family's beloved pet hung from the low ceiling by baling wire wound around its neck.

She had been gutted from her head to her tail. Her insides were strewn everywhere. And the puppies were dead—all except one. Blood spattered, the delicate creature crawled in circles, mewling weakly. Still blind and searching for its mother.

With care, Tim wrapped the tiny animal in the old bath towel the homeowner had given him and held it against his chest. Grimly, he walked across the deck, and after wiping his feet on the coconut fiber mat, passed through the sliding glass door into the den, where he found Elizabeth Chernov holding her daughter in her lap.

When the little girl saw the bundle he was carrying, she wriggled loose and went to see.

"One of them is still alive," he said.

Tim opened the towel and showed the little girl the puppy. Slowly, she moved her hand over the shivering creature and touched its tummy with the pink tip of her finger.

"Cover him," she said. "He's cold."

Tim did as he was told and stood in front of Mia's mother. When she looked up at him, he saw an emotional wasteland in her eyes. It was the same emptiness he had felt since that horrible night at the women's shelter when two fellow officers died.

"Have you called your husband?" he said.

"I've tried. He's out of the country on business."

"I can take the little guy to the vet. They'll bottle-feed him until he's a bit bigger."

She didn't answer. Instead, she continued looking toward the glass door, waiting for some new horror to make an appearance.

"It's okay, Mommy. We can visit him every day."

"If you can find some garbage bags, paper towels, and liquid soap, I'll clean things up for you out there."

She continued staring at the glass door. "No, I—"

"It's no problem. I think you should remain here with your daughter."

She looked at him intently, her expression uncomprehending. "Who would do this?"

"I don't know. We've had other reports of..." He glanced at the little girl. "Similar incidents."

"Flossie was so sweet. She wouldn't hurt anyone. I don't understand."

He looked around, then decided to take a seat on the sofa next to the distraught woman. The little girl squeezed in between them and laid her tiny hand on the towel, as if protecting the animal.

"I'm naming him Mikey," Mia said.

"Mrs. Chernov, I need to ask you some questions." Then, to Mia, "Do you think you could hold Mikey so I can take notes?"

He placed the fragile creature in the girl's lap and got out a small notebook and pen. As he was about to begin, she pulled on his sleeve.

"Those mean people had funny eyes," Mia said.

A light rain fell as Tim finished cleaning up the shed. He had placed the heavy duty plastic garbage bags containing the dogs' remains and bloody bedding in the wheelbarrow. And he'd made sure to clean and disinfect the shed's interior to remove every trace of blood. When he had finished, he admired his work.

Tim placed the cleaning supplies in the wheelbarrow. He paused when he heard someone whispering very close. The voice had come from behind. But when he turned around, no one was there. Ignoring the distraction, he grabbed the handles of the wheelbarrow and headed for the gate.

He walked around to the front of the house and knocked on the door. Elizabeth Chernov answered.

"I left the wheelbarrow and supplies by the side of the house," he said. "I'm ready to take Mikey now."

"I appreciate you doing this, Officer."

"Call me Tim."

She pressed herself to his chest and wept, her body shuddering. He glanced at her perfect nails as she gripped his shoulders. Unsure what to do, he patted her back.

"I'm sorry," she said, pulling away. "I've gotten your shirt wet."

"Don't worry about it."

She nodded and left him at the door. When she returned, she was cradling the puppy wrapped in the towel. Gently, he took it from her.

"Is Mia okay?" he said.

"She's taking a nap. Children don't remember things like this, do they?"

When Tim was eight, he had joined the Cub Scouts with his father. They'd gone on their first hike together, and he could still see the clearing in the forest where the troop had chosen to stop for lunch. It was a warm day. He'd had to pee. His father pointed to an outcrop of boulders. As he made his way around to the rear, he saw what someone had done.

They'd arranged small rocks in a circle in the dirt. In the center was a mourning dove that had been cleaved in two. Lying in a little depression between the two halves was a mound of ashes and blackened flesh. He never told anyone, not even his father.

"No, they don't," he said.

---

Tim left the vet's office and returned to his police cruiser. After an examination, they told him the animal was strong and healthy. They promised to provide Mrs. Chernov with regular updates. And they had agreed to take the other dogs' remains and incinerate them.

He unlocked the car door. His phone vibrated. When he saw who it was, he answered immediately.

"Hey, Chief. Tonight? No problem. If it's okay, I'd like to take the afternoon off."

He told Chief Fiore what had happened at the Chernovs' house and how he had rescued the lone remaining dog.

"Thanks, Chief. I appreciate it. I'll be at the cemetery later."

Tim had just started the car and checked the rearview mirror when he heard the whispering again. The words were indistinct and sounded as if more than one person were speaking.

Nervous, he glanced to his left. A middle-aged woman,

in a hurry and holding a cat carrier, entered the vet's office. There was no one else around.

He needed to go home and lie down. The carnage at the Chernov house had affected him more than he realized. His head pounded, and he felt nauseous. Awkwardly, he climbed out and vomited in the boxwood hedge that lined the parking lot.

Putting his car in reverse, he backed out. The last thing he wanted was to spend the night at a cemetery. But he had a duty.

---

After reading her daughter her favorite bedtime story, *Goodnight Moon*, Elizabeth laid the book on the nightstand. She smoothed the covers of the small white bed and tucked the purple-and-white polka dot sheets just below Mia's chin. Then, she dabbed the little girl's nose with her index finger, making the child giggle.

"Time to go to sleep now."

"Do you think Mikey is sleeping, too?"

"I'm sure he is. Safe and warm."

"I can't wait to see him tomorrow. Do you think he misses us?"

"Yes. And we miss him, right?"

"Uh-huh. Night, Mommy." Mia rolled onto her side and closed her eyes.

"Night, punkin."

Elizabeth turned out the light. The moon-and-stars nightlight with Mia's name written in script stood on the dresser, giving off a comforting glow.

"Mia honey?"

"Whah…?"

"Do you remember when you said you'd seen that man before?"

"The devil?"

"Yes. Where did you see him?"

"At the park."

"You mean, this week?"

"Uh-huh."

"But how do you know he's…what you say he is?"

"*They* told me."

"Who?"

"Those other kids." Yawning, she snuggled deeper under the covers. "I'm tired."

"Sweet dreams, my love."

Elizabeth was very cold. She remembered that day clearly. It was afternoon. And though she had seen an old car in the parking lot, she couldn't recall seeing a man there. But that's not why she was frightened. Other than Mia and her, the park had been deserted.

There were no other children.

———

Eddie Cruz carried the old cardboard storage box from the kitchen to the garage and set it down on the work bench next to a can of lighter fluid and a plastic lighter. He opened the garage door and placed a metal waste basket in the middle of the driveway. The rumble of distant thunder made him look up. He could smell the rain, but it hadn't begun coming down yet.

He returned to the garage and stared at the storage box. The yellowed, brittle packing tape no longer held it shut. He pulled back the dog-eared flaps. Inside, he found a pile of old letters partially covering a photo album. On top was a single black-and-white photo with scalloped edges. One corner was torn. He took out the photo and looked at it.

The picture was of a pretty young Latina. She wore an old-fashioned maid uniform with a wide lace collar and lace cuffs. In front of her was a small girl looking off-camera at someone. She had bright eyes and a huge smile. They stood in front of a Spanish-style mansion.

Eddie flipped the photo over and read the notation. *Dolores with Lelo. June 1925.* Clearing his throat, he tossed the photo back in and closed the flaps. He was about to carry the box outside when the door to the kitchen opened.

Rachel stood in the doorway, her arms folded against the cold.

"I thought I heard you out here," she said. "What are you doing?"

He glanced at the waste basket in the driveway. Then, he retrieved it and closed the garage door. Grabbing the box, he headed back into the house, past his daughter.

"Nothing," he said. "I wasn't doing anything."

## Eight

It was pouring rain by the time Sarah pulled up to the curb in front of the apartment building. Wearing a hooded rain jacket, Carter trotted down the steps, where she almost slipped. Laughing with embarrassment, she climbed in.

"I wonder how long this storm is going to last," she said.

"Supposed to go all night."

Sarah checked her mirrors and pulled into the street. "Joe's meeting us there, by the way."

"What for?"

"He said he learned his lesson after the women's shelter and wasn't letting me out of his sight."

"Hey, so, here's some news. I gave my notice."

"Really? Things are that bad over at The Cracked Pot?"

"The job keeps getting in the way of what you and I need to do. Looking at it from their point of view, I guess I haven't exactly been a model employee."

"What are you talking about? You've been great. I think it's your manager who has the problem."

"Maybe. He said if I wanted, I could finish my shift and be done. Anyway, my furniture will be here soon. I'm really excited to start decorating my house."

"Whoo-hoo! Which means, I get to help."

When they arrived at the cemetery, the street was lined with cars, vans, and trucks with generators. Eventually, Sarah found a parking spot marked with a temporary No Parking sign. She and Carter pocketed their phones and tossed their purses in the trunk. As an afterthought, Sarah tore the paper sign off the streetlamp and sent it sailing into the trunk.

"If I get a ticket, I'll let my future brother-in-law make it go away," she said.

"So, you think Lou and Rachel will get married?"

"Yeah, I do."

Zipping up their rain jackets, they scooted along the road, careful to avoid the water sheeting across the asphalt. As they passed through the gates, a sharp pain at the base of her skull made Sarah stop.

"What's wrong?" Carter said.

"I don't know. I felt the same thing before, when I was here with Gillian."

They continued across the grounds toward the mausoleum. Sarah spotted Tim standing guard outside. He wore a long black rain jacket with a high collar. His hat was covered in plastic. Puffs of warm air shone white as he breathed.

"Hi, Tim," Sarah said as she looked around. "Have you seen Joe?"

"He's inside. Hey, Carter."

"Everything okay out here?"

When he didn't answer, Sarah touched his shoulder. "I

wasn't going to say anything, but I like you better without the moustache."

"Thanks. I guess."

The mausoleum's interior was bright with artificial lighting and filled with people running cables. Gillian stood off to the side, talking to one of the crew members. Joe was down on one knee with his toolbox, fiddling with a light stand. *They're putting him to work?*

As soon as Sarah walked in, the pain in her head increased. Joe was stationed near the great iron door and, the closer she moved toward him, the more her vision blurred. Soon, she could no longer make out distinct voices. All sound had become a low, sonorous hum.

"Sarah Greene?"

Holding her head, she looked up and saw Donnie Fisk. Wearing a parka, he had on his coke-bottle glasses. She tried responding, but no words came out. For a second, the nighttime sky appeared overhead, glowing hot from a descending flare. Blood ran from her nose. She wiped it and, looking at her hand, made a weak groaning noise.

"Hey, can we get some help over here?"

By the time Joe reached her, Sarah was lying on the cold, damp floor on her back, twitching uncontrollably. Crouching opposite Joe, Carter held her hand tightly.

"Sarah, it's gonna be okay." She looked desperately at Joe. "What's wrong with her?"

"Someone call 911!" he said.


Donnie, Debbie, and the rest of the crew stood in front of the mausoleum, watching as the ambulance drove off, its siren piercing the stillness. Carter followed Joe to his truck. As he was about to climb in, she touched his arm.

"I really wanna come with you. But someone needs to be here."

"It's okay. I'll look after her." He began backing out.

"Call me when you know something, okay?"

But he didn't answer.

---

Wearing the clothes she had on at the cemetery, Sarah walked on duckboards below ground at twilight. They led her through a winding path whose walls were made of sandbags.

Somewhere, men's voices shouted. A rat-a-tat-tat noise from behind startled her. It sounded near, intense, and unrelenting.

She arrived at a dugout and looked inside. A weak yellow light illuminated the space where a lone soldier lay, breathing erratically. He was young, dressed in a khaki tan wool uniform. Blood seeped from his bandaged chest.

Raising his head with difficulty, he reached out his hand. Starting toward him, she tried to say something.

"Sarah?"

When she opened her eyes, Sarah found herself in a hospital room and wearing a gown. She expected to see Joe, but it was Alistair Goolsby who stood near the bed. She almost didn't recognize him in his jeans and black leather bomber jacket.

"Where's Joe?" she said.

"He nipped out to find some coffee. How are you feeling?"

Groaning, she sat up. Though the pain in her head was

gone, her muscles ached. She wiped her hand under her nose. No blood.

"I think I'm okay. What are you doing here?"

"Carter called the house. I came straight away."

"How's Harlan?"

"I'm more worried about *you* right now. Can you tell me what happened?"

"There's something in that mausoleum. And I must be sensitive to it, because it didn't even affect Carter."

"Can you describe how it felt?"

"Like someone driving an icepick into my skull. I had a dream just now. I was somewhere far away. Maybe another country? It was some kind of trench. I heard guns. And men shouting."

He came closer. "Did you see anyone?"

"A soldier. His uniform was old fashioned. He… He was seriously wounded in the chest."

"Sarah, this is very important. Did he see *you*?"

She stared at him. "He reached out to me. I was about to ask him his name when you woke me."

Alistair's face became as smooth and blank as a stone in a Japanese garden. He went silent and cast his eyes down.

"What is it? Do you know something?"

He looked at her sharply. "Someone's trying to draw you into the past. *Their* past."

"I don't understand."

As Joe walked in, Sarah grabbed one of the rails and shook it.

"What're you doing?" Joe said.

"I can't stay here. Can you find my clothes?" Frustrated, she rattled the rail again. "How does this thing work?"

"Sarah, they want to observe you overnight."

"But Carter's still in that place. I can't leave her there by herself. What if something happens?"

Alistair zipped his jacket. "I'll go. You need to rest."

"But I'm fine," she said. "Really. Why don't men ever believe a woman when she says she's okay?"

Joe took her hand. "Sarah, please."

Alistair went to the door. "I'll check in with you in the morning. Tell me if you have that dream again, won't you?"

"What dream?" Joe said, craning his neck. But Alistair was gone. Then, to Sarah, "What dream?"

"It's nothing. Just a stupid nightmare." She stared at her hospital gown. "Did you put me in this thing?"

"No, it was a nurse."

He sat next to her and took her hand. Pouting, she avoided eye contact.

"Listen," he said. "You had a seizure. They did a CT scan. You have a slight brain injury. That's what caused your bloody nose."

"A brain injury? That's ridiculous."

"Sarah, you are the most stubborn woman I know. You need to take this seriously. I'm staying with you tonight."

She groaned dramatically, then touched his face. The old Joe was back. And true to form, he wanted to protect her. Letting go of her anger, she realized she loved him more than anyone in the world.

"Okay, I promise I won't go anywhere. Go home and get some sleep. Besides, Gary probably needs attention." He didn't move. "Really, I'll stay here. Besides, I'll sleep better knowing you're getting some rest, too."

"I *will* ask the nurse to use restraints if necessary. I love you."

"That's what keeps me going, you know."

He kissed her and went to the door. "I'll be here first thing in the morning to drive you home."

After Joe had gone, Sarah remained sitting up. Outside her room, it was quiet, except for a distant noise. It was the persistent echo of machine gun fire.

---

Carter stood outside the room that held the tomb of John Dos Santos. Donnie and Debbie had shot most of the episode and were now focused on getting the sarcophagus open. But they were having trouble and couldn't budge the heavy stone lid.

The plan was for them to open the tomb dramatically and film the remains, all the while making wisecracks about vengeful ghosts and curses. These people had no clue. They were like naïve children at a tea party in a graveyard. She wanted to warn them, but what was the use?

So far, Carter hadn't experienced anything unusual— not like Sarah. Only the biting cold inside the damp building. Outside, the rain had let up, and the moon was out. She saw something out of the corner of her eye and turned toward the exit.

Tim was staring at her, his eyes strangely vacant. She tried smiling to break the tension. His mouth moved, but she couldn't hear what he was saying. Then, Alistair Goolsby appeared. Excusing himself, he slipped past the cop.

The moment the Englishman set foot inside, a milky-looking force assaulted him in sickening waves. When he didn't move, it retreated into nothingness. Instinctively, Carter gripped her St. Benedict bracelet.

"Alistair?" she said.

"Quiet on the set!"

A crew member glowered at her. Embarrassed, she made her way silently out of the building and joined the Guardian. They drifted away from Tim and stood under a tree, whose leaves dripped steadily.

"What are you doing here?" she said, shivering against the cold. "I thought you were with Sarah."

"She's resting. I'm afraid she was trying to come back here."

Carter smiled self-consciously. "She was worried about me, right?"

"Very. It seems you two are as thick as thieves."

"So, what's wrong with her? She was in pretty bad shape."

"Carter, you've got to listen. Sarah is in danger."

"What?"

"Someone's attempting to communicate with her. I believe it's why she had that episode. Whatever this entity is—The Darkness—it's extremely powerful. I felt it as soon as I entered the mausoleum just now."

"I saw something when you walked in. It tried to attack you. But why is Sarah in danger? I thought Harlan was protecting her."

He looked away. A short distance off, an old groundskeeper with a leathery neck and face watched them, letting the filterless cigarette butt he was holding burn down to nothing in his fingers.

"Harlan, as you know, is unwell," the Englishman said.

"Then, *you* have to protect her against The Darkness. Right?"

"I can try. The thing is—and I mean no disrespect to Sarah—I'm not sure she has the strength to resist it."

"'Resist it'? You make it sound as if, as if it's trying to possess her."

"Not possess. *Kill.*"

She covered her mouth with both hands. "No. No, I won't let it." She grabbed his arm. "Alistair, you have to help me. *Please.*"

"I will. But first, I need to prepare. And so do you. I know now everything that happened with you and that demoniac. Harlan told me."

She started to walk away when he grabbed her arm.

"That creature wasn't nearly as powerful as what Sarah is facing," he said. "If you want to help me defeat The Darkness, you need the right weapons."

Carter felt faint. How had she gone from neighborhood wahoo to full-blown demon hunter? The whole thing was insane. Alistair and Harlan were the Guardians. Why weren't *they* taking care of it? She thought of Sarah again. And when she'd composed herself, she looked the Englishman in the eye.

"Tell me what I need to do," she said.

---

Det. Dan Martens had been at it for days, poring over case files and reports. He hadn't seen his family for two nights, and he felt as if he was coming down with something. Since the grisly discovery by Sarah and Carter in Mt. Rainier National Park, he and his team had worked tirelessly to identify the twenty bodies.

*Twenty.* Boys and girls, all sixteen and under. After researching missing persons databases, CSI had used a combination of dental records and genetic genealogy to identify the victims. All of them were from Washington State. All were runaways.

Martens had a teenaged son of his own—just thirteen. He thought of his boy as he began the heartbreaking task of notifying parents that the remains of their long-lost children had been found. What would *his* reaction be to such a call? Relief? Anger? Most were grateful for the news; they'd gotten closure.

One man from Marysville—an attorney—threatened to sue the police department for dragging their heels. The detective wanted to laugh in his face. He hadn't even been born when the kids went missing.

After testing the soil around and under the skeletons, CSI determined that the bodies had been buried sometime between the late sixties and early seventies. And because the estimates varied depending on the victim, that meant the killer had gone back repeatedly to dispose of fresh victims.

He drained the last of the tepid coffee in the mug his son had given him last Father's Day. Printed on the front was WORLD'S COOLEST DAD. KEEP THAT SHIT UP. It still made him laugh.

Setting the cup aside, he flipped open the ME's report. In every case, cause of death was from sharp force trauma at the base of the skull. The ME found nicks in the vertebrae consistent with a weapon such as an ice pick. It was likely all were murdered by the same individual—someone who was right-handed.

Martens recalled that, when he was a child, the Green River Killer had been sentenced to life in prison for forty-nine murders in Washington. Some of his victims were underage runaways. Whoever killed these children, though elderly, might still be out there somewhere.

His mobile phone rang, startling him. He checked the number and answered.

"Charlie. What's going on? No, still at the office." He laughed. "I'll sleep when I'm dead. What? *Now?*"

. . .

Martens grabbed two bottles of a local IPA from the bar and walked across to a booth where Charlie Beeks sat. His friend wore a flannel shirt and ski vest.

Though there were nicer establishments closer to Seattle PD Headquarters, the veteran homicide detective liked dive bars—especially Linda's Tavern. Supposedly, the neighborhood venue had been the last place Kurt Cobain was seen alive. But Martens didn't care about that. He felt comfortable here. Anonymous.

"I was surprised to get your call," he said.

He handed over one of the beers and slid into the booth opposite the private investigator. They clinked bottles, and each took a swig.

"Just passing through?"

Charlie examined the bottle's label. "I'm stopping over on my way back to LA. My flight leaves in three hours."

"Can I ask where you're coming from?"

"Guatemala. Business, you know."

"Yeah. And here I thought you were retired."

"Me, too."

Charlie waited for a couple to make their way past. He reached into his black leather messenger bag and removed what looked like a police file.

"A present?" Martens said.

"I thought it would help with your investigation."

"Well, we've identified all the bodies. So, unless you're handing me the killer..." His friend's expression didn't change. "No shit, you know who did this?"

Charlie opened the file to a particular autopsy photo and handed it to Martens.

The homicide detective examined the photo. It was a closeup of a man's right profile. The eye was missing, and there were small lacerations all around, as if made by...a bird? But it was the avulsion-type bite mark on the cheek that caught his attention. That had been made by a human. The skin was ripped open, exposing the flesh.

Another patron passed by, and Martens deftly hid the photo. He took a long swallow of beer and looked at his friend.

"His name is Leon Wayne Vogel," Charlie said, his voice matter-of-fact. "Fifty-five. His body was discovered in the forest in Dos Santos, California, in 1970."

"What happened to his eye?"

"*Eyes.* He was attacked by ravens. But it's the bite mark that's important."

He handed Martens the file and gave him time to go through it as he drank his beer.

"I'd advise you to compare the DNA found on every victim's teeth to what's in this file."

"You're saying one of them bit him," the detective said. "1970. That corresponds to the dates the victims were buried. But how did you—"

Charlie sighed. "I'm sorry, Dan. That's all I can tell you. Thanks for the drink."

He closed his bag and slid out of the booth. Martens followed him outside. A wet wind assaulted them at the door. They walked a little ways up the street, away from a group of laughing locals entering the bar.

"Can I give you a lift to the airport?" Martens said.

"Sure. But don't expect any more information."

"Fair enough. I'm parked up here."

## Nine

Harlan sat up in bed staring at the morning light streaming through the large windows. He breathed with difficulty. Soon, it would be time for Mary to drain his lung. He knew in his soul death was approaching; he felt it all around him. But it wasn't what he thought—the dark, soulless reaper some people believed in, pursuing us from the day we were born. No, it was something else. It was silence.

There was a soft knock at the door. Mary entered and immediately crossed to the window and opened the sheer curtains.

"How are you feeling?" she said.

When she saw the smoothie sitting untouched on the nightstand, she made a face. He looked at the glass and folded his arms.

"Not hungry."

"Harlan, we talked about this. You need to keep up your strength. I suppose you don't want your coffee either?"

"I would like some water."

A stainless steel table stood against the wall. On one of the lower shelves was the equipment needed to perform a thoracentesis. On top sat a pitcher of water. She poured out a glass and gave it to him.

"Carter's here," she said.

"Does she want to see me?"

"She's here for Alistair. What are you two cooking up for that girl?"

Harlan bristled. "She has a gift. And we need her help."

"It's she who's going to need the help."

"Sorry, what did you say?"

She wheeled around to face him. "I said Charlie's back from Seattle."

"Good. I want to see him."

"Are you sure you…" When she noted his expression, she decided to let it go. "I'll send him in."

She got as far as the door when she heard her name. Harlan looked at her intently.

"I realize I'm a terrible patient," he said. "Thank you for putting up with me."

"It's all right, Harlan. I consider it my penance for having left the convent."

She walked out before he had a chance to come back with a well-rehearsed bon mot. Moments later, Charlie walked past her and closed the door. Mary stood on the landing, which afforded a perfect view of the garden. Carter and Alistair were walking together, deep in conversation.

"Please, Blessed Mother, protect her," she said, and continued down the stairs.

"Well, I made it back in one piece," Charlie said.

He looked around the room, spotted a chair, and brought it over next to the king bed where Harlan sat, sipping his water.

"I take it all went well with Ana's mother?"

"You can't imagine how happy she was. She especially wanted me to thank you for bringing her daughter home."

"I'm glad." The attorney set the glass down. "And Det. Martens?"

"I gave him the file as instructed. There's something I don't understand. The autopsy report doesn't mention the bite mark."

"Correct."

"That photo. Was it part of the original file?"

The lawyer smiled. "Still pretty sharp, I see. No. The medical examiner withheld it."

"On whose authority?"

"Mine. The ME and I were quite good friends. He's since passed on."

"Harlan, I hate to ask this. Did you know the victim?"

The attorney thought a moment. "I'll answer your question. But first, I want to tell you about Leon Vogel."

---

Gillian awoke with a headache that started at the base of her skull and crept upward like tentacles squeezing her brain. She'd felt ill ever since that godawful night in the crypt room. They said death had a smell, and it was true. But this was worse.

The intense odor hanging invisibly around them reminded her of rotten eggs. But it was Donnie's tirade at three in the morning that had gotten to her. After repeated attempts to remove the sarcophagus lid, they had to give up. He was furious, screaming in that nasal voice of his and blaming everyone within sight for the failure.

John Dos Santos. She'd heard so many stories lately. Was it possible he was as evil as they said? Before entering the crypt room, Donnie and Debbie had played up the legend, to be sure.

While the camera inspected every inch of the outer chamber, the wisecracking hosts played off each other. They took turns recounting episodes from Dos Santos's life that involved wild parties with underage girls and boys. The whole performance was like a tennis match between the brother and sister, each lobbing a new story across the net even more lurid than the last.

Apparently, there was a war going on between the corrupt mayor and the editor-in-chief of the *Dos Santos Weekly*, Thaddeus Pruitt. Also the owner of the newspaper, Pruitt was a frequent critic of the mayor. And he proved it regularly in his op-ed pieces.

At one point, some FOJ—Friends of John—men threatened Pruitt, one of them giving him a black eye. But the grizzled newspaper man was undaunted and continued his attacks. Then one night, he was found dead in his bathtub, a victim of drowning. The police chief declined to investigate, concluding that Pruitt had died from natural causes.

Near dawn, when they had finished packing everything up, the film crew headed back to Burbank. Donnie and Debbie stayed on at the motel. Gillian planned to have breakfast with them before they returned to the *Dubious* offices to supervise editing of the footage.

In a few days, they would reappear with the crew to shoot the final episode at the former home of John Dos Santos. Meanwhile, Gillian was told to stay and explore the

The Blood She Wore

mansion. For the first time since joining the show, she felt afraid and dreaded what was still to come.

---

It was warm and sunny when Joe pulled his truck into Sarah's driveway. Before getting out, he took her hand.

"I was so worried," he said.

"The doctor told me there wasn't any permanent damage."

"And the seizure?"

"He explained about that. It's—"

"A sudden, uncontrolled electrical brain disturbance. I know. But what caused it?"

"I think it has something to do with that mausoleum."

"Well, you're never going back there if I have anything to say about it."

She smiled as he got out and trotted around the other side to open the door for her. He waited for her to give him her hand.

"Is all this necessary?" she said.

"Can you *please* let me take care of you?"

"You're right—I'm sorry."

As he helped her out, he grabbed her purse and walked her to the front door. A woman of around seventy stood on the corner, staring at them. She was dressed plainly, with straw-like hair. She wore a large wooden cross around her neck.

"Joe?" Sarah said.

"Go inside."

"What are you going to—?"

"Please do as I ask."

Gary waited for her in the foyer. Sarah dropped her purse and picked him up. Joe had closed the front door after her. She went to the window and, stroking the cat's head, looked out.

Her ex-husband was crossing the street, saying something to the stranger as he approached. She said something back to him, and the next thing Sarah knew, Joe was shouting. Something about "the police." Chastened, the woman scurried away. Joe returned to the house.

"Who was that woman?" Sarah said.

"I don't know her name, but I've seen her around. She's a loony."

"What did she say to you?" He walked toward the kitchen, and she followed. "Joe, tell me what she said."

He took the cat from her arms and set him on the ground. He laid his hands on her shoulders.

"She told me you and I are living in sin and that there's going to be a reckoning for every sinner in Dos Santos."

"A reckoning? You mean, like *punishment*?"

"I don't know. Like I said, she's crazy. I warned her to leave us alone or I'd call the cops."

"You did the right thing."

"I left my phone in the truck."

He walked back outside to retrieve it. Cold, Sarah enveloped herself in her arms. According to her faith, she *was* living in sin; sleeping with a man who was not her husband. She thought of the Samaritan woman at Jacob's well in John's Gospel.

"But I love Joe," she heard herself say.

---

Gillian was the first to arrive at The Cracked Pot. Donnie and Debbie Fisk rarely slept. Over the past few hours, they had carried on an intense email thread with the editor in Burbank, who was going through the recent footage.

Gillian had been copied on everything. It was only now she'd decided to read the emails on her phone while sipping her macchiato.

From what she could piece together, there had been problems with the footage. Unexplained lens flares and flashes of light had appeared throughout the video taken inside the mausoleum. And worse, in places, the sound had cut out.

The editor, Tyler, said he could probably work around the visual anomalies. But Donnie and Debbie would have to loop some of their dialogue. Delays like this cost money. And Donnie and Debbie loathed spending money.

The *Dubious* hosts walked in together. Ignoring the stares of locals who recognized them, they passed between tables and slid into the booth opposite Gillian.

"Morning," Gillian said.

The brother-sister team were not morning people, and she hadn't expected a response. A server came by and laid down two menus.

"Coffee?" he said.

Donnie answered him without looking up. "Sounds great. Whatever you have that's strong."

His sister nodded her agreement, and the server left them. After glancing at it, Donnie laid the menu aside and leveled his myopic gaze at Gillian.

"So, how's Sarah Greene doing?" he said.

Absently, she wondered if he was worried about a possible lawsuit. "I haven't been in touch with her."

Debbie folded her hands on the table. She was the picture of self-satisfaction and primness. Gillian had a pretty good idea of what was coming.

"I think it's an act," Debbie said. "She's always had it in for us."

"They took her to the hospital, Debbie." Gillian realized too late she'd snapped at her employer.

"Well, I still say—"

Donnie scoffed. "Look, it doesn't matter." He grinned at his sister. "Hey, who was that tall English dude that showed up? Is he mixed up in this thing, too?"

"I never saw him before. He is kinda cute, though."

"Shut up."

"No, *you* shut up."

Gillian rolled her eyes. The server reappeared with two mugs of coffee and took everyone's order. Later, as they ate, Donnie ran down the agenda for the UPM.

"So, I'm probably going to have to sit with Tyler the whole time to make sure he doesn't screw this thing up any worse than it already is."

"Have you tried looking for a new editor?"

Debbie scoffed. "Gillian, you know as well as I do, good editors cost money."

"I wasn't aware."

"Anyhoo," Donnie said. "Make sure you cover the entire house. And send us lots of pictures. Hey, what do you guys think about a séance?"

Gillian bit her lip until it bled. "We've only done that, like, forty times."

"I know, but the fans love it."

"Hey, maybe Sarah Greene could conduct it," Debbie said, tee-heeing. "Or that little tattooed sidekick of hers. What's her name?"

Gillian looked at her evenly. "Carter. And they're not mediums."

"Sor-*ree*. I just thought it might be fun. Why are you so grumpy, anyway?"

"Look, guys," Gillian said. "There's no way I'm hiking up to that mansion by myself."

Debbie waggled her fingers in front of her. "Scared?"

"It's an old house. What if I get hurt? Besides, you don't want me filing for workers' comp, do you? All that red tape? Think of the delays."

Donnie side-eyed his sister. "Yoshi can go with you."

Pouting, Debbie tugged on his sleeve. "But he was going to drive us back."

"I can drive."

"You suck at driving."

They slid out of the booth, leaving Gillian to pick up the check, as usual.

"Later," Donnie said. "We'll let you know when we arrive." Then, to his sister, "I do *not* suck at driving."

Gillian sat there, drinking her coffee and contemplating what Sarah had told her about John Dos Santos. At some point between leaving the cemetery the night before and coming to the restaurant, she had decided she'd had enough.

When shooting wrapped at the mansion, she would put in her notice. There was plenty of work in LA. She had a sterling reputation and was confident she could find another regular gig in television.

As she brought the coffee mug to her lips, she saw the thing floating on top—a blow fly, huge and angry. Sickened, she flagged down a busboy.

He waited while she slid the mug over to show him. He stared at it, uncomprehending. When she looked at it again, there was nothing amiss. Just a regular macchiato.

She laughed helplessly. "I need some sleep."

---

Lou traveled fast up the long, curvy road that led to Harlan Covington's mansion. Angry as hell, he almost hit a squirrel but kept going. When he reached the house, he screeched to a stop and marched to the front door. Mary answered. He took a breath and smiled professionally— none of this was her doing.

"I'm here to see Charlie Beeks," he said.

"Is he expecting you?"

He showed her the folder he was carrying. "He sent this over by messenger. I need to discuss it with him."

She glanced behind her, then let the police chief in. "Wait here, please."

He checked his phone for new emails as he shifted his weight from one foot to the other. He felt fat. With everything going on these past few weeks, there'd been no time to exercise, other than a brisk walk to the espresso machine several times a day.

"Chief Fiore?"

Lou looked up and found the investigator with his hand out. His manner took some of the wind out of the cop's sails.

"Sorry to show up unannounced. I received your report, and I have some questions."

"Sure." Charlie glanced toward the library door, which was shut. "I believe the library's in use right now. Why don't we go into the garden? It's a nice day."

Lou followed the investigator outside. Some of the rose bushes were beginning to show green buds. Birds chirped happily in the bare branches of the trees that also displayed signs of spring.

Charlie found a stone bench he liked and sat. Lou took a seat next to him and laid the report open on his lap. He took a breath. Though he was still furious, he didn't want to alienate the investigator.

"What I want to know is, why are you sending me these

papers now? It seems to me I could've used this information days—*weeks*—ago."

"Chief—"

"You can call me Lou."

"Lou, I realize Harlan hasn't kept you in the loop as much as I'd like. Believe me, I know where you're coming from. I used to be a homicide detective."

"Yeah, I heard."

"And I don't like secrets either."

"Okay, so, why didn't I get this report sooner?"

Charlie sighed, the beginnings of exasperation seeping into the folds of his furrowed brow.

"I've been pretty much in the dark as to some of the details myself," he said. "Harlan Covington is a curious man. He shares only what is necessary to deal with the situation at hand. Nothing more, nothing less. Believe me, I'm as frustrated as you are."

Lou got to his feet and began pacing.

"I need to know everything. Since those two officers died, there's been a rash of animal mutilations. A couple nights ago, we found a body just off the freeway. He was a kid. I'm pretty sure he'd been ritually sacrificed."

"I wasn't aware."

"No, but I'll bet Harlan was." No reaction. "And now, I've got this film crew in town. And all they want is to dig up some ancient history concerning the town's founder. And if that isn't bad enough, I come to learn that Ana Robles was *found*."

"Yes, I can see how that would—"

"I've been tearing myself up with guilt, thinking that crazy woman had killed Ana." He was shouting now. "And all this time, she's safe and sound in Guatemala?"

"Lou, I…"

The police chief sank onto the bench and rubbed his eyes with the heels of his hands. The men sat in silence.

"God, I'm tired," Lou said. "Look, I know this is not your doing. But I can't be left in the dark anymore. It's *my* job to protect the town—not Harlan Covington's."

"Okay." Charlie got to his feet. "How do we fix this?"

"I want to know what Harlan knows the minute he finds out. I realize he has a stake in Dos Santos. He's done a lot for us over the years. I'll commit to keeping him informed of my activities."

"That sounds fair."

"And he can start by telling me everything he knows about Leon Vogel."

"Okay, I'll set up a meeting."

"Thank you," Lou said. "So, how long were you in Homicide?"

"Twelve years. I've seen a lot. But the worst is—"

"When it happens to a kid."

"Yeah," Charlie said. "There's no forgetting something like that."

---

Bethany Pruitt lifted the steaming kettle from the range top with difficulty and filled the teapot. The house was cold and drafty, and her gnarled fingers ached. She sat at the rude wooden table to wait for the tea to steep.

Before her lay her bible, open to Jeremiah. The cover was worn, and some of the pages were stained with old blood. The book had been a gift from her preacher father. He'd given it to her on her seventh birthday. Seven, he had advised her, was the age of reason.

Fingering the wooden cross lying against her breast, she thought back to earlier in the day and chastised herself.

She should never have confronted that man. Though a sinner himself, he really had nothing to do with it. It was the woman—Sarah Greene. She was the one who had brought the evil to Dos Santos, when she discovered the mirror.

Bethany poured herself a steaming cup. She reread the dog-eared pages she'd printed off at the library. "The Girl in the Mirror" by Carter Wittgenstein. The old woman had read the story many times. She was convinced the ravens had been meant for Sarah, as well as the man who died. But inexplicably, Sarah had escaped death.

She rose stiffly and stuffed the paper in the trash can that stood under the sink. Making herself comfortable at the table, she blew on her tea and took a sip. She removed the hatpin she kept inside her worn, faded blouse.

With a fluid, practiced motion, she drove it into her palm. Almost at peace, she watched as the blood dripped onto the pages of the Good Book.

# Ten

"Sarah?"

She looked up to find Joe staring at her in a way that suggested she had food stuck in her teeth. They were sitting at the butcher block table in her kitchen. Her wine glass was full, and she'd barely touched her pasta.

"I've been babbling away for ten minutes about the new property. I didn't realize you'd left the building."

"Joe?" she said. "How would you feel about getting married again?"

Almost spilling his wine, he set the glass down. "Is this a test?"

She laughed. "I'm being serious."

"Look, forget about that crazy woman."

"She has nothing to do with it. I've been thinking about this for a long time."

He got up and pulled down the bottle of Talisker from the cupboard. Grabbing two glasses, he started toward the living room.

"Coming?" he said.

She looked at the dishes. "What about dinner?"

"Leave it."

She made herself comfortable on the sofa, tucking her legs under her. Like a cat. He handed her a glass and clinked his against it as they faced each other. Sarah hadn't meant to go down this road. Not now. She had wanted to discuss her feelings with Fr. Brian first. But then, it all came out as naturally as a spring rain.

"Okay, now that we're settled," he said. "I seem to remember it was you who called this thing off the last time."

"I know."

"Let's see. There were two things. Okay, I was guilty of the first. I gave you the impression that I was on board with having kids. And I'm really sorry. But the second thing—"

"Joe, I never asked you to convert."

"That's right, you didn't. But I know you, Sarah. You love being Catholic. Remember in college when we were just friends? You told me you saw yourself marrying a Catholic and raising a huge, noisy family."

"Back then, I wished that for you. Of course, I had to mess everything up by falling in love with you."

She took his hand. "Okay, yes, I was upset about the possibility of never having children. And I guess that's what made me decide on the divorce.

"I was angry with you. And the second thing? Honestly, I never expected you to convert."

She set down her glass and laid her head on his shoulder as he stroked her hair.

"But there's something that's never changed," she said. "And it's why, after everything we've been through together, I chose to live in Dos Santos. *I* chose. Because I still love you. And I can't ever imagine being with anyone else."

Defiant, she straightened up.

"Look, I don't care that you're not Catholic. You're a good person. A man who, for better or worse, gets me. How can I say no to that?"

"What about children?"

She looked away. "Maybe that's not my destiny."

"Are you absolutely sure about this? Because I am *not* going through another divorce. I care about you too much."

"I'm sure." She kissed him on the lips. "I'm so sure."

---

Carter sat on her loveseat in her apartment and opened the book Alistair had given her. The prayers had been transliterated from the original Hebrew. It had been years since Carter studied the language, and she felt frustrated and angry at her disconnectedness with her Jewish heritage. Struggling, she made her way through the sacred words, using a dictionary on her phone for reference.

Alistair assured her that, in time, things would become easier. To get her started, he taught her one of the prayers phonetically, and she said it to herself now, all the while keeping her eyes closed and clasping the St. Benedict bracelet.

She repeated it a second time, then a third. Before she was finished, a faint image appeared in her mind. It was an old man with a crooked staff.

Abramo Levy was speaking to her.

---

It was early morning when Sarah heard the knock at the front door. Right on time. When she answered, she found

Carter, wearing a Nike hoodie, sweatpants, and shoes—all black.

"That's some outfit," Sarah said.

"Like it? I bought it last night. Come *on*, let's go."

"You're chipper this morning."

Dressed in her shorts and hoodie, Sarah shut the door and locked it. They began stretching. Then, they headed out to the street, past Carter's MINI Cooper. The neighborhood was quiet as they made their way north.

Carter had decided not to say anything about training with Alistair. She told herself she was doing it to protect her friend; Sarah didn't need to know.

"You feeling better now?" Carter said.

"Outstanding."

Sarah was bursting to tell her friend about her conversation with Joe at dinner. But they had agreed not to say anything until Sarah had talked it over with her priest.

"So, Alistair called me last night," Carter said.

"Really? I think that guy has a thing for you."

"No way. He wants us to come to the house tonight. Said there's something important we need to discuss."

"I remember the good ol' days when *I* used to get the bat signal."

"Don't be jealous."

"I'm not. It's just that, ever since Alistair arrived… Forget it. I'm thinking about Harlan, that's all."

"Me, too. Hey, let's take a right up here," Carter said, accelerating. "I can't believe I'm not winded yet. I—"

When she realized she was alone, Carter stopped and, her hands on her waist, turned around.

Sarah was standing in front of a run-down Craftsman house. Weeds covered the lawn. The paint was peeling. The white picket fence surrounding the front of the property was falling down in places, and several of the ball post caps were missing.

"What's going on?" Carter said.

She followed her friend's gaze. A severe-looking woman with straw-like hair stood on the porch, a broom in her hand. She wore a large wooden cross. The way she watched the two of them unnerved the girl.

"Do you know that woman?"

Sarah started toward the house. As she got closer to the gate, the old woman retreated inside and shut the door. Sarah rejoined her friend on the sidewalk, reading the name on the mailbox. The lettering was worn and weathered. PRUITT. And there was something else.

Next door, a low chain-link fence surrounded the yard that fronted the modest Craftsman house. Unlike their neighbor's property, the lawn and shrubs were well tended. Two cats watched Sarah from the porch. But it was the vehicle parked in the gravel driveway.

It was a 1966 Buick Skylark GS. The beige paint was dull, and one of the taillights was broken. The car belonged to an elderly couple Sarah had seen off and on since she had moved to Dos Santos. She recognized the faded "Don't Worry Be Happy" bumper sticker with the yellow smiley face.

The last time she had spotted the vehicle, she thought she saw a desperate child staring out at her through the rear window. As she and Carter jogged past, Sarah took note of the mailbox. THE WALTONS. *Oh, come on.*

"You're acting a little weird," Carter said.

"Who, me?"

Picking up the pace, the women rounded a corner and found themselves heading north again. Soon, they would reach San Marcos Pass Road.

"Hey, isn't this the way to my house?" Carter said.

"Yep. Thought we'd get in an extra couple of miles."

"So, are you going to tell me what happened back there? Who was that woman?"

Over the next quarter-mile, Sarah told Carter what happened near her house and what the woman had said to Joe.

"Don't pay any attention to her," Carter said. "It sounds like she's a nutcase."

"I don't know. There's something about her."

"And the neighbors?"

"It's probably nothing," Sarah said, not believing her own words.

Lou strode toward the autopsy room, where he found the assistant Annie waiting for him. Without speaking, she used her badge to unlock the door and let him through. He continued toward one of the autopsy tables, where he found Dr. Franklin Chestnut, the Santa Barbara Sheriff-Coroner, and Tiffany Gersh.

The body of the young man was covered with a blue disposable sheet up to the abdomen. The body block underneath the corpse made the chest stick out as if the teenage boy were trying to impress a girl. Which might have worked except for the Y-incision glistening under the lights.

"Hey, guys," Lou said. Then, to Franklin, "Fancy sheets now?"

"Thought I'd class up the place."

The ME handed over the folder he was holding. Lou flipped it open and began reading the report. Waiting for him to finish, Frank and Tiffany observed the police chief. Examining one of the autopsy photos, Lou looked up. He came around the table and leaned in close to the victim's upper left arm, where he noticed a dark red puncture wound.

"They injected him with something?" he said.

The ME nodded. "Succinylcholine chloride. It acts as a neuromuscular blocking agent. Hospitals use it for things like tracheal intubation in surgery."

"So the patient can't move around."

"Exactly. Whoever did this administered the drug first, then went to work."

Lou glanced at the report again. "Cause of death was cardiopulmonary arrest from massive bleeding." He looked at his colleagues gravely. "And while they were cutting him, he was conscious the whole time."

"Conscious and immobile," Tiffany said. "He couldn't even scream. And there's something else."

She crossed the room and retrieved a clear plastic evidence bag, which she handed to Lou. The cop examined the contents closely. It appeared to be soil with small, smooth pebbles and bits of vegetation mixed in. Nodding, he looked at Tiffany, a smile breaking across his face.

"You two trying to play Stump the Police Chief again? You got this off the victim's shoes, right?"

"Uh-huh…" she said.

Grinning, the ME nudged her with his elbow. She frowned and pushed him away.

"And now," Lou said, "you're going to tell me it doesn't match the dirt where the body was found."

Chuckling, Franklin shook his head. "He's still got it. Pay up, Gersh."

Lou laughed. "Tiffany, when are you going to learn never to bet against me?"

"Give me another twenty years, Lucky Baldwin," she said, handing the ME a twenty.

"If you can afford to live that long." Lou held up the bag. "So, tell me about this."

Tiffany was serious now. "That soil is characteristic of a freshwater biome. It's what is known as riparian."

"Meaning…?"

"Soil that is adjacent to rivers and streams. Our team found traces of silt and clay. Not only that. We found microfauna that's also characteristic of riparian soil."

"Lou, they compared the soil to that found under the victim," Franklin said. "Vastly different."

The police chief handed over the evidence bag and began pacing. He stopped and looked at the body.

"The victim wasn't from around here. Could he have been brought in?"

The ME nodded. "Quite possibly. And whoever escorted him into town traveled near a stream."

"But why not just drive?" Tiffany said to Lou.

"I guess they wanted to avoid detection."

Lou's phone vibrated in his pocket. He removed it and, when he saw the number, answered the call.

"Hey, Mary. Tonight?" He glanced at his colleagues. "Uh-huh. Okay, I'll be there. Thanks."

He put away the phone and grabbed the file. "Seems I'm needed at Harlan Covington's house."

"I heard he isn't doing so well," Franklin said.

"No. Do you remember that file you showed me last year? The guy they found in the forest with his eyes pecked out?"

"The John Doe from 1970?"

"What's he got to do with it?" Tiffany said.

"His name is Leon Vogel. Tiffany, I need you to do me a favor. I'm going to try to find his shoes from the evidence lockup.

"It's a longshot, but I'm betting they're somewhere in

storage. I want you to do a soil comparison, the same as you did for this victim."

"What do you expect to find?"

"I don't know, it's just a hunch. Can you help me out?"

"Sure." Then, to the ME, "Maybe I can win back that twenty."

"Oh, and Frank," Lou said. "Keep the body on ice. I want—"

"Sarah Greene to work her mojo on it?"

"Exactly."

"I don't get it," Tiffany said. "Who's Sarah Greene?"

"Someone who might be able to tell us where that kid came from. She, uh… She senses things."

*"A psychic?"*

Lou leveled his gaze at them, his expression deadly serious. "A friggin' godsend."

---

Gillian met Tim Whatley at the gate. Her SUV was acting up, and she had to park down below about a half mile. By the time they reached the top of the rise where the Dos Santos mansion stood, she was winded and dearly wished they'd taken Yoshi's Toyota Forerunner.

Yoshi Kuroda, the annoying intern who had accompanied her, put away the joint he was about to light when he saw the cop.

"Officer Whatley?" she said, putting out her hand. "Good to see you again."

She wasn't sure, but the police officer's face looked drawn—like he hadn't been sleeping. She knew the feeling. Ever since coming back to this town, Gillian felt tired and irritable. Like a battery with all the juice sucked out. Though she didn't remember her dreams, she found herself awakening each morning with a niggling sense of dread. That's what this guy looked like now—dread in the flesh.

"I have a key for you," he said.

He dug it out of his pocket and handed it to her, side-eyeing the intern.

"I guess you should keep it until you've finished shooting. You can return it to the police station after."

"Thanks. So, what do you know about this place?" She was merely making conversation and didn't expect him to answer.

Looking past the gate, he took in the crumbling façade of the sprawling two-story Spanish-style house. Many of the tiles were broken, not to mention some of the windows. He recalled that before the city erected the fence, kids used to throw rocks, seeing if they could break every piece of glass on the property.

A voice whispered something to Tim, just behind his left ear. He turned sharply and stared at Yoshi, his eyes accusing. The kid wore an unbuttoned plaid shirt. He had on a faded red T-shirt underneath featuring some old Japanese punk band Tim had never heard of. And he smelled like weed.

"What did you say to me?"

Yoshi stood there, confused. "Nothing."

"I'm going to check out the grounds."

Tim started down the hill, following the remains of the crumbling driveway covered in pine needles. As he moved out of sight, he swatted at something invisible circling his head. Yoshi brought out the hotstick and lit it. Took a deep drag, then let it out slowly.

"There's something wrong with that guy," he said.

Gillian inserted the key into the padlock. "Put that thing out. You could start a fire up here."

When Sarah entered the autopsy room, Lou and Franklin greeted her. She still wasn't sure she should have come. The last thing she needed was another episode like what happened in the mausoleum.

"Sarah, thanks so much," Lou said. "Normally, I wouldn't have bothered you with this. But—"

"It's okay. Hi, Frank."

"Always good to see you, Sarah."

After shaking hands, Sarah approached the body. Lou and the ME made room as she moved in to touch it. The odor hit her at once, and she had to concentrate to keep from getting sick. She remembered what Frank had said on another occasion, that it took a few minutes to get used to the smell.

Closing her eyes, Sarah breathed normally and waited. Soon, her muscles relaxed. No nausea. Opening her eyes, she pressed her St. Michael medal, said a silent "Glory Be," and reached out her hand to touch the cold, pale flesh.

The inside of the tunnel was dark and smelled of earth and vegetation. Sarah felt as if she were in the gullet of some huge, terrible monster. It took a minute for her eyes to become accustomed to the darkness.

Several figures approached. Though she couldn't see their faces, she knew they were men.

Their conversation was muted. They came closer. Sarah was sure that one of them was the dead boy. Had he been abducted? No, his hands weren't bound. And no one carried a weapon.

"When do I get my money?" the boy said to an older

man behind him.

"Told ya. Soon as we're done with ya."

The man speaking had a horrible countenance—intense and filled with vileness.

Sarah pressed herself against the moist wall as they made their way past. The boy stopped and looked at her.

"James Stark," he said. "Tell my mother."

"Did you see anything?" Lou said.

Sarah glanced around the autopsy room and realized she was safe. Frank handed her an antiseptic wipe for her hands.

"His name is James Stark," she said. "I don't know where he's from." She looked from one to the other. "He begged me to let his mother know."

Lou wrote down the name. "I'll take care of it."

"Listen, I need to go now. These visions are exhausting."

"Can't even imagine," the ME said. "Will you be okay?"

"I just need some fresh air."

"I'll walk you out," Lou said. Then, to the ME, "Frank, I'll let you know what I find out. Maybe you can locate the dental records."

"Looking forward to that. Thanks, Lou."

When they were outside, Sarah sighed with relief. Though the sky was overcast, the cool air revitalized her. Lou touched her arm.

"Sarah, have you got a minute? There's something I need to ask. It's not related to the case."

"Sure. What is it?"

"Not here. Can we meet for coffee tomorrow? It's important."

## Eleven

It rained steadily as Sarah drove through the wealthy neighborhood toward Harlan Covington's house. Carter sat next to her, reading something on her phone. They had started out as they often did, cheerful and talkative. But now, a gloom hung over them like a sheet fashioned from dirty ice. Sarah thought again of that odd Pruitt woman in the run-down house. She was sure she'd never met her and wondered why the stranger hated Sarah so much.

"It's right there," Carter said, pointing.

"Wow, how could I miss it? It's not like I haven't been here before."

"You're just nervous."

"You're right. You?"

"Same."

Sarah passed through the gates and continued up the long lighted driveway. "Let's keep a positive attitude. Maybe there's been some progress."

"Sarah, have you noticed that every time we get one answer, it leads to more questions? More mysteries?"

"It's almost as if we're in this giant maze. And each time we think we've found the way out, we hit another dead end."

"And usually there's an angry ghost waiting for us."

Sarah parked next to Lou's police SUV. The women ran to the door and out of the rain. Sarah rang the bell. A moment later, Elsa answered.

"Hi, Elsa," Sarah said. "Are we late?"

"No. But everyone else is here."

Sarah and Carter removed their jackets and handed them off. Everyone was in the living room—except Harlan. Sarah took in the room. The huge monitor the lawyer had used previously in the library stood at one end.

Without asking, Mary handed Sarah and Carter each a glass of wine.

"Thanks, Mary," Sarah said. "If I didn't know better, I'd say we were having a party. How's Harlan?"

"He'll be down later."

Carter giggled as she nudged her friend. "Check out Lou. Does he look nervous or what?"

The police chief stood with Charlie and Alistair. He had on dress slacks and a new sport jacket. Sarah expected to see the price tag hanging from it. Though he wore no tie, he kept tugging at his collar as if he were being strangled.

"Poor Lou," Carter said. "I wonder if he wishes he were back in Santa Barbara."

But Sarah wasn't thinking about that. She recalled the conversation they'd had outside the Sheriff-Coroner's offices. What was so important that Lou couldn't come out and say it? Could it be about Rachel and him?

When the Englishman saw the women, he came over to greet them.

"Hi, Alistair," Sarah said.

"Hello, Sarah. Everything okay at the house?"

"Everything's normal. Thank you again."

He smiled broadly at Carter. "Nice to see *you* again." Then, to Sarah, "Excuse us a minute."

Putting an arm around the girl's shoulder, he guided her to one of the floral sofas as she looked back apologetically at her friend.

"Is this guy for real?" Sarah said sotto voce as Charlie walked up to her.

"And how are you? I understand you had a little trouble at the cemetery."

"That sounds like a line from a movie. And I suppose I should say, 'Nothing I can't handle.'"

He clinked glasses with her. "Well, I'm glad you're here."

"I see you guys finally decided to include our dear police chief."

"Way overdue, if you ask me. But you know Harlan."

"Ladies and gentlemen," Mary said above the noise. "Let's make our way into the dining room."

Some of the others filed past while Carter and Alistair remained seated. The Englishman did all the talking. She nodded repeatedly, as if listening to a set of instructions. He said something, and they got up. Alistair walked ahead, joining the others.

Sarah touched her friend's arm. "You okay?"

"Fine. Why do you ask?"

―――

Dinner was unlike anything Sarah had experienced at Harlan's house before. Instead of the carefully prepared menu of organic ingredients that excluded red meat and pork, they enjoyed what she could only describe as comfort food. Ribeye steak, mashed potatoes, macaroni and cheese, and vegetables. And for dessert, apple pie with vanilla bean ice cream. Harlan had not joined them, and Sarah worried he might be getting worse.

When they had finished, everyone left the table to return to the living room. Sarah excused herself. Though she was aware the guest bathroom was downstairs, she trotted up the stairs.

She made her way down the unfamiliar hallway, telling herself she shouldn't be up here. But she desperately needed to see Harlan, if only to assure herself that he was alive.

After trying several doors, she arrived at a room at the end with double doors. Certain this was the master bedroom, she knocked softly. When no one answered, she turned the knob and pushed the door open, just enough to see inside.

There was nothing unusual, other than a table filled with prescription medications and medical equipment. But it was the cloying odor in the room that reminded her of her mother's last days when she lay dying in a hospice room. It was the smell of death.

Sarah entered quietly and made her way to the king bed, where she found Harlan dozing. Though his breathing was labored, his chest hardly moved. She stood next to him and laid her hand on his.

He opened his eyes, and almost immediately, he began coughing. Sarah looked around the room and saw the water pitcher. She poured him a glass. He was already sitting up when she handed it to him.

"Thanks," he said. Then, smiling, "How did you make it past the guards?"

His voice was weak. But in his eyes, she saw that his sharp, crystal-clear mind was intact.

"I'm worried about you," she said. "Mary said you'd be joining us."

"I had planned to. But I don't think I have the strength."

She found a chair and set it next to the bed. Taking a seat, she squeezed his hand.

"Harlan, I'm just going to ask. Because, well. Because it's driving me crazy. Why is Alistair here?"

"I think you know why."

"Because you're dying?"

Though she had thought it often, she'd never said the words aloud. And when she did, the tears sprang from her eyes. Now it was his turn to provide comfort, and he patted her hand.

"Everyone dies, Sarah. I had hoped to defeat the evil in Dos Santos once and for all. I'll tell you something about Guardians. All of us have the gift, but to varying degrees.

"Since the beginning, there have been great ones and those, like me, who serve but do not excel."

"I've seen the things you've done," she said.

"It's no longer enough. The Darkness is too much for me."

"Why?"

He hesitated. "I suppose it's because my faith isn't strong enough."

"And Alistair?"

The old man took a sip of water. "His faith is absolute. It's why he was able to rescue Ana Robles. I believe he has the power to stop this evil."

"Harlan, there is one other thing. It's about Carter. Why is Alistair so interested in her?"

"You must know that she has an extraordinary ability. Something she is only now realizing."

"But why him?"

The door opened. When Sarah turned around, she found someone standing in the doorway. She was in shadow, backlit by the light from the hallway.

"Sarah? We've been waiting for you." It was Mary.

"Coming," Sarah said. Then, to Harlan, "I'm praying for you."

She kissed the attorney on the forehead. Before she could leave, he took hold of her hand.

"Sarah, don't stand in Carter's way."

"I'm sorry, I don't—"

"You must let her go."

She pulled her hand away and stared at him, her anger rising. Then, she left the room, not bothering to acknowledge Mary as she brushed past.

---

In the living room, Sarah sat next to Carter. *You must let her go.* After everything that had happened, she'd been confident that she and her friend were a team. And now, Sarah had been deemed some kind of *obstacle*?

Everyone sat in a semicircle around the monitor. Sarah looked over at the Englishman and realized she loathed him. Sensing her, he turned and gave her a wan smile. Mary dimmed the lights as Charlie took the stage, standing next to the monitor.

"I feel like the emcee at a benefit concert," he said. "Look, I think we all know what's at stake. Alistair and I will take you through the evidence we've collected so far. Feel free to ask questions."

Mary started a slide presentation on her laptop. A

black-and-white closeup of a man's face appeared on the large monitor. Sarah studied the face, unnerved by the smallish, dead eyes that reminded her of a predator. There was violence in those eyes, she could feel it coming off the monitor in waves.

"This is Leon Wayne Vogel," the investigator said. "A pedophile and human trafficker from Renton, Washington. He molested young boys for years. Eventually, he gathered a group of other like-minded individuals, and they began abducting children—mostly runaways.

"Sometime during the late sixties, Vogel decided that trafficking these kids wasn't enough. And he started killing them. Unfortunately, his crimes went undetected. In 1970, he arrived in Dos Santos, where soon after, he was found dead in the forest, a victim of a raven attack."

Charlie looked at Sarah and Carter, his expression grim. "It took you two to connect the dots for us. When you went poking around Mt. Rainier, you discovered twenty bodies, all children. We believe they were Vogel's victims."

A chill ran through Sarah as she recalled that awful, freezing night. She and Carter held hands.

"What was he doing in Dos Santos?" Lou said.

Alistair rose and stood on the other side of the monitor. "We think he was planning to move his base of operations."

"You mean, trafficking kids?"

"And killing them, yes."

"But why Dos Santos?" Sarah said.

Carter cleared her throat. "Because he was called."

Alistair gazed at the others. "Precisely."

Lou stared at the women. "I don't understand. What do you mean 'called'?"

Charlie pointed at Mary, and she brought up the next

slide, which showed a line graph with dates, beginning in 1925.

"If you go back to the death of John Dos Santos, you can see a pattern. Those spikes indicate periods of increased activity."

"What kind of activity?" Lou said. "You mean, crime?"

"I'm just an ex-cop from New Hampshire. I think Alistair can explain it better."

The Englishman unbuttoned his suit jacket.

"As I'm sure you know, there's been a massive growth of evil in Dos Santos, beginning with the death of the town's founder." He pointed to the monitor. "Those spikes indicate eruptions where the forces of darkness are particularly strong.

"This for example. 1939. A busload of children from Dos Santos is en route to an Easter egg hunt in Santa Barbara. They never arrived, and no trace of them—or the bus—was ever found.

"1951. Eight children turn up missing whilst on a hike. Once again, no bodies were recovered. 1960. A family reunion ends in tragedy when they become trapped in the barn in which they were celebrating. They burned to death in a fire whose cause was never explained."

"There was one survivor," Charlie said, "A thirteen-year-old girl. She suffered from third-degree burns over most of her body. She lived just long enough to tell the police what she saw."

He referred to his notes. "'There was a man standing near the locked doors. He had black hair that was combed back and bad eyes.'"

"I saw him in the mausoleum," Sarah said, blanching.

Lou scoffed. "Okay, you guys are talking Harry Potter now. Next, you'll be telling me Voldemort exists."

"This is no joke, Chief," Alistair said. "Ask Sarah. The Darkness is real."

Sarah turned to Lou. "Didn't Tim tell you the things he saw at the women's shelter that night? And the fact that you thought you had Laurel Diamanté in custody? When in fact, she was never really there?"

"Yeah, but…"

Carter groaned. "Lou, can't you see? We're under attack. And it's not something you can shoot bullets at."

Sarah pointed at the monitor. "Alistair, what about those later events?"

"Ah yes. 1970. Leon Wayne Vogel arrives in Dos Santos. Chief, if you check your police records, I think you'll find four children went missing within weeks of his arrival.

"After Vogel's death, Dos Santos enjoys a period of relative calm for twenty years. Then in 1990, things start happening again."

"Peter Moody," Sarah said.

"Yes. Harlan was well acquainted with the family, as you know. 1990 was the year the boy murdered his parents and his cousin."

"So Laurel Diamanté was a part of this?" Carter said.

"Laurel was also called. And she brought Ana Robles, a possessed girl, to the women's shelter."

Sarah stood. "But to what end? I still don't see where this is going."

"At first, we couldn't work out why," Alistair said. "But Harlan and I know now. It's, without a doubt, John Dos Santos."

"But what does he want?"

The Englishman looked at each of them gravely. The silence was almost unbearable.

"To destroy the town," he said.

Sarah sat in the library next to the fire. Carter was slumped in the other Chesterfield chair, her head resting on her arm. Alistair leaned against the desk. The mood was somber, and no one felt like talking. Setting aside her anger toward the Englishman, Sarah decided to focus on getting answers to the questions she still had.

"But how can he destroy a whole town?" she said.

Alistair poured himself a whiskey neat. He offered the bottle, but there were no takers. He drained the crystal glass and poured another. Sarah was confused. Weren't Guardians supposed to abstain from alcohol? Come to think of it, he'd also enjoyed wine with dinner.

"In answer to your question," he said, "John Dos Santos is already doing it. He's been at it since his death. But he requires others, which is why people like Leon Vogel, Peter Moody, and Laurel Diamanté were essential to his plan."

"And all those demoniacs we keep seeing?" Carter said.

"They come from far and wide, drawn to the town like hounds to the fox."

"What do you intend to do?" Sarah said to the Englishman.

"Harlan must've shared with you that there are certain rituals we perform."

"But what do you intend to *do*? I'm sorry, but are rituals enough? When I visited the mausoleum that last time, I felt the evil. It brought on a seizure, something I've never had in my life."

"That's because this is not only about the town."

Sarah bowed her head. "Peter Moody warned me, The Darkness *is* after me."

"I'm afraid that's true."

"Harlan said you have the power to defeat this thing. Was he wrong? And what about that film crew? They're still planning to shoot at the house."

"Then, we'll have to be there, too."

Carter's eyes went wide. "What?"

He drank the last of the whiskey and set the glass aside. "The three of us. We have to work together."

"Okay, I guess I can go with you. But not Sarah. That *thing* put her in the hospital."

Alistair took a seat on the sofa opposite them.

"Carter, can't you see? It's why Peter Moody made such a strong connection with her." Then, to Sarah, "And why you had that dream."

Alistair waited patiently as Sarah told her friend about the soldier in the dugout. When she had finished, Carter looked at the Englishman.

"You see?" he said. "Sarah *is* at the center."

"No—"

"You know what I'm saying is true."

Carter's eyes glistened. "But she could *die*."

"Possibly."

Sarah wrung her hands. All she could think of now was Joe and her family. Was she really ready to give up her life for this? And if she didn't, how many more would perish?

"What happens if I refuse?" she said to Alistair.

"Sarah, this evil won't stop pursuing you. You saw how easily it got into your home. Next time, it could harm you and those you love. Yes, you can refuse. But The Darkness isn't done with you."

"Carter, I…"

"Sarah, *no*. You need to leave Dos Santos."

"That won't stop it," Alistair said.

"Shut up—just shut up." Carter sprang to her feet and

jammed a finger in his face. "Either you leave Sarah out of this, or I don't help you."

"Carter, be reasonable."

"I *am* being reasonable. I'm protecting my friend."

For a long time, Alistair stared into the fire. Then, he got to his feet.

"Sorry. It's just that I'm not used to people disobeying."

"And by 'people,' you mean women."

He laughed weakly. "Okay." Then, to Sarah, "Can you at least help with our research?"

"Of course."

He picked up a book from the desk and showed it to her.

"The housekeeper's journal," Sarah said.

He addressed the others. "It belonged to a woman who worked for John Dos Santos, a childhood friend of his."

"Where did you get it?"

"Harlan acquired it some time ago. Apparently, it was part of a wealthy doctor's private collection."

"Did something happen to the housekeeper?"

"Not that I'm aware of. I want you to study—" He caught himself. "Sorry, old habits. *Please* let me know if you find anything interesting."

As soon as Sarah took it from him, she fell into a swoon.


Sarah stood in the shadows in a well-appointed dining room at night. In another room, people carried on multiple conversations. Some were laughing.

Following their voices, she found the parlor. Seven heavyset men sat in a circle in Spanish Revival chairs with carved turnings. Wearing double-breasted wool suits in grays and blues, they held cigars and glasses of Canadian whiskey.

In the center, a frightened girl who couldn't have been more than fourteen stood there, wearing nothing but a white bandeau and knickers. A blue silk party dress lay at her feet.

One of the men addressed the others. "What do you say, gents? I'm starving."

The others grunted their approval. They got up and unbuttoned their jackets.

A woman in her forties hurried into the room. She wore a black beaded flapper gown and a silver filigree comb in her hair. Sarah recognized her as the disagreeable woman from her dream.

"Pay no attention to them, dear," the woman said.

The men glared at her as she picked up the blue dress. Taking hold of the girl's hand, the woman walked her out. Sarah followed them. One of the men had come after them, barely able to control his indignation.

"How dare you," he said.

Unafraid, the woman stared him down. "You know very well he wants her for himself."

The woman hurried her charge upstairs.

"Please," the girl said. "I don't want to."

"Shush. You'll do as you're told."

Sarah placed her hand on the banister to follow when another woman came down in tears. She was in her late twenties. A pretty Latina, with long chestnut hair and large brown eyes. She wore a modest maid uniform with a wide lace collar and lace cuffs.

As she brushed past the other two, the disagreeable woman said, "You know better than to come up here."

Someone put on jazz music in the parlor. The men became boisterous, their voices louder.

"Dolores, we need more ice! Where is that miserable wetback?"

"Coming," she said, wiping her eyes.

After she had gone, Sarah looked at the floor. A wooden spool of scarlet thread lay at her feet.

Someone touched Sarah's hand. It was Carter, looking at her with concern.

"What did you see?" the girl said.

"I can't talk about it right now." Then, to Alistair, "I'd like to go home."

"Of course." He slipped the journal into her purse.

"Please thank Mary for dinner."

Outside, the rain had stopped. Sarah got out her keys and looked at her friend.

"Really wish you knew how to use a stick."

"Sorry," Carter said. "Are you okay to drive?"

"I think so. Good thing the rain stopped."

Sarah passed through the gates and made her turn. That's when she saw them. This time, there were around a dozen. Like all the other demoniacs she had seen, they were disheveled and unwholesome looking.

"Why are they here?" Carter said.

"Harlan is dying." Sarah hit the gas.

"Wait. Pull over up there."

Sarah drove past the demoniacs and parked under a streetlamp. "What are you going to do?"

Carter looked at her bracelet. "Maybe I can get rid of them."

She opened her door. Sarah grabbed her arm. "Are you sure you want to do this?"

Carter looked over the roof of the car at the seedy

group. One of them turned to face her. Her pulse rising, she closed her door.

"I can't do it," she said. "Let's get out of here."

As they drove off, Carter took out her phone and dialed. "Hey, it's me. I think you need to see what's waiting outside the gate."

"Alistair?" Sarah said when Carter had disconnected.

"I'm sure he can deal with it."

# Twelve

Sarah and Carter sat in the Galaxie in front of Carter's apartment. The windshield had started to fog up, making the interior claustrophobic. In her head, Sarah replayed the conversation in the library. *The Darkness isn't done with you.* Why her? What had she ever done to bring about this fate?

"What did you see?" Carter said.

"Carter, please, I—"

"I don't want you to carry this burden alone."

When Sarah saw the sincerity in her friend's eyes, she softened. She held her St. Michael medal between her fingers.

"I felt so sick after. There was this group of men. And a young girl. They were going to…"

Carter shuddered as the memory of her rape came back stronger than ever. On the way from Harlan's house, she had decided to ask Sarah to let her see the journal. But now, after hearing about the child, Carter was worried about what the resulting visions might do to her.

"A woman wearing a dress that was way too young for

her showed up," Sarah said. "She took the girl before those men could do anything."

"Who was she?"

"The woman? I don't know, but I've dreamt about her."

Sarah watched the rivulets moving down the glass, her anger building. Carter touched her arm.

"There was another woman wearing a maid uniform," Sarah said. "I think she may have been the housekeeper."

"That means she wrote the journal. Do you know her name?"

Sarah saw the disagreeable woman's face again. *You know better than to come up here.*

"No."

"Was John Dos Santos there?" Carter said.

"I didn't see him. But I'm pretty sure that bitch was delivering the girl to him." She squeezed Carter's hand. "I'm sorry."

"You have a right to be upset."

"Tomorrow, I'll read the journal and hope I don't have any more visions."

"I know I'm gonna regret this," Carter said.

She stroked her St. Benedict bracelet, then grabbed the book from Sarah's purse.


Carter stood alone in a void, a place she was well acquainted with. Holding out her right arm, she felt her way forward.

Shadows with sharp angles sailed overhead like soaring birds. Far off, a tearing noise broke the silence.

"Hello?"

The sound stopped. Carter's breathing quickened. She wished she hadn't taken the journal.

Gathering her nerve, she continued forward into a faint glow that revealed a bed. A bloody maid uniform lay on top, the fabric in shreds.

The pool of light expanded, revealing a woman with long chestnut hair, wearing a coral chemise and holding a pair of sewing scissors.

Like a movie reel running in reverse, the woman dressed herself in the bloody uniform, which was no longer torn.

In an instant, the ghost was next to Carter, her face and hands covered in blood.

Afraid, Carter showed her the St. Benedict bracelet. Shrinking away, the woman let out a deafening wail.

Then, the ghost dissipated into gray smoke and was gone.

"Carter? *Carter.*"

The girl looked around and realized where she was. As Sarah's hand moved toward her, Carter flinched. For a time, she sat there, unable to respond. She looked down. The journal was no longer on her lap.

"I put it away," Sarah said. "Had to use my scarf. Want to talk about it?"

"I saw her—the housekeeper."

"Did you speak to her?"

"No. I was too scared."

"What did she look like?" Sarah said.

"Long brown hair. She had on a uniform. I couldn't tell anything else about her because of the blood."

*"Blood?"*

"Sarah, she was covered in it."

"What in the world are we dealing with? Shit, it's eleven-thirty. Joe's going to think I died."

Carter grabbed her purse and got out of the car. "I need sleep. Can we get together tomorrow? You know, to talk? I feel like we need to stay close now."

"Sounds good. I have to look at a new property with Joe first thing in the morning, so I won't be able to join you for a run. Lunch?"

"Done. See you."

"Night, Carter."

Before her friend closed the car door, Sarah extended her arms toward her. The girl came back inside, and they hugged.

"Good night, Sarah."

Driving home, Sarah thought again about the vision and the housekeeper coming down the stairs. And that other awful woman. To take her mind off things, she switched on the radio. Chet Baker played the haunting "Stella by Starlight."

"Perfect," she said. "More ghosts."

---

Gary slept comfortably in a ball on Sarah's side. She moved him to the foot of the bed and slid under the covers. Usually, Joe would wake whenever she came to bed. But he was out. Leaning over, she kissed him on the ear. He moaned softly.

She was about to close her eyes when the temperature in the room plummeted. Something on the opposite wall twinkled.

Alyssa, Sarah's ghost friend, appeared, dressed as she always was—in the white dress and gold crucifix she'd been buried in. Sarah looked over at Joe. Sound asleep.

"Alyssa, thank God," Sarah said. "Am I going to die?"

The apparition glitched, then came back more intense. "You know I can't answer that."

"What does John Dos Santos want of me?"

"He's afraid of you."

"Of *me*? But it's Carter who has the power."

"Carter has a great capacity to vanquish—more than she realizes. But Sarah, you have the power to *love*. And that is what he hates more than anything."

"I don't understand."

"You were called here, to this place."

"What about Carter? Was she called, too?"

"Yes."

"So, we're destined to fight this thing together?" Alyssa glitched again. "No, please. Don't go."

"Faith is your greatest weapon, Sarah. Never forget. Find the slender thread."

Light streamed from the window as Sarah opened her eyes. Purring, Gary kneaded his paws next to her. The bathroom door opened, and Joe stepped out in his boxer shorts, his skin glistening.

"Morning," he said. "I didn't even hear you come in last night."

"What time is it?" She ran her fingers through her hair, then rubbed her temples.

"A little after six. You'd better get up. I want you to get a look at the house before Manny and the guys get there. How's your head?"

Yawning, she probed her face and ears with both hands. "Still attached. What time are they coming?"

"Eight."

She threw back the covers, making the cat scamper off. "I'll jump in the shower now."

He leaned in and kissed her. "Want some company?"

"You just showered."

"I missed a spot."

She patted his clean-shaven face. "Tonight, okay?"

She kissed his lips. Without saying anything, he continued dressing as she went into the bathroom and closed the door.

---

Sarah blew Joe a kiss from the front door as he drove off in his truck. She turned to go back inside. Something stuck out from under the mat. It was a plain envelope. She picked it up, noticing that it was addressed to her.

On the street, the woman with the straw-like hair was stealing away. Sarah opened the letter. Inside was a single piece of lined paper torn from a spiral notebook. There were only two words printed in heavy, dark pencil.

SAVE US.

Angry, Sarah stomped into the house. "That's it, bitch. You're messing with the wrong psychic."

Grabbing her purse, she headed to the door leading to the garage when she kicked something. It was the journal.

"Alyssa, if you're trying to tell me something…"

She was about to reach for it when she stopped and grabbed a tea towel. Careful not to touch it, she picked up the book and laid it on the counter. For a time, she stood staring at it. It was seven-twenty. She got out her phone and texted Joe that something had come up. She would see the property later. He replied with a sad-face emoji.

Sarah retrieved a pair of driving gloves from her car. When she returned to the kitchen, she found her cat drinking water. She put on the gloves and settled on one of the barstools as Gary rubbed himself against one of the legs. Tentatively, she reached for the journal. Sensing nothing, she flipped it open.

The handwriting was small and neat, written in elegant cursive. The pages had yellowed, and the once-black ink had faded to a dark brown. The entries began in the summer of 1925.

Sarah turned to the last page and saw that it was blank. Working her way back, she located the last entry, dated September 13. She returned to the beginning, where at the top of the page the author had inscribed JUNE 1ST MONDAY.

I am keeping this journal at the recommendation of my dear friend Eliza Warrington. She has assured me that if I unburden myself on these pages, the dreams will cease. And so, with God's help and mercy, I am doing what I must to bring peace to my daughter and myself.

My name is Dolores Lopez and I am 28 years old. I have my own room in the house of John Dos Santos, a man I have known since we were children. Only I do not truly know John. That is, he is not the person I remember from our youth.

I accepted the position of housekeeper because my husband, Nesto, died. He was killed in an accident at the Loughead Aircraft Manufacturing Company. The fuselage he was working on suddenly fell, killing him and injuring two other men. They told me it never should have happened.

Not long after taking up this position, the dreams started. In them, I see terrible visions and often wake up with a sick headache. I do not know what these nightmares mean or why they are happening to me. But I do know they are not of this earth.

*Que El Señor me proteja.*

When Sarah entered The Cracked Pot, she found Carter sitting at a back booth, sharing a laugh with one of the servers. Sarah sidestepped a group of people just leaving and slid in opposite her friend.

"Coffee?" the server said to Sarah.

"Sure." Then, to Carter, "Let's order, okay?"

Sarah waited for the server to leave, then reached across the table and took Carter's hand.

"So, I read the journal."

"Aw man. Bad?"

"Really bad. Her name was Dolores Lopez. And she was literally in a living hell. There's something else. I think she may have been psychic."

"No way."

"It was how she described her dreams. *I* could've written those words."

When the food came, Carter took a bite of her sandwich. "Imagine having that ability and living in a place like that."

"Right? After finishing the book, I got a real sense of who Dolores was. She was sweet and good and devoted to her daughter."

"And did John Dos Santos ever harm her?"

"Not according to the journal. I got the sense that, in some twisted way, he may have been trying to protect her."

"What about all that blood I saw?"

"That's what puzzles me," Sarah said. "I do know those awful visions were tearing her apart. Maybe..."

Sarah bit into her sandwich and took a sip of water.

"There's something else that's bothering me," she said. "The journal only covers a short period during the summer of 1925. It stops abruptly on September 13th."

"Maybe she became ill."

"She did suffer from migraines," Sarah said. "Hey, what have you got going on this afternoon?"

"Are you kidding, I'm all yours. What are we doing?"

"Let's just say I could really use a good researcher."

---

Sarah parked in the civic center lot and waited for Carter to pull in next to her. She thought of how often she had been here to see Lou and wondered how he was getting along. When they met for coffee that morning, she had been convinced he wanted to get her blessing to marry Rachel. She was way off.

There was no doubt the man was suffering through a spiritual crisis. No wonder. Nothing that happened recently in Dos Santos made sense when looked at through the lens of the criminal justice system.

He had asked her—begged her, really—to tell him how she'd kept her faith through everything. The answer, she had told him, was always the same. It was the advice the saints had provided over the centuries. There was only one path out of the darkness: prayer.

The public library was located in the same complex as police headquarters and City Hall. Sarah and Carter walked briskly through the courtyard past the large fountain and entered through the main doors.

There weren't many people inside. The last time Sarah had been here was when she'd first arrived in Dos Santos. She wanted to learn something about the town's demographics for her real estate business.

The women headed straight for the research desk, where Sarah found a pretty young woman with long, wavy brown hair looking intently at her computer monitor.

"Excuse me," Sarah said, reading the woman's nametag. "Shannon? Not sure you remember me. Sarah Greene."

"Sure. What can I do for you?"

"We're looking for everything you have on the town's history. We'd also like to look through old newspapers."

"We're specifically interested in the 1920s," Carter said.

She leaned over the counter to get a better look at the brightly colored tattoo on the librarian's forearm.

"Aw man, I've been wanting to get a Sailor Moon tattoo. That looks amazing."

Shannon reddened. "Thanks, um… My cats like it, too."

She got out a pad and paper and made a list, circling the first entry. When she was finished, she tore off the sheet and handed it to Sarah.

"A lot of those papers are archived online now. I would start with Newspapers.com."


Sarah and Carter sat opposite each other at one of the long tables in the middle of the library. While Carter searched old issues of the *Dos Santos Weekly* on her laptop, Sarah pored over a pile of history books.

She was disappointed to see how little had been written about John Dos Santos. There were several short articles listing his birth, military service, tenure as founder and mayor, and his death from heart failure in 1925. But little else.

Frustrated, she looked at her watch. Her sister had texted Sarah, asking where she was. She got out her phone and exchanged a few more texts when Carter stepped away. When she returned, she was carrying a pile of printouts.

"I hope you had better luck than me," Sarah said.

Carter took the seat next to her and laid out several pages, each featuring the editorial page from different weeks in the spring and summer of 1925. Sarah began reading.

All had been penned by Thaddeus Pruitt, owner and editor-in-chief of the *Dos Santos Weekly*. Without exception, each op-ed piece was a stinging indictment of the town's mayor, his administration, and the local police force. Carter had also printed a few rebuttals, written by prominent businessmen, valiantly defending John Dos Santos.

"Donnie and Debbie were right," Carter said. "There *was* a war going on that year."

"No kidding." Sarah pointed to something. "This guy had some balls. Wait a minute. *Pruitt.*"

"You've heard of him?"

"I was just wondering if he has any descendants still living in Dos Santos."

"Like who?"

"You remember that strange woman we saw the other day?"

"The crazy lady in the falling-down house?"

"Yes, her. Can you do a search on Thaddeus Pruitt? I'm looking for his obituary. And whether he had any children."

"I think I know where you're going with this."

Carter began typing on her laptop as Sarah continued paging through her books. It wasn't long before the girl had disappeared, then reappeared, carrying more printouts. She handed one to Sarah.

"I think I found her."

"That was fast," Sarah said while reading. "Bethany Pruitt."

"The great-granddaughter of Thaddeus. She's an only child. *And* she lives in Dos Santos."

"Wow, Carter. You really *are* good."

"Just say it, I'm a nerd. Her mother died when she was little, and she was raised by her father. There isn't much I could find on him, except that he was a street preacher and got arrested a lot for being drunk and disorderly."

Sarah sat back and looked at the pile of books she still hadn't gotten through.

"Well, you did way better than me," she said. "I say we pay Bethany Pruitt a visit. You up for it?"

"Let's do it."

## Thirteen

The women walked up to the door of the dilapidated Craftsman house. Carter eyed the pink cake box Sarah was carrying.

"I still say you went a little overboard," she said.

"You catch more flies with honey."

"Right. Look, the door's open."

Sarah pushed it the rest of the way and found the old woman lying on the floor.

"Oh no."

Handing the box to Carter, she went in. She knelt and felt the woman's cheek, which was warm.

"Come and help me."

Carter set the cake down on a side table and assisted her friend as they got the woman into a sitting position.

"Bethany Pruitt?" Sarah said.

Slowly, the woman opened her eyes and, disoriented, stared at the women with alarm.

"What...?"

"You must've passed out. Can you walk?"

"I think so."

. . .

Bethany sat at the kitchen table with Sarah. Carter poured boiling water into a teapot. She'd already placed the cake on a plate. Looking for a cake knife, she dug through one of the drawers when she saw an old utility knife. The blade was curved, and it had a wooden handle. She kept digging around for something suitable. Then, she set everything on the table.

"Do you want to see a doctor?" Sarah said.

"Doctors are of no use to me. I get these spells sometimes. What are you doing in my house?"

"We need to talk to you."

The old woman eyed them warily. "What about?"

"You're the great-granddaughter of Thaddeus Pruitt, is that right?"

The old woman lowered her head. "Yes."

"What do you know about him?"

Carter handed Bethany a cup of tea.

"Thank you. Just stories, mostly. After Thaddeus died, his assistant took over. Then later, the paper shut down. Someone else bought it eventually."

"I read that Thaddeus Pruitt drowned in the bathtub," Carter said.

Bethany glared at her as if the girl were insane. "That's a lie. He was murdered."

"How do you know?" Sarah said.

"Because my great-grandmother knew the men who did it. When she told the police, they said it was better she forget the whole thing. Otherwise, there might be more trouble.

"She never mentioned it again. But she wrote a letter. After she died, her son—my grandfather—found it as he was packing up the house."

"Do you have the letter?" Sarah said.

"I got a whole box."

An open hat box sat on one of the kitchen chairs. Sarah read the letter written by Bethany's great-grandmother. The words were filled with anguish. She described the outrage her husband felt over the corruption from the mayor on down.

After the thugs hired by Dos Santos had roughed up Thaddeus, his wife begged him to stop attacking the mayor. But he wouldn't listen and continued to publish op-ed pieces. *In a way, he was responsible for his own death*, she had written.

"Were the murderers ever punished?" Sarah said to the old woman.

"No. You see how in the letter his mother warned her son about the police. He decided to return to his Protestant faith. He was baptized and devoted the rest of his life to the Lord."

"Is that why your father became a preacher?" Carter said.

Bethany gripped the edge of the table. "My father was a sick man. He did the best he could, that's all."

"I'm sorry," Sarah said. "Would you mind if we borrowed these letters? We're trying to learn more about the history of this town, and these would really help."

"I don't care."

"Would you like a piece of cake?"

Bethany looked at her warily. Then, a smile broke out on her face.

"It's been a long time," she said.

Sarah looked at Carter, who began cutting the cake

and handing out pieces. She sipped her tea as the old woman tried a bite.

"It's good. Fresh."

"Bethany, this is Carter Wittgenstein."

"I know who she is."

"I need to ask you something," Sarah said, side-eyeing her friend.

"What about?"

"I'm pretty sure we've never met. Yet you seem focused on communicating with me. Why?"

All at once, the old woman's manner changed. She slid her plate aside and drank her tea. Sarah reached over to pat her arm. Bethany shrank back.

"Please understand," Sarah said. "I'm not angry with you. But I need to know. Why did you send me that letter?"

"Letter?"

Sarah opened her purse and dropped the handwritten note on the table.

"Don't you remember?" she said.

"Course I remember. I may be old, but I still have my faculties."

"What is it you're asking me to do?"

Bethany's fingers were swollen and arthritic. Her hands trembled slightly as she took a sip of tea.

"Repent," she said into her cup.

"Why? Did I do something wrong?"

"Besides living in sin?"

Sarah glanced at Carter, who rolled her eyes. "What has my personal life got to do with anything?"

Bethany set down her cup. "That's not why I wrote the note. You opened a door. It was you who brought all this suffering. You must repent!"

The old woman was practically hysterical. This wasn't

working. Sarah remembered what Alyssa had said about love. She pushed the teacup closer to Bethany.

"Don't let your tea get cold," she said.

Bethany's lower lip trembled. She burst into tears, shaking with a grief Sarah had never seen before. She got to her feet and, crouching in front of her, held Bethany in her arms.

"Maybe you should lie down."

"Okay." Bethany sounded like a child.

They helped the old woman into bed. Sarah removed her shoes and covered her with a pink-and-yellow crocheted blanket. She knew she couldn't hate Bethany even if she wanted to. She saw real suffering in her eyes, and it stirred a deep compassion in her. When she looked at Bethany's hands, Sarah noticed the dried blood on the fingertips.

The minute she closed her eyes, the old woman was asleep. Carter left the room to clean up the kitchen while Sarah remained. The well-maintained furniture was old fashioned and dark. On the dresser lay a white lace dresser scarf that had yellowed over the years.

On the wall hung a plain wooden cross. Next to it was a framed needlepoint that looked as if it could have been made by a child. It featured a shepherd, and next to him, a small white lamb. In bright yellow thread were the words THE LORD IS MY SHEPHERD. I SHALL NOT WANT.

On the nightstand sat a worn black bible. Taking it, Sarah grasped the ribbon marker and opened the book to the Second Letter of Paul to the Thessalonians. Ignoring the droplets of dried blood, she read what had been highlighted.

Who shall be punished with everlasting destruction from the presence of the Lord, and from the glory of his power.

Sarah found Carter in the living room, examining a wall of black-and-white photographs.

"What are those?" she said.

"They're mostly of Bethany and her father. Look at this one. She couldn't have been more than five."

In the middle of the photo stood a man wearing a black suit and fedora, his fist in the air. In his other hand, he clutched a Bible. He was frozen in the midst of a fiery speech before a small group of men and women. Dressed all in white and wearing a veil, his daughter stood meekly at his side. Sarah thought of touching one of the frames but didn't think she could handle another vision right now.

"What do you think she meant about opening a door?"

"This may sound crazy," Carter said. "But she might be talking about that conjuring mirror you discovered."

"I guess that makes sense." Sarah looked around the room. "She would've had to read your story, though. Have you seen any newspapers?"

"None. And I'm pretty sure she doesn't own a computer."

"Maybe someone told her," Carter said.

"Okay. But why does she think *you* started all this? We know it's been going on a long time."

"Judging by the way she was raised, she probably sees sin around every corner."

"So, what are we going to do? We can't stay here."

"I think I'll try again another day," Sarah said. "Maybe next time she'll be more receptive."

She walked out the front door, carrying the box of letters, and gazed into the next yard. An old woman was bent over a flower bed, roughly turning the soil with a hoe. Her hair was white, and she wore a faded flowered dress, a sweater, socks, and slide sandals. The Buick Skylark with the faded paint was parked in the driveway.

"What are we looking at?" Carter said.

"Nothing."

As they walked to the street, Carter glanced back at Bethany's unkempt yard.

"Do you think she's dangerous?" she said.

"Bethany?"

Sarah stopped and took a last look at the dilapidated house.

"If anything, she's a danger to herself. Come on. I could really use a drink."

---

Tim Whatley dropped the storage box on the floor and climbed down the ladder. He'd been searching through physical evidence for two hours, and so far, had come up with zip. Like all the others, the box was numbered. But because the contents were so old, no one had bothered to enter the information into the evidence tracking system.

When he removed the lid, he saw them. Worn, dusty men's black boots inside a plastic evidence bag. The chief would be pleased he had found what he was looking for. Taking hold of the bag, he stood. Someone whispered just behind him. When he turned, no one was there. He swung back around and dropped the bag.

A man with small, mean eyes stood before him, glowering. He was dressed poorly. Tim thought he might be a vagrant. But how could he have gotten in? The door was locked.

"What're you doing in here?" the cop said.

When the man opened his mouth, thousands of black flies poured out in an angry swarm. Screaming, Tim fell back, striking his head against the ladder.

Lou reread the autopsy report, thinking again of his conversation with James Stark's mother in Buellton, the home of Pea Soup Andersen's. She hadn't seemed shocked at the news of her son's death. In fact, she had been expecting it for years.

Like Dos Santos, Buellton was a small town, and the boy had hated it. According to Mrs. Stark, James had been running away since he was eleven. A single mother, she was no longer able to manage and reluctantly agreed to place him in foster care. After only three weeks in his latest group home, he was gone. She never saw him again.

The police chief had let Franklin Chestnut know about the victim, so he could order dental records. Eventually, the body would be returned to the boy's mother. The last thing she said on the phone was, *I don't know how I'll pay for a funeral.*

Hearing a knock, Lou looked up and saw Tim standing in the doorway, clutching a plastic bag.

"I found them," he said. He looked shaken.

"Good work. Leave them on the chair."

The chief worried about Tim. Ever since the murders at the women's shelter, the kid had become sullen and withdrawn. Lou thought about placing him on administrative leave, but now was not the time. He needed every able-bodied person on the force, even if they weren't a hundred percent.

"Tim—"

"I'm fine," the cop said.

He walked out, leaving Lou to wonder whether he had

lost another good officer the night those other two were killed.

———

Sarah and Carter found themselves back at Rich, a hipster bar that had opened recently in Dos Santos. As she waited for her drink, Sarah pointed to a wall featuring mostly Great Depression era black-and-white photos.

"Looks like they're branching out," she said.

Carter set down her Guinness and took a look. "The Marx Brothers? Wait, I thought there were only three."

"The fourth guy is Zeppo. He didn't last very long."

The bartender placed a dark-looking drink in a crystal glass in front of Sarah. She tried it.

"What's that thing called again?" Carter said.

"A Negroni. Here, try a sip."

Carter tasted the drink and, making a face, handed it back. "Enjoy."

"So, what do you think? Is Bethany Pruitt connected to what's happening in this town?"

"Hard to say. But she seems to know what's going on."

"I don't know," Sarah said. "I feel like there's something she's not telling us. Did you know she self-harms?"

"Is it bad?"

"She had these puncture wounds on every finger and in the middle of her palms. They look like they were made by a needle."

"Is it possible she's diabetic?"

"I found blood stains in her bible. I'm pretty sure she's punishing herself."

"That poor thing. I wonder if her father had something to do with it."

"Who knows? Look, I'm done sleuthing for today.

What do you say tomorrow we tackle that box of letters? Maybe there's something in there about John Dos Santos."

"Great." Carter raised her glass. "Here's to stopping the evil overlords."

They clinked glasses. Outside, sirens wailed, one after the next. Sarah counted three.

## Fourteen

"This is a surprise," Fr. Brian said as Sarah settled into her chair. What can I do for you?"

She was familiar with the priest's schedule and knew that, one night a week, he liked to work in his office late into the night. Taking a chance, she showed up unannounced.

"Sorry about the pop-in, Father. You've been a hard man to get ahold of."

"Yes, I was at a retreat."

"Something happened at the house a few days ago. I'm hoping you can say Mass there as soon as possible."

"When you say 'something'…"

"Someone hid a cursed object. I got rid of it, though."

"Got rid of it, how?"

"I took it to Harlan. But he wasn't the one who disposed of it."

"I understand he has another houseguest?"

"Alistair Goolsby. He's from the UK and very tall."

"Mm. I might've seen him at Mass. Blond, black suit?"

"That's the guy. Father, whoever did this disguised it as

a cat toy." She looked away. "I saw what was inside. And ever since it got into our house, Joe…"

The priest chuckled. "You said, '*our* house.' I get the feeling you have something else on your mind."

Blushing, she covered her face and shook her head. "I never could fool you."

"Don't forget, I've known you your whole life."

When she looked up, her eyes were glistening. He came around the desk and took her hand.

"I need to stretch my legs."

It was chilly as they followed a floral-scented path behind the magnificent old church. She loved it here. It always gave her a sense of comfort—and safety.

"I really need you to cleanse the house," she said. "Can you come by tomorrow?"

"Sure. How about right after morning Mass?"

"Perfect." Sighing, she stopped and faced the priest.

"And the other thing?" he said.

"Okay, I want you to keep an open mind. Do you promise?"

"Sarah, when have I not—"

"Do you promise?"

"On my grandmother's paisley shawl."

"Your grandmother's been dead for fifty years."

"It was worth a try."

"Joe and I want to get married."

---

Sarah turned into her driveway, anxious to tell Joe the news. An SUV was parked in front of the house. She pulled into the garage and walked into the kitchen, where she found an open bottle of wine on the counter. Two voices drifted in from another room.

"Hello?"

"In here," Joe said.

Sarah found her ex-husband and Gillian Davies on the sofa, each with a glass of wine. She did her best to keep the momentary jealousy out of her voice.

"Gillian? What are you doing here? How did you—?"

Embarrassed, the other woman rose to shake hands. "I'm really sorry. I got your address from the police chief. When I explained why I needed to see you, he said it would be okay."

Joe got to his feet and headed for the kitchen. "I'll get another glass."

Disconcerted, Sarah took Joe's seat. "Did something happen?"

"Sarah, I…" She grabbed her glass and took a swallow of wine.

"Okay. I went out to the Dos Santos mansion today. And you were right. There's something wrong with that place. I could feel it. It was malevolent.

"I've been with Donnie and Debbie from the beginning. And we've gone to all kinds of haunted houses, graveyards, and such. But I've never felt anything like this before."

Joe returned with the wine and a glass, and poured a drink for Sarah.

"Thanks, honey," Sarah said. Then, to Gillian, "Have you ever had these kinds of feelings before? What I mean is—"

"You mean, am I psychic? No, I don't think so. The thing is, *Dubious* is meant as entertainment. Most of the places we visit, we *know* there's nothing there."

Sitting in another chair across from them, Joe looked disappointed; he loved the show.

"If there's one thing Donnie and Debbie are good at,

it's research. Well, that and putting on a good show. We make sure to always go to places where there's lots of urban legends and no credible paranormal activity.

"On camera, they make a big deal of using EMF detectors and spirit boxes. But we already know we're not going to find anything."

Sarah narrowed her eyes. "I knew it. You guys are gaming the system. No wonder those two can make fun of it."

"Exactly. And most of the time, we pull it off. But, like that funeral home I told you about, every once in a while, we stumble onto the real deal. Then, we have to ignore the phenomena and blame it on drafts and tricks of the light."

Sarah took a swallow of wine. "What a way to make a living."

"The show has a lot of fans. I think most of them get that it's not real."

Sarah smirked at Joe. "Yeah, *most.*" Then, to Gillian, "Basically, you guys are the paranormal version of fake wrestling."

"Like I said, it's meant as entertainment."

"So, what happened out there? Did something try to harm you?"

"No. But I saw something. A woman wearing a maid uniform. She was only there for a second. But I definitely saw her."

Wary, Sarah set down her wine. "Can you describe her?"

"She had long, brown hair. And she was covered in blood."

"Did you go there alone?"

The woman scoffed. "I might as well have. I went with our intern Yoshi."

"Did *he* see anything?"

"No. He was probably high."

"Well, what do you want to do? Aren't Donnie and Debbie coming back soon?"

"Right now, they're stuck in Burbank. A lot of the footage we shot at the mausoleum is unusable. And they never did get the sarcophagus open."

Gillian took another sip of her wine. Sarah tried topping up her wine, but she covered the glass with her hand.

"I don't know what to do," Gillian said. "I sure as hell don't want to go back there."

"Well, we've arranged for Carter and that other blond guy you saw to be there when you film."

"What good will that do?"

"Both are used to dealing with the supernatural. Trust me, you'll want them there."

"What about you?"

"I'm bowing out of this one." She smiled at Joe. "I don't want to risk another trip to the hospital."

"Sure, I get it." Gillian got to her feet. "Listen, I'm sorry I showed up unannounced."

"Don't worry about it."

Sarah walked her guest to the front door. They stood on the front porch where a heady perfume filled the air. Closing her eyes, Gillian breathed it in.

"I love jasmine," she said. "It reminds me of my Dad's house."

"Gillian, I want you to call me if you experience anything weird tonight."

"What do you mean?"

"It's hard to explain. But if you hear any strange noises, or you see anything out of the corner of your eye."

"Is that what it's like for you?"

"Pretty much. Anyway, call me, okay?"

"I will." She touched Sarah's hand. "And thanks."

They hugged, and Gillian walked toward her car.

Sarah and Joe sat on the living room sofa, sipping wine. Ben Webster's "My Romance" played in the background. Gary had joined them and was curled up on Sarah's lap, purring loudly. Stroking his head, she debated the best way to bring up her conversation with Fr. Brian.

"Did I tell you?" she said. "I made an appointment to get an alarm system installed." *Smooth, Sarah.*

"Good idea."

"Oh, Fr. Brian is coming tomorrow morning to say Mass here." *Just tell him already!*

"Great. Do you mind if I hang around for that?"

"Are you kidding? I would love it." She took his hand and swung it playfully back and forth. "I also talked to him about us getting married again."

His face went slack. "That was fast."

"Joe, I told you, I'm serious this time. I want us to be a married couple."

"Okay. Look, don't get mad. But I keep wondering if this has anything to do with Bethany Pruitt."

"You know, at first, I thought it might. But no. It's what I want. And I hope—I pray—you want it, too."

He took her face in his hands and kissed her. "What do you think? Come here."

He started on her ears and neck when she wriggled free and struggled to her feet, flush with passion.

"What's wrong?" he said.

"There's something I forgot to mention."

"Uh-oh."

"We're not supposed to have sex again until we're

married. I've already been to Confession and received Communion."

Sighing, he got to his feet. "Okay, I'll move my things into the guest bedroom." He noted her expression. "No good?"

She scrunched her nose. "I'm sorry, but it's just too much of a temptation for me. I'll get scared in the middle of the night. You'll come running. And the next thing you know…"

"So, you want me to move out?" She looked at the cat. "Well, it's a good thing I have a place to stay. I'll leave tonight. Can I still come by in the morning for Mass?"

"Of course," she said.

Her arms open, she went to him and pressed her head against his chest. "I love you."

"I just hope you're not planning a fall wedding. I'm not a monk, you know."

"Fr. Brian promised to work with the archdiocese to fast-track us. We'll be married before you know it."

"Better get moving."

"Joe? Thank you."

"Don't mention it. Lucky for you I don't meet a lot of women in my business. I wonder if that checker over at the Rite Aid is seeing anyone."

"The one with the lazy eye?"

"Beggars can't be choosers."

"Whatever you decide, I don't want to know about it."

Blowing her a kiss, he walked off to pack.

---

Bethany Pruitt stood by the sink, drying the dishes. The whispering had become more frequent. And though she tried ignoring it, the chatter was unbearable. She'd heard those same voices in the past, right after her father died from cirrhosis of the liver.

She was only eighteen when it happened, preparing to go to college. Despite his drinking, he had managed to save a little money—just enough for her to bury him. After the funeral, instead of going to school, Bethany found an entry-level job with Santa Barbara County and remained in Dos Santos, living in the house she was born in.

But now, after all those years, the whispering had started up again around the time Sarah Greene discovered that damned mirror. The voices plagued her as she did housework, went for walks, and slept. There were times when she managed to make out a word or two. *Suffer* and *eternal*. And *legion*.

What were they trying to tell her? Bethany didn't know. But whenever they spoke to her, she became more agitated —afraid that she would lose her last shred of sanity and become like her father at the end of his life.

Ever since she was a little girl, she had heard him preach about a new day when the righteous ruled the earth and the wicked were punished in the eternal fire. He believed that with all his heart and soul.

At the end, just before closing his eyes for the last time, he told her something that would haunt her forever, even as she tried to live a good and pure life the way she had been taught. Three final words.

*I was wrong.*

A smacking sound followed Bethany from the kitchen as she fluffed cushions, turned out lights, and retreated to her bedroom. She slept little these days and knew she would lie in bed for hours in the still of a broken night, listening to the ungodly noises that had decided to visit her after the sun went down.

After brushing her teeth, she opened the plastic bottle

of medication and shook out two tablets. The doctor had prescribed fludrocortisone acetate, explaining that she was suffering from vasovagal syncope, which resulted in occasional fainting spells. In many people, this condition was triggered by the sight of blood. But in Bethany's case, there was no obvious cause.

She climbed under the covers and reached for her bible. Tonight, she would read Psalms. Opening the book, she thought of Sarah Greene. Despite everything, the woman and her friend had shown her kindness. But their actions had changed nothing.

A sacrifice was required—something to drive away the evil before it consumed the town. Sarah would need to make that sacrifice. And soon. Or all would be lost.

Something moved in the corner of the room. That particular place behind the door was always filled with shadows that were alive. Often, they were indistinct and did not present a threat. But now, the old woman was afraid.

She observed the figure of a man lurking there like a wraith. Though she couldn't see him clearly, she knew he had dark, shiny hair, and eyes like live coals that glowed red in the darkness. Thinking she was protected, she began reading Psalm 1 aloud. As she did, something invisible cut her arms.

Ignoring the assault, she went on. But before she could finish, the book was torn from her fingers and flung into the hall, where it struck the wall.

"No!" she said, clutching her cross and saying the words she knew by heart. "'For the Lord knoweth the way of the righteous: but the way of the ungodly shall perish.'"

A whooshing sound preceded a hurricane-like wind that sent everything in the room flying. The force lifted the frail old woman out of bed and pinned her against the wall.

Valiantly, she recited Psalm 2 as the demonic force sliced mercilessly at her arms and legs, splattering blood across the bed. When she wouldn't cease praying, the attack stopped. She fell forward onto the mattress and looked up at the shadows.

She was alone.

---

Sarah stood inside the dugout. The wounded soldier lay motionless on his back on the Army cot. His eyes were open and his skin was like wax.

Filled with an unnameable fear, she ran out and found herself in the tunnel, walking among a group of teenage boys and girls who were silent. She sensed their fear.

She turned to look at one of them—a girl of perhaps thirteen or fourteen. Her eyes and tongue were missing. She realized all of them had been mutilated in one way or another. Just like the animal she'd found at her front door.

Somewhere far off, Sarah heard Bethany's voice, the words ringing in her head. *For the Lord knoweth the way of the righteous: but the way of the ungodly shall perish.*

Sarah sat up straight in bed, her heart pounding. Taking a series of calming breaths, she gazed around her bedroom and felt very alone, now that Joe was no longer in the house.

"Gary?"

She heard a faint thump. In a moment, the cat trotted into the bedroom and leaped onto the bed, purring.

Relieved, she stroked his back and scratched behind his ear, which he loved.

"Guess it's just you and me now."

Dolores Lopez's journal lay on the nightstand next to Sarah. She didn't remember bringing it into her bedroom. Reminding herself, she got a clean washcloth from the bathroom and used it to open the book. She turned to the page dated July 5.

I remained overnight at the house again. John had arranged a picnic and invited local businessmen and their families. Though he had hired extra help, there was so much to do. The hour was late by the time we cleaned everything up. John insisted I stay until morning.

Though he is a strange man, I never feared for my own safety. But it was the others—the boys and girls he and his friends would bring to the house. On the nights I slept there, they arrived after dark and left before morning. Often, I heard them crying. Last night, one of them screamed.

Does God punish those who stand by idly while others suffer? Do they, too, bear the guilt of sin? Please Lord, tell me. What is the right thing to do?

Sarah set aside the book and lay back down. Closing her eyes, she said an "Our Father." She got as far as *Give us this day* when she drifted off, her hand resting on the contented cat.

## Fifteen

After Mass in the living room, Fr. Brian walked through every room of Sarah's house, including the garage, reciting prayers and sprinkling holy water. When he had finished, they returned to the kitchen.

"Can we buy you lunch, Father?" Joe said. He was holding Sarah's hand and felt happier than he had in weeks.

"Thank you, but I have a number of appointments."

Sarah hugged him. "We'll take you to dinner, then. I'll check your schedule with Mrs. Ivy."

"That sounds good. I am so pleased at your decision. And Joe, you have my solemn promise I won't try to convert you."

Joe laughed. "It's Sarah I'm worried about."

"Well, you both seem very happy. I'm looking forward to performing the ceremony. Again."

"We're in it for good this time," Sarah said.

Outside, a UPS truck pulled up to the curb. The driver trotted around to the rear, grabbed something large, and set it on a hand truck. As he headed up the walkway, Sarah let out a squeal.

"It's here!" she said to Joe.

"The painting? I'd completely forgotten about it."

While she signed the paperwork, Joe directed the driver to leave the package in the foyer.

Inside, Sarah stared at the tall box. "I really want to open it."

"Let's wait till we get it to Carter's house."

"Yeah, you're right. Can't wait to see her expression. Do you think she'll love it?"

"Guaranteed. It's from you."

"From *us*."

"So, it's official." He took both her hands. "We're getting married. Does this mean I need to go out and buy another engagement ring?"

"Not necessary. I still have the old one. Somewhere."

"Oh."

He started to walk away when she grabbed his arm. "What 'oh'?"

"Nothing. Hey, we'd better—"

"What did you do?"

"I, um…"

He dug something out of his pocket. It was a black velvet ring box. Her eyes went wide.

"Guess I'll have to take this back," he said.

"Oh my God, Joe. You didn't."

"I did."

"I don't know what to say."

Taking his time, he opened the box. Nestled inside was a one-and-a-half carat emerald cut diamond engagement ring that glinted in the late-morning light.

"Wait," he said, and got down on one knee.

Giggling, she tapped his shoulder. "You don't

need to—"

"Sarah, I just want you to know. I'll always be here for you."

"Joe…"

She held out her left hand and chewed her lip as he slipped on the ring. When he was on his feet again, she kissed him.

"I love you so much," she said.

"I love you, too. Hey, what's Rachel going to say when she finds out you got engaged before her?"

She admired her ring. "Well, I *am* the big sister."

Sarah got a call. It was Carter. She walked into the kitchen and grabbed her phone lying on the counter.

"What's up?" she said. "What? Joe and I will be right over. Later."

"Trouble?"

"Carter's furniture arrived. She's heading over there now to meet the movers."

"Great. We can give her the painting. I'll get a dolly."

"Wait. I have a better idea."

"You're the boss."

She dropped her phone in her purse and followed him to the front door.

"Oh crap," she said.

"Did you forget something?"

She looked at him with a serious expression. "Rachel. I have to tell her before Carter sees the ring."

"I'll start the truck."

Sarah locked the front door and, standing on the porch, dialed her sister.

"Rache? No, everything's good. Hey, um. There's something you should know."

Gillian stood in the Ramada parking lot, clutching her jacket closed. Ever since the mausoleum, she felt cold all the time. She spoke into the driver-side window of Yoshi's Toyota Forerunner. It annoyed her that the intern always wore the same faded red T-shirt.

"Are you sure you're okay doing this by yourself?" she said. He gave her the stink eye. "Oh, here's the key to the padlock. Make sure to lock up when you finish."

He dropped the key into his shirt pocket and checked his rearview mirror.

"Yoshi?" she said. "Thanks. I don't want to spend another minute in that place until the shoot. Be careful."

*"Ki ni shinaide kudasai."*

She stepped back as he threw the truck in reverse and shot out of the parking lot. He had told her not to worry. Though she wasn't crazy about the kid, he was right. She *was* worried.

"He'll be fine," she said, and returned to her room.


The Forerunner made it easily up the hidden driveway to the fence surrounding the Dos Santos mansion. Yoshi set the brake and climbed out. The wind had kicked up, blowing pine needles and debris across the property. Bits of dirt got into his eyes. He used his shirttail to wipe his face and walked around to the rear of the vehicle to get his camera bag and tripod.

He unfastened the padlock and gazed at the sky. It was an odd color of yellow. Grabbing the camera, he took a few shots of the house's exterior. He unlocked the gate and went inside.

The house looked creepy in the shadows created by the surrounding trees that stood like sentinels. He could appreciate why Gillian had been reluctant to return. The last time they were here, she'd claimed to have seen a woman inside.

*Covered in blood*, Gillian had told him. Donnie and Debbie would love that. Maybe he would see if he could draw her out again and capture her image. It might provide the inspiration he needed to finish his horror screenplay.

He walked up to the house and set his things down. Remembering what Gillian had said, he decided to smoke outside. With everything inside dry and rotting, there was a very real chance he could start a fire.

Inhaling the Blue Dream he had bought in Koreatown in LA, he thought he saw something glide past one of the upper windows. *Trick of the light*, he told himself, channeling Donnie Fisk. The effects of the cannabis were mild, and when he'd finished, he felt a pleasant head buzz. Grabbing the bag and tripod, he walked in through the front door.

Gillian had asked Yoshi to get shots of the cellar and, if he was able, the attic. On their prior trip, they had avoided those places because she'd been too nervous. So, they concentrated on the downstairs areas and the upstairs bedrooms.

"Well, here goes," he said, laughing.

Once inside, he crossed to the staircase riddled with dry rot and made his way up. A faint tearing noise got his attention. Curious, he continued past the landing and stopped in front of an arched window covered in grime. Outside, he could see his truck. On the ceiling was the attic access door. He would have to find a long pole to open it.

He whipped around. The sound he had heard earlier now seemed to be coming from below. Excited, he trotted back down the stairs, when one of the steps broke, pitching him forward.

*"Chikushō!"*

The camera bag fell to one side, and the tripod slid down the stairs. Furious, Yoshi sat on a step and examined his foot. Blood leaked through his sock where the skin had been scraped raw.

Wincing, he flexed his foot. Nothing broken. Shaking his head in disgust, he got to his feet, snatched the bag, and proceeded to the bottom of the stairs, where he retrieved the undamaged tripod.

The tearing noise seemed louder down here and more rhythmical. Limping a little, he followed it through the dining room, into the kitchen, and toward a room in the back. He remembered that this had been the housekeeper's quarters and the place where, supposedly, Gillian had seen the ghost. Part of him hoped the spirit was still there.

Setting his equipment on the floor, he removed the camera. He would take pictures and send them to Donnie and Debbie. The sound continued as he approached the door and grabbed the doorknob. Taking a breath, he turned the knob and swung the door open.

The tattered remains of a maid uniform lay on the bed, covered in fresh blood. Exhilarated, he raised the camera and focused the lens. He took several photos in rapid succession.

Outside, a fierce wind had kicked up. The sky darkened, and the room fell into shadow. Yoshi moved closer. Now, the only sound came from tree branches brushing the side of the house. A flicking noise startled the intern. His eye still looking through the lens, he swung around to see what it was.

---

It was nearly two when Gillian walked into the police station and approached the desk officer, who was at the computer typing with two fingers.

"Is the police chief in?" she said.

He didn't bother looking at her. "He's out. Is there something I can help you with?"

She didn't like his attitude and glanced around the lobby. "How about Officer Whatley?"

He looked up, his expression neutral. "I'll check."

The officer stepped away and, using a phone that was farther away, made the call. A minute or two went by, then Tim came out of the back and entered the lobby.

"Gillian? What's going on?"

"It's Yoshi. I'm worried. He went back to the mansion to take more pictures. But that was hours ago. He should've been back by now. I tried calling several times, but he doesn't answer."

He thought a moment. "I guess I can take a ride out there." Then, to the desk officer, "I'm going to the Dos Santos mansion."

"I'll log it," the other cop said without enthusiasm.

"Can I come?" Gillian said.


By the time they reached the house in the forest, the wind had died down. The Forerunner was parked outside the fence where Yoshi had left it. Tim peered inside the cab, then walked over to the chain-link gate, which was unlocked.

"I hope he's not hurt," Gillian said.

"I'm going to check it out. You should probably wait here."

"No, I'm coming with you."

Tim opened the gate and let her through first. As they got closer, he stopped and looked at the upper windows. He thought he saw Yoshi looking down at them. But then, the image was gone. On his last trip, Tim had heard the whispering voices. He hoped they would leave him alone this time.

He switched on the industrial Xenon flashlight he was carrying and passed through the front door. Gillian followed. Inside, the floor was covered with debris. In places, he could make out footprints.

At first, he thought they might be Yoshi's. But now, it looked as if multiple people had come through. Careful not to disturb potential evidence, he went around them, advising Gillian to do the same.

"Could someone have gone in with him?"

"I don't think so. I'm pretty sure he doesn't know anyone here."

"Yoshi!" he said, using his command voice.

The quiet inside the house unnerved the cop. It reminded him of that deadly night at the women's shelter. The air had a certain quality. Rather than silence, it seemed there was something missing—an *absence* of sound.

"Let's start with the cellar," he said.

He found a door toward the front of the kitchen. He pushed it open. The first thing that hit him was the smell of carrion.

"What is that?" Gillian said, covering her mouth and nose.

"Some animal probably got trapped down there and died."

Shining his beam inside, he saw the unfinished wooden stairs leading down into the darkness.

"Wait here."

This time, she didn't argue. As he descended the stairs, she was unaware that she was digging her nails into her palms.

When Tim reached the bottom, he swept the flashlight

beam past piles of old furniture and wooden crates. But it was the floor that caught his attention. It was covered in dead animals, bloated and rotting. All had been mutilated.

"What the—"

One of them moved. He inched toward the carcass and, using his toe, pushed it aside. Hundreds of flesh-eating beetles fanned out. Stumbling backward, he found the stairs. When he emerged, out of breath, he slammed the door shut behind him.

"Did you see something?" Gillian said.

He looked at her with a blank expression. "He's not down there. Let's try upstairs."

As they ascended, he pointed out the broken step. When he had gotten three-quarters of the way up, he saw a pair of legs dangling lifelessly in the air.

Gillian screamed and nearly fell backward down the stairs. Tim caught her in time and helped to steady her.

"Go back to the vehicle," he said.

Nodding, she trotted down the stairs, feeling as if she were starring in a horror movie. Only this was real; Yoshi was dead. And it was all her fault because she had been too afraid to come with him. She thought of the last thing he'd said to her. *Ki ni shinaide kudasai. Don't worry.*

Standing next to the police cruiser, she looked at the sky. Something moved out of the corner of her eye. She turned sharply and stared into the trees.

Someone was there, watching her. She climbed into the vehicle and locked the doors.


Tim stood staring at the body that hung from the attic access door. Like Elizabeth Chernov's dog, the kid had been strung up with baling wire.

The eyes and tongue had been cut out. The shirt was

unbuttoned, and underneath, the red T-shirt had been shredded to reveal a long gash across the abdomen, where intestines dangled like link sausages in a butcher shop window. The dark blood that continued to drip formed a shiny pool on the rotting carpet.

He turned and read what was scrawled across the wall in Yoshi's blood.

TRICK OF THE LIGHT.

---

The sun had gone down by the time the ambulance carrying the intern's body left the scene. Lou waited outside as Tiffany Gersh conducted her investigation. His vehicle and another police car were parked inside the fence, their flood lights pointed at the house. Gillian Davies had gone home. Lou would let her get some sleep and interview her in the morning.

A Land Rover appeared at the crest of the hill. It came to a stop just outside the fence. Charlie Beeks climbed out. Recognizing Lou, he waved genially and walked over.

"Thanks for coming, Charlie," Lou said.

"I'm glad you called."

Lou ran down the situation. A cop wearing gloves trotted down the stairs carrying a camera bag and tripod.

"Chief, we found these in the bedroom behind the kitchen." He opened the bag. "The camera was lying on the floor."

Also wearing gloves, Lou reached in and removed the camera. He switched it on and cycled through photos as Charlie watched over his shoulder. He recognized Stearns Wharf in Santa Barbara. The photos seemed random— shots a tourist might take. A park, the Botanic Garden, a mother with her small daughter in a stroller.

He continued until he found photos of the house. The kid had taken several in the back bedroom. There was nothing unusual about the bed. Why had he photographed it? He advanced to the last photo and almost dropped the camera.

"Jeez," Charlie said.

A man's face in extreme closeup scowled at them, his eyes black.

"Looks like someone followed the kid into the house," Lou said.

"Had to be more than one person to be able to string him up."

Tiffany trotted down the front steps and walked over. She didn't look happy.

"Hey, Tiffany," Lou said. "This is Charlie Beeks. He's a private investigator."

"Pleasure. Lou, it didn't help that Tim and that other woman trampled my crime scene. Still, I'm pretty sure there were three men. Based on the shoe prints, I'd estimate two were at least six feet. The other was short.

"Could that have been a woman?" Charlie said.

"Possibly." Then, to Lou, "I found a puncture wound on the vic's neck."

Lou glanced at the PI. "Don't tell me. Succinylcholine chloride."

"The toxicology report will tell us for sure. I think they immobilized him, then carried him up the stairs, where they hanged him by the neck. We found a ladder in one of the bedrooms."

"He was alive when they cut him open?" Lou said.

"That would be my guess."

"There were no signs of another vehicle. They must've walked in from the forest and went back the same way."

Tiffany peeled off her gloves. "I've gotta get home to

my kid. I'll have my full report for you first thing in the morning."

"Thanks. Oh, what about those boots I sent over?"

"Oh, yeah. You wanted me to compare the soil from those to what we found on James Stark's shoes, right? Sorry, we've been swamped. I'll start on that tomorrow."

"Really appreciate it, Tiffany."

She looked him in the eye. "You've got a real shitshow here." Then, to Charlie, "Nice meeting you."

Lou waited for the forensic science technician to leave. He looked around to make sure no one else was listening.

"Charlie, I hope you don't mind my asking. But are you still on Harlan's payroll?"

"As a matter of fact."

"Do you think he'd mind if you helped me with my investigation? I'm up to my ears, and the department doesn't have a detective."

"I can't imagine Harlan having a problem with it. I'll ask him, though, to be sure." He looked at the house. "Mind if I take a look inside?"

"Not at all."


On his way back to the police station, Lou began to tick off what he would need to do in the morning, starting with canceling the filming permit. As far as he was concerned, Donnie and Debbie Fisk were done in Dos Santos. Good riddance.

And the second thing, an emergency meeting with the city manager. Lou wanted that house of horrors in the forest torn to the ground asap.

## Sixteen

It had taken Charlie only forty-five minutes to reach Buellton, a town of fewer than five thousand people. Though slightly out of the way, it had been quicker to take the 101. When he exited at East Highway 246, he was amused to find OstrichLand, a sprawling park featuring not only ostriches but emus. The roadside sign depicted a gigantic bird, with the tagline FEED THIS BAD BOY. In another few minutes, Charlie saw his turnoff and followed it to the address on Google Maps.

The house was a ranch style, with redwood siding and a sturdy roof. He parked in the gravel that fronted the property and passed under a white trellis with pink climbing roses. An old navy Saturn sat parked alongside the house under a blue plastic canopy.

He rang the bell and waited. When no one answered, he rang again, then knocked. A woman appeared from around the corner, dressed in overalls and holding a hand trowel.

"Hello?" she said.

"Mrs. Stark?"

.   .   .

They sat in a tidy, modest living room. Charlie held a mug of chamomile tea in his lap. The woman looked to be in her mid-forties. She had a kind face lined from the sun and years of worry.

A framed photograph stood on the end table. In it, a much younger Mrs. Stark, wearing a sun dress, crouched in the front yard with James, who looked to be around three or four. His hand shielding his eyes from the sun, he looked intently into the camera lens.

"I'm sorry I don't have coffee," she said. "Doctor says it's bad for my blood pressure."

"Tea's great. I just have a few questions. Shouldn't take long."

He took a sip and set the mug down on a coaster on a side table. Then, he got out his notebook.

"When was the last time you saw your son?" the investigator said.

"It was after they moved him to the new group home. His case worker asked me to visit. She was a lovely woman. I think she wanted James to know that I was…" Her voice broke. "That I was still here, and I cared."

"I see." He referred to his notes. "And how long until he left?"

"Not even a month."

"Your ex-husband. You don't think James might've gone to stay with him?"

"No. He left us when James was three. My son hated him."

"Did James have friends? Somewhere he could stay?"

"Not that I'm aware of."

"So, you don't think he might've formed any attachments at any of the homes he lived in?"

"He was always a loner."

"Do you have any of his things?"

Charlie followed the woman into a small bedroom, where he found a twin bed with a beige coverlet, a maple desk and chair, and a bookcase. Photos of wildlife adorned the walls.

"I keep everything the same," she said. "Except, I added those pictures. He always loved animals."

Charlie took a look around, starting with the bookcase. There was nothing unusual. He slid the closet door open and glanced at a few clothes and shoes. A basketball was tucked in the corner, along with a shoebox containing a game console and cartridges.

"Interesting he didn't take the Nintendo," he said.

"He was afraid someone would steal it."

Satisfied, he closed the closet door and left the room.

"Can you write down the name and address of that last group home?"

Mrs. Stark lingered at the front door with Charlie. Flipping to the front of his notebook, he removed a cashier's check. He handed it to the startled woman.

"My employer would like to pay the funeral expenses."

"But I don't—"

"It's all right." Charlie smiled. "He can afford it."

Mrs. Stark waited at the front door as the investigator descended the steps. He got into his car and was about to drive off when she hurried after him, waving the check.

"Mr. Beeks, I just remembered. There *was* someone. An old man who used to visit the group home, dropping off books and such. James liked to call him Grampa."

"Do you happen to know his name?"

"I'm sorry, I don't."

Charlie wrote something in his notebook. "That's very helpful. Thank you again, Mrs. Stark. And God bless you."

"God bless you, too," she said, and folded her hands in front of her as he drove off.

---

Charlie hopped on the 101 and headed south toward Las Cruces, an unincorporated community in Santa Barbara County. He exited a few minutes later and headed to his destination, a private facility located off San Julian Road. The Spanish-style building was sprawling and surrounded by fruit trees. The investigator headed up the long driveway. A group of teenage boys played touch football on the lawn. He parked near the other vehicles.

Entering the lobby, he gazed at his surroundings. The place reminded him of a senior living facility. Groups of boys passed, well groomed and wearing clean clothes— completely unlike the residents of the places Charlie used to call on when he was a probation officer in New Hampshire.

The woman behind the front desk eyed him as he pulled out his ID.

"May I help you?" Though she was smiling, her eyes betrayed suspicion.

"I'm a private investigator. I've been hired to look into the disappearance of one of your residents, James Stark."

He detected a reaction as he handed over his ID. When she had copied down the information, she returned it.

"I'll let the director know you're here," she said.

He crossed the room and took a seat on a sofa upholstered in burnt orange fabric. While he waited, he wondered why James was so eager to leave. The place seemed pleasant enough. In a few minutes, an African-American man wearing jeans, flannel shirt, and black-rimmed glasses, approached, his hand extended.

"Mr. Beeks? I'm Carl Rollins. I understand you're looking for information about a resident?"

Charlie was about to answer when a group of boys entered, fake-punching each other and laughing.

"Why don't we talk in my office," the director said, eyeing the kids.


The men sat next to each other on a long corduroy sofa. The director's office felt comfortable. There were books and plants everywhere. And in the corner, a stack of board games. A small desk and chair stood in the corner. Ignoring his coffee, Charlie laid the notebook on his lap.

"This place is pretty nice," Charlie said. "Are the kids happy here?"

"For the most part. We have a few who…require a little extra attention."

"Was James one of those?"

"Yes. To be honest, Mr. Beeks—"

"Call me Charlie."

"James was a mystery to me." He pointed to the wall. "I have a master's degree in Sociology and a PhD in Psychology. I've been around kids like James for most of my career.

"Usually, it's their home life that shapes them. James's father left when he was little, leaving his mother to raise him."

"Yes, I've met her."

"Unfortunately, it's all too common. Poor thing. How is she?"

"She's as well as can be expected, I suppose."

"I'll tell you, we try to make every one of these kids a success. But sometimes… This was James's fifth home."

"Did he make friends here?" Charlie said.

"Oh, he hung out with a couple of the boys. But they weren't what you'd call friends. He was pretty withdrawn. Didn't like group activities.

"We have a game night every week. The boys really look forward to it. I always encouraged James to attend. But he preferred to remain in his room. The others tried getting him interested, too. Eventually, they gave up."

Charlie glanced at his notes. "Mrs. Stark mentioned that James may have been acquainted with an elderly gentleman who visited here."

The director thought a moment. "Oh, she must mean Bud. Yes, he's been coming by for years. He brings donated books, and also toys for the younger ones. I believe he visits a number of the group homes in the area."

"Would you happen to know if he was here the day James disappeared?"

"No, but I can check the visitor's log. Wait here."

Charlie gazed out the window, watching the boys playing football. He thought of the baby he and his wife had lost due to a miscarriage. It had been a boy.

"Charlie?" the director said. "You really have a nose for these things. Bud *was* here that day."

The investigator got to his feet. "What time did he leave?"

"He signed out around two p.m."

"And when did you notice James was missing?"

"At five. That's when we serve dinner."

Charlie wrote everything down. "Do you recall what kind of car Bud drives?"

Carl chuckled. "An old Buick. The boys refer to it as The Tank."

"Do you think there's any chance he might've returned and given James a ride somewhere?"

"If he did, no one reported seeing him. The rules here

are strict, and Bud is well acquainted with our procedures."

Something nagged at Charlie. Knitting his brow, he looked at Carl.

"It's quite a coincidence, don't you think? Tell me, has Bud been back since?"

"You know, that's interesting. I haven't seen him in a while. Are you seriously suggesting he might have had something to do with James's death?"

"I'm not suggesting anything. But I would like to interview him. Can I get a name and address?"

Carl walked over to his desk and flipped open the laptop sitting there. He copied something down on a piece of paper and handed it to the investigator.

"Bud Walton." Astonished, Charlie looked up. "He lives in Dos Santos?"

"I believe he retired there after a long career in aerospace."

"Okay, thanks. I'll let you know if I turn up anything. Can you do me a favor? Please ask the boys and the staff whether they remember anything unusual that day concerning Bud Walton."

"The police interviewed everyone, but I guess it doesn't hurt to ask again."

The director walked Charlie out to the lobby, where he found the boys lining up for lunch.

"You'll let me know if you find out anything?" the director said.

"You can count on it."

"Tell me, Charlie, your honest opinion. Do you think Bud Walton is involved?"

"Let's just say he's a person of interest."

· · ·

Driving back, Charlie experienced a feeling of falling. He often felt this way when he had a hunch. It took him only thirty minutes to reach the 154. Soon, he was in Dos Santos, making his way toward the neighborhood where Bud Walton lived. When he turned onto the street, he noticed the tan Buick Skylark GS parked in the driveway.

He walked up to the front door and knocked. Inside, someone shuffled along the floor. When the door opened, an elderly woman regarded him with an annoyed expression. Her hair was short and white, her eyes a piercing blue. She wore a housecoat and slippers and looked unusually pale. Faintly, Charlie smelled sweat and wondered when she had last bathed.

"Mrs. Walton?" he said.

"Yes, I'm Karen Walton."

Charlie showed her his ID. "I'm looking for your husband. It's related to an investigation."

He caught the look of concern in her eyes, which was fleeting and soon vanished.

"He's not here," she said.

"But his car is here."

The old woman craned her neck and looked at the vehicle. "He likes to walk."

She was about to close the door when Charlie inserted his foot. She looked at it, then at him.

All at once, her expression changed. Her eyes went dark, and her teeth grew sharper. An insect buzzed near the investigator's ear. In an instant, he had come face to face with a malevolent force he had no ability to understand. An unnamed fear washed over him like a red tide. He had an overwhelming urge to run.

"You have no business with my husband," she said. Her voice was colorless.

Charlie stood there unable to move as she shut the

door in his face. It took him a full minute to revive. Something urged him to get out of there and find somewhere safe. It was an irrational feeling—primitive and all consuming.

He hurried across the street, climbed into his car, and pulled out. His cold, shaking hands were barely able to control the wheel.

"Jesus," he said. "Oh my dear Jesus."

---

It was approaching noon when Gillian pulled her SUV into the parking lot of Bad Blonde Productions. Traffic had been heavy the whole way, and to keep herself from losing it and ramming her vehicle into a concrete overpass support, she'd filled the interior with classical music.

She sat there motionless for a time, her eyes unfocused, thinking of Yoshi Kuroda. He was dead, and nothing would change that. When the police chief interviewed her in the early morning, he'd mentioned the kid had been eviscerated. Thankfully, the cop didn't show her the crime scene photos.

She still couldn't believe it. Climbing out of her SUV, she felt a dull ache in her guts. Her legs were numb. She wanted to curl up somewhere and sob like a child who had lost everything. She hadn't felt this kind of grief since her mother passed away when Gillian was twenty.

Trudging into the offices, she found the assistant Lillian making coffee.

"Hey, stranger," the older woman said. "Welcome back."

"Thanks. Are they in?"

"Debbie's around here somewhere. And I think Donnie's with Tyler."

Gillian poured herself a cup of coffee and walked back. A few people were on the phones in the bullpen. She continued toward the editing suite. The door was closed. She knocked once and went in.

The soundproofed room was large, with six black leather lounge chairs for viewing. A large monitor was mounted on the wall, displaying a freeze-frame of the iron door that led to the crypt where John Dos Santos's sarcophagus stood. In front was a long, curved birch table with three smaller monitors, a computer keyboard, and a mouse.

Standing, Donnie fidgeted next to the seated editor. He pointed at the large monitor.

"Cut it there. When we get back to Dos Santos, I'll record another segment. I'm pretty sure we can get it to match."

"What about that lens flare earlier?"

"Leave it," Donnie said. "Then, to Gillian, "I guess we should talk."

Donnie and Debbie shared a large corner office. Most of the furniture had been scrounged from various productions around town. Debbie had decorated the room tastefully with plantation shutters, potted plants, and framed movie posters. The effect reminded Gillian of a bungalow she'd visited years ago on the Paramount lot.

Donnie was stationed behind a large mahogany desk that faced another identical one. Debbie sat on the black leather sofa with Gillian.

"So, bad break," Donnie said the way someone might bring up a minor fender-bender.

Gillian took a breath before speaking. She was aware that neither Donnie or Debbie ever expressed sympathy or concern for anyone. In fact, she was convinced they were psychopaths. Though they'd never mistreated her or anyone on the crew, their manner was detached and uncaring. She was used to it, though, and usually let it go.

"Do you know if Yoshi had any family here?" she said.

Debbie tilted her head back as she applied eye drops. "He doesn't."

"We'll notify whoever is on his emergency contacts list," Donnie said. "Don't worry about it. How are you holding up?"

"Honestly? Not so good."

"Why don't you take the rest of the day off. We're planning on getting everybody back up there tomorrow, and I need you rested."

Gillian's head snapped up, and she gawped at them both. "Didn't they call you?"

"Who?" Debbie said.

"I don't know, someone from Dos Santos? They've canceled the permit. We can't shoot there anymore."

Donnie got to his feet, letting go a string of f-bombs that rang saltily through the office and into the hallway.

"They can't do that!" he said, his face and neck crimson. "I just convinced a bunch of nervous execs at the Discovery Channel that all was well." Then, to Debbie, "We'd better call the lawyers."

Gillian was reluctant to tell them the rest of the bad news. Looking away, she cleared her throat.

"They're tearing down the mansion," she said.

"Oh, no way." Now, Debbie was on her feet. "Donnie, we need to get back up there before that happens."

"Debbie, it's *over*," Gillian said.

The brother and sister stared at her, their mouths hanging open as if on hinges.

"Yoshi *died* in that house. But not before they cut him

open so he could bleed to death. Don't you get it? He was alive when it happened. No one is permitted to go there ever again. For God's sakes, they probably saved our lives by keeping us away."

Donnie massaged the back of his neck. "But we gave them a deposit."

Disgusted, Gillian opened her purse and removed an envelope. She dropped it on his desk.

"There's your money." She stomped to the door and, her shoulders slumping, faced them.

"I quit," she said, and walked out.

But they'd barely heard her. They were already plotting how to return to Dos Santos and shoot the remainder of the two-part episode they had promised the network.

---

Lou sat at his desk, rereading an email the city planner had sent, confirming that demolition would begin on the Dos Santos mansion within days. He wanted to kick up his heels. This was the first time in weeks he felt he was in control of the situation. Maybe he couldn't stop all the bad things happening in his town. But at least, he could shut down one source of evil.

His computer chimed as a new email arrived. It was from Tiffany Gersh. He read the subject line: Soil Sample Analysis. He opened the email message.

> You were right. Again. The soil taken from Leon Vogel's boots matches what we got from James Stark. Both are riparian and contain the same traces of microfauna. Nice hunch.
>
> I guess I owe you twenty bucks. :(

Tiffany

Lou found her analysis attached and sent it to the printer. Now, all he needed was to find the exact location both men had visited. If he was lucky, it would lead him to the killers.

## Seventeen

Sarah had just finished washing the last of the Williams Sonoma cookware and arranging it in Carter's kitchen cabinets when the doorbell rang. Excited, she ran to the foyer and opened the front door. Joe stood there with the painting on a hand truck.

"Just in time," she said. "I hope those wheels are clean."

He turned the hand truck around and pulled it inside. "Where's Carter?"

"I sent her on a snipe hunt. Right now, she's searching for organic Turkish cotton bath towels. Can we get this hung before she gets back?"

"Just need the ladder. Can you bring in my tools?"

Before long, Joe was standing on an extendable ladder, drilling a hole in the wall for the flat-mounted hook and anchor that would support the painting. Sarah stood below, her hands on the ladder to steady it.

"Are you sure that's high enough?" she said.

"Any higher and no one will be able to read the signature. Okay, I'm ready."

He came down the steps to help her. She cut the top of the box open. They slid out the wrapped painting. She took her time removing all the bubble wrap. When that was done, she pulled off the cardboard corner protectors. Then, she put on the nitrile gloves the gallery had provided and removed the glassine.

"It's stunning," Sarah said.

She opened a manila envelope and removed the paperwork. Her breath caught.

Joe gazed at it over her shoulder. "Yes, dear, you did spend that much."

She pointed at the name. "Frannie Jacobson."

"Do we know her?"

Sarah's eyes moved down the painting to the artist's signature. *F. Jacobson.* "No, but Carter does."

"I don't get it."

"If this is the same Frannie Jacobson—and I think it is —then, they were childhood friends in Sausalito. That's why the subject looks so much like Carter."

"The painting should really be special to her, then."

"I don't know. They had a falling out and never spoke again. Maybe this was a bad idea. Let's pack it up before she gets back."

Joe took her hand. "You're being ridiculous. She's going to love it."

Sarah scrunched her nose. "Are you sure?"

"Yes."

He grabbed a long piece of bubble wrap and set it on the floor next to the ladder. They carried the artwork over and set it down. Joe climbed the ladder, and Sarah handed the painting up to him.

"Careful," she said.

He straightened the frame and, using a soft cloth,

wiped it off. Then, he came down the steps and pointed at the ceiling.

"I'm going to have Manny install a small spotlight right about there."

"That's a great idea. Let's clean everything up before Carter gets back."


Carter walked through the front door carrying huge plastic bags from Bed Bath & Beyond.

"Sarah?" she said. Then, operatically, "I'm back."

She continued into the living room and stopped when she saw the painting.

"What in the world…"

Sarah emerged from the kitchen. She placed her hands on Carter's shoulders, closely observing her reaction as she admired the artwork.

"I told you I was getting you a housewarming gift," Sarah said. "This is from Joe and me."

"I… It's so beautiful." She hugged Sarah. "Thank you."

"We found it during that little weekend trip up north. The second I saw it, I thought of you."

Carter moved closer. "Why does she look so much like me? And the other girl in the window. Is she a ghost? She…"

Carter ran into the kitchen and returned with an aluminum step ladder. She set it up near the painting and climbed up to better read the artist's signature.

"No, it can't be. It…" Without thinking, Carter stepped off and hit the floor.

"Carter!" Sarah knelt and took her friend's hand.

"That was stupid."

"Are you okay? Let me help you up."

When the girl was on her feet again, she was pale. She moved the step ladder aside and gazed at the painting.

"Where did you say you got it?" she said.

"In Half Moon Bay. Carter, I promise you I didn't know when I bought it. It wasn't until I looked at the invoice just now."

"What's it called?"

Sarah put her arm around Carter. "*The Lost Friend*," she said.


In the kitchen, Sarah poured two glasses of red wine and handed one to Carter, who was slumped on a bar stool next to the island.

"All these years," the girl said. "Don't you think it's strange that *you* were the one to find the painting?"

"It is, kind of. Look, if that thing is going to upset you, I'll send it back. I'm sure I can find—"

"No, I wanna keep it. I guess I was just in shock for a second. Please, I love it."

Sarah patted her friend's hand.

"I never stopped thinking about her, you know? And I suppose she's still thinking about me. I mean, why else would she paint it?"

"Why don't you contact her?" Sarah said.

"What? No, I don't think…"

"I'm sure I can get her information from the gallery."

"Not right now. Let me get used to the idea first." She took a sip of her wine. "Hey, thanks for everything you've done. The house looks amazing."

"Joe suggested installing a spotlight for the painting. What do you think?"

"Definitely." She reached over and wiggled Sarah's engagement ring. "I still can't believe you guys are getting married."

Sarah laughed. "Neither can I. I guess there was only ever one man for me."

"That's sweet. Okay, we're having the engagement party here—no arguments."

"Are you sure?"

"Yes. It's my gift to you. Wait here. I wanna show you all the cool bathroom stuff I bought. I think I went a little overboard."

While Carter went off to retrieve her bags, Sarah thought about all the pain her friend had suffered in her life. Recently losing someone she cared for to suicide at the women's shelter. And at thirteen, the father of Carter's best friend raping her. And as if that wasn't enough, Carter losing her best friend when the rapist—Frannie's father—committed suicide. And yet—through all of it—the girl had survived.

Closing her eyes, Sarah thanked God for leading her to that art gallery in Half Moon Bay.

---

The Englishman stood in the middle of what used to be a parlor, his arms extended downward and his eyes closed. Before stepping into the house, he had prayed a psalm. Now, his entire being was a conductor, listening for the slightest vibrations of the evil that lurked in the electric atmosphere.

Day became night. A tearing noise repeated rhythmically. He opened his eyes and followed the sound to a small room off the kitchen.

As he got closer, luminous hands with sharp black fingernails burst through the walls, trying to grab him. But they were helpless to touch the Guardian, and he moved past them without a glance.

The door was partway open. He stood outside, listening. The sound continued. When he pushed the door open, he saw her—Dolores Lopez.

She was barefoot, wearing a coral chemise. Her long hair was unpinned and flowed loosely down her back. In her right hand, she clutched a pair of sewing scissors. Hovering over the bed, she tore repeatedly at her maid uniform, which lay there covered in fresh blood.

The room looked as it must have in Dolores's time. The furniture was polished, and the curtains looked crisp. A hair brush lay on the dresser, along with perfume and the housekeeper's journal.

As he approached the specter, she faced him. At first, fear shone in her eyes, then, curiosity. He reached out and took the scissors from her. Still, she didn't move.

"Dolores?" he said. "Whose blood are you wearing?"

She continued to stare at him, the fear gathering in her eyes once again. She glanced at his ring. Her face contorted into a horrible, screaming mask.

"NO!" And then, she was gone.

Alistair returned to the parlor, which he found furnished. A group of well-fed men in suits sat on chairs in a circle. They looked intently at a pile of naked boys and girls, their arms and legs splayed and smeared with blood. All dead.

In unison, the men turned their faces toward the Englishman, their eyes like coal and their mouths snarling. He raised his arm.

Howling, they cowered as a blast of light shot out of his palm and enveloped them. Burning with blue fire, they dissolved into black ash and floated away into nothingness. All that was left were the chairs and the children's bodies.

The Englishman raised his arm again and, whispering a prayer, directed a warm, comforting white light at the dead. Turning white themselves, they rose from the ground and floated up through the ceiling into eternity.

Brushing off his Bogner quilted vest, Alistair emerged from the house and trotted down the stairs. Someone was hiding among the trees. He continued past the gate and locked it behind him. But instead of returning to the Land Rover, he followed an invisible path into the forest.

———

Sitting in the Chesterfield chair, Charlie took another swallow of brandy. Though he was next to the fire, his hands were like ice. The last time he had felt this way was years ago when he was a homicide detective. He'd been alone in the interview room with a serial killer—a woman who, Charlie was convinced, was a victim of demonic possession.

Harlan sat next to him, a mug of steaming coffee in his hand. He practically swam in the camel cable-knit wool cardigan he wore. His eyes were sunken, his breathing labored from dyspnea. He wore a nasal cannula attached to a portable oxygen concentrator. As usual, the Englishman was behind the desk. The attorney cleared his throat.

"All right," Harlan said. "We know The Darkness requires humans to carry out actions on its behalf. Charlie, with the Waltons, you may have stumbled onto something important."

"Fallen into is more like it," the investigator said. "I still don't understand what happened. One minute, I was talking to Karen Walton. And the next, I'm running for my life."

"Alistair, what do you think?" Harlan said.

"It's curious these people live in Dos Santos and that Bud knew James. Charlie, how keen are you to continue your investigation?"

The investigator made a face. "Not very. I'll start again tomorrow. And I'll update the police chief."

"Good," Harlan said. "He can check to see if our friends the Waltons have ever been arrested."

The Englishman poured himself a drink and took a seat on the sofa. Almost as an afterthought, he told the others about his ghostly encounter at the mansion.

Charlie topped up his drink. "I don't feel so bad now."

"There's something else," Alistair said.

His face took on a neutral, unemotional aspect. The others leaned forward in anticipation.

"Someone was watching me outside. I followed him through the forest for a long time, though I never saw him again."

"Could it have been a specter?" Harlan said.

"Possibly. I ended up somewhere behind Montecito. It was getting dark, and I had to turn back. But not before I found something."

"Please don't say another body," Charlie said.

"A tunnel. I think it's how these demoniacs have been entering Dos Santos without being detected."

Harlan set his coffee aside. "There are tunnels that have been around since the 1800s. They used to supply water to the city of Santa Barbara."

Charlie finished his drink. "So, these demoniacs are simply *walking* into town?"

"That would explain how they come and go as they

please. Call the police chief and let him know. I'd like Alistair to accompany him when he goes up there."

The investigator rose and went to the door.

"And Charlie?" Harlan said. "As you observe the Waltons, do *not* make contact. Is that understood?"

"Don't worry. I'm going to have nightmares as it is."

After the investigator had left, the Englishman took a seat next to Harlan.

"How are things going with our protégée?" the lawyer said.

"She's a quick study. But she's willful."

"Be patient with her, Alistair. Carter has experienced great tragedy in her life." He patted the Englishman's arm. "You of all people should understand what that's like."

"And what about Sarah? She's the key."

"I know. So long as I'm alive, I'll protect her."

"And after?"

"That'll be Carter's job. I hope she'll be ready."

"As do I," the Englishman said, and finished his drink.

---

It felt strange being in the dining room. For as long as Sarah could remember, her family had always gathered around the kitchen table to eat, except for Christmas and Easter. Stranger still, Joe was with her.

"I'm still mad at you," Rachel said to her sister, laughing in spite of herself. "How you pulled this off, I'll never know."

Sarah patted her hand. "Sorry, Rache."

Joe glanced around. "So, where's Katy?"

"She's having dinner with a friend," Rachel said. "I thought it would nice, just the four of us."

Sarah's father seemed to be in better spirits than she had seen him in a long time.

"So, Eddie," she said. "No words of wisdom for me?"

"Don't screw it up this time."

The others laughed—including Sarah. "Okay, I deserved that. Seriously, though."

Her father took a swallow of beer. "Seriously? I couldn't be happier. Now maybe Joe will finally take me to a Lakers game."

"It would be my pleasure."

"And also, I'm very happy for you two. Sarah, I never told you this because, well. Because you're a grown woman and can live your life the way you want."

"Not sure I'm ready to hear this," Sarah said.

"It's nothing bad. I always had faith that you and Joe would work things out. You belong together."

Sarah squeezed her father's hand. "Thanks. That really means a lot to me."

"But I will say—"

"Uh-oh."

Eddie looked at Joe. "Kids. Just think about it."

Sarah turned to her fiancé, embarrassed.

Joe took her hand. "I have."

"Come again?"

"I'm not the guy I used to be. I'm not saying I'm ready for a family yet. But I'm also not saying I won't be someday."

"I'm pretty sure that's the wine talking," she said.

"Yeah, we'll see."

Eddie pushed his empty beer bottle aside. "And now, as long as we're discussing everyone's future, I'd like to hear from my *other* daughter."

"What?" Rachel said. "I don't have any news."

"Still in love with that cop?"

"Guilty as charged."

"Then, tell that *cabrón* to get off his ass. I don't plan on living forever."

That brought down the house.

Rachel stood outside with Sarah and Joe. She kissed her sister. "Thanks for doing this. You made Eddie very happy."

"I'm glad," Sarah said. "Is he doing okay?"

"He worries about you."

"Why?"

"I think you know. After that business at the women's shelter. And then, you ending up in the hospital. Promise me you won't do anything crazy."

"I won't let her," Joe said.

Rachel gave him a hug and embraced her sister again. "I'm freezing out here."

"Night, Rache," Sarah said. "I love you."

"I love you more." She disappeared into the house.

"I'm worried about you, too," Joe said as they walked to the truck.

Sarah thought of Dolores and the journal, and of the horrible things that had occurred at that wretched house in the woods. And she thought of her recurring dream of the dying soldier and how he was drawing her to him. Then, she smiled in that practiced way of hers.

"I'll be fine, Joseph. I promise."

The basement was dark, except for the white desk lamp that illuminated the long wooden work table. The only sound was the gentle whirring of an old Singer sewing machine. Sisal balls in various color combinations lay at one end, next to a pile of patterns, skeins of brightly colored yarn, and swatches of printed dress fabric. Under the table on the dirt floor sat a small plastic cat kennel.

Karen Walton bit off the thread and, adjusting her reading glasses, examined the tiny doll dress under the intense light. Her fingers were stiff from the cold and her back hurt. Ignoring her discomfort, she reached over to the naked cloth doll lying near the sewing machine and placed the dress next to it. The doll's chest had been hollowed out, the white cotton filling set aside in a small pile.

Scooting back the chair, the old woman got up and walked to the end of the table, where something small, dry, and dark lay on a paper towel. She reached behind her head and, using her shears, snipped off several strands of white hair. Then, she laid them on the paper towel and brought everything over to where the light was better.

Taking her time, she wound the hair around the dark object in a crisscross pattern until its surface was completely obscured. Using black thread, she secured everything in a neat package. Something nudged her foot.

When she looked down, she found one of the cats she had adopted. He looked at her with squishy eyes and maowed laconically. Ignoring the animal, she placed the object inside the doll's chest.

She reinserted the stuffing and, using flesh-colored thread, expertly sewed the chest closed. Then, she picked up the tiny dress and placed it over the doll, working the soft little arms through the sleeves. She smoothed out the fabric, turned the doll over, and sewed the dress in such a way that it couldn't be removed easily.

Across the room, Karen's husband, Bud, lay on a cot, dead. The smell was getting stronger as female blow flies laid their eggs in the ears, nose, and eyes. The sound of their buzzing grew more frantic as they discovered new nesting places.

Sitting the doll up against the base of the lamp, Karen admired her work. The long reddish-brown hair made of yarn. The hand-painted face and the tiny plastic shoes. Perfect for a little girl.

"Happy birthday, Mia," she said, and turned out the light.

## Eighteen

"And how long has Mia been having the nightmares?" Fr. Brian said.

Weary, Elizabeth Chernov met the priest's gaze. She turned to her daughter and tried a smile.

"Since we lost Flossie and her puppies."

The little girl frowned. "Somebody killed them."

"Yes," the priest said. "But one was saved, wasn't he? How's Mikey doing?"

Swinging her legs, Mia brightened. "Good."

"Glad to hear it." Then, to her mother, "What does her doctor say?"

Elizabeth sighed. "She recommended a psychologist."

"I think that's a good idea. If you need a referral, I can—"

"No." She looked behind her, then at Fr. Brian. "Can I speak to you in private?"

"Sure. Just a moment."

He left the office. The little girl picked up a pen. Her mother coaxed it from her and laid it back on the desk. When the priest returned, he addressed Mia.

"I need to speak to your mother alone. And I'm going to ask you to sit outside with Mrs. Ivy. She'll give you a lovely coloring book and crayons. Is that okay?"

Mia's mother nodded to her encouragingly. "I'll only be a few minutes, honey."

"But before you go," Fr. Brian said, "I have something for you."

He picked up a holy card from the desk and gave it to Mia. Knitting her brow, she studied it.

"That man has wings," she said.

"It's St. Michael. Each night, I want you to pray for his protection, okay?"

"Okay." She turned the card over. "These words?"

"Uh-huh. Your mom can say them with you."

Fr. Brian took the little girl's hand and led her outside, where the assistant was waiting for her. He closed the door and sat behind his desk.

"Mia doesn't need a psychologist," Elizabeth said. "She needs a priest."

He tensed. "Why do you say that?"

"My daughter is convinced she's seen the devil. She says he was the one who killed the dogs. Before you say anything, let me explain. We don't keep any kind of scary books in the house. And we don't ever watch those kinds of shows on television."

The woman let out a weak laugh. "My husband doesn't even swear around the house. So, I don't think Mia is being influenced by negative things."

"I see," he said. "Has she described this person to you? Told you where she's seen him?"

"At the park. I didn't see him, but she said he was old and fat, with white hair. She even described his car. Said it looked old fashioned."

"And why does she think he's the devil?"

"That's what has me so confused. She said some other kids told her. But we were the only ones there that day."

"And as far as you know, there's nothing to connect what happened at your house to this stranger?"

"No. I don't know anyone like that. I called my husband and—" The priest looked at her sharply. "He's away on business. He had no idea who the man could be."

"Tell me about the nightmare."

Elizabeth hesitated. "It's disturbing and always the same. Mia told me she sees three people—two men and a woman—standing in a circle." Her voice cracks. "They're looking at Flossie. She and her puppies are dead."

"And the old man?" he said.

"He's there, too. She said he's controlling them."

Fr. Brian toyed with his pen. "She might be trying to work out what happened. Often in dreams, the mind takes bits of information and tries to form connections, to make sense of things."

"There's something else," Elizabeth said. "Last night in the dream, Mia told me the people looked right at her." She gripped the arms of her chair. "And their eyes were black."

The room fell silent. In his head, the priest heard his own heart beating.

"Father, do you think the house is haunted?" she said.

"How long have you lived there?"

"We moved in a year ago from the Bay Area. Aren't realtors supposed to disclose it when something paranormal has occurred?"

"That's my understanding. Who sold you the house?"

"Sarah Greene. She's always been very nice to us. And she adores Mia. You don't think she would've lied to us about—?"

"No, I don't. I know Sarah very well. She's what I

would call guileless. Considering what's happened, I'd like to come and bless your house. And I want your daughter to see me do it.

"Also, I'm going to ask that you pray the Rosary as often as you can, starting today. Make sure Mia is aware that you're doing it.

"And for now, I want you to keep your daughter away from that park."

They rose and shook hands.

"Thank you, Father," she said. "I feel better."

"You look like you could use some sleep."

Elizabeth brushed the hair from her face. "Maybe now I'll be able to."

He held out his hands and said a blessing over her, ending with the Sign of the Cross. She was about to open the door when he touched her arm.

"How old is Mia?" he said.

"Four. She'll be five on Saturday."

"Please wish her a happy birthday for me. You can arrange for the house blessing with Mrs. Ivy."

She hugged the priest and walked out. When Mia saw her mother, she proudly held up the coloring book to show her what she had done.

"Can I keep it?" the little girl said.

Outside, Mia skipped along the sidewalk, clutching her coloring book and holy card. She stopped when she saw Sarah Greene approaching.

"Sarah!" Elizabeth said. "Oh my gosh, how funny. Wait, you're engaged?"

"Yep. Just dropping off my baptismal certificate." She crouched and dabbed the little girl's nose. "Hey, you."

Mia pretended to be mad. "Why does everyone do that?"

"Because you're so darned cute," Sarah said. Then, to Elizabeth, "Are you okay?"

"I haven't been sleeping very well. Sarah, do you think…? Forget it, it's stupid."

"What?"

"I just thought maybe if you had time for coffee. Mia has a play date later, and…"

"What time?"

"I'm dropping her off at eleven."

"I can meet you at The Cracked Pot. I'll head over from the office."

"Thank you so much. See you soon."

Walking to her car, Elizabeth's shoulders were slumped, and, to Sarah, she looked as though she were carrying the weight of the world.


Fr. Brian sat at his desk with the door closed. That was no ordinary nightmare, he was sure of it. The little girl was in danger. The sickness that had befallen Dos Santos was spreading. And now, to the children.

He said a "Hail Mary." Before he could finish, something crashed. His framed photo of Pope Francis lay on the floor, the glass shattered. Using his mobile phone, he selected a name from his contacts. As the number rang, he picked up the photo and shook off the broken glass over the wastebasket.

"Mary?" he said. "It's me. Yes. I need to see him right away."


Lou and the Englishman made their way out of the brush toward the tunnel entrance. Each carried a flashlight.

Dappled sunlight fell on the washed stone face, revealing the words written across the top: Santa Barbara Cold Spring Tunnel. Below, stood a black wrought iron gate that fit perfectly in the archway.

Lou examined the gate and found that it was unlocked. Kneeling, he used a stick to poke around the vegetation until he found an old padlock. Someone had taken bolt cutters to the hasp. Pulling a plastic evidence bag from his jacket pocket, he hooked the lock with the stick and dropped it into the bag. He got to his feet.

Before embarking, the police chief had researched the tunnel and learned that it extended five thousand feet through the mountain. He had hoped Charlie Beeks would want to accompany him and was disappointed when the investigator suggested Alistair. Though polite, the tall man wearing expensive outdoor clothes seemed formal. And that made Lou uncomfortable.

"Shall we?" the police chief said.

Using his jacket, he pulled the gate open and walked through. He stopped and found his companion examining the gate.

"Be careful where you touch. We might want to dust for fingerprints."

Alistair leveled a gaze at him. Reaching high, he placed a flattened palm on the cold wrought iron.

Hundreds of bedraggled men and women paraded past him, pouring out of the tunnel into the bright light.

They paid no attention to the Englishman as they shuffled into the forest and out of sight, the sound of buzzing flies following them.

. . .

Snapping on their flashlights, Lou and the Englishman proceeded into the darkness. The ground was covered in rotting vegetation, leaving a powerful smell. Lou crouched to take a closer look.

"What do you know?" he said. "Riparian soil."

The cop collected a soil sample and placed the bag in his pocket. They continued deeper into the darkness. Alistair spotted the outline of a figure looming in the distance.

'Wait here," he said. "And put out that torch."

Confused, Lou complied. The tall man disappeared, his light beam playing along the walls. Enveloped by a cloying silence, the police chief stared at his sweating palms. Taking slow breaths, he waited.

Alistair shone his light straight ahead. Nothing but emptiness. A man materialized in front of him, barely two feet away. He was elderly and overweight, with white hair and blue eyes. He glared menacingly.

"Bud Walton?" the Englishman said. "You appear to be dead."

The specter made a coughing sound. When he opened his mouth, a viscous black liquid poured down his chin and clothes, forming a pool all around him. In it were hundreds of words chiseled out of a shiny crystalline material resembling coal.

They were *names*.

Hearing something, Lou switched on his flashlight. When he saw the Englishman approaching, he let out a relieved breath.

"Find anything?"

"I need to call Charlie," Alistair said.

Fr. Brian had just arrived at Harlan Covington's house when Carter Wittgenstein came out the front door.

"Carter?"

"Hey, Father." She glanced around nervously. "What are you doing here?"

"Visiting an old friend. You?"

"I, um. I needed to use the library. I'm helping with some research." He glanced at the Hebrew books. "Well, I'd better go. Nice to see you."

"Same," he said. "I hope you'll come by my office. I miss our discussions."

"I will."

She practically leaped into her car and drove off. He continued toward the front door and rang the bell. In a few moments, Mary answered.

"Hello, Father. He's waiting for you in the library."


Harlan nodded gravely as the priest finished telling him about the little girl. They sat on the Chesterfield sofa, each with a cup of strong coffee. The priest hadn't seen his old friend in a while. He was astonished at how dramatically the attorney's health had deteriorated.

"How is it possible, Harlan?" Fr. Brian said. "Could it be that Mia is—"

"Psychic?" His voice had lost all its old resonance. "How did she seem to you?"

"She's a bright child. Well spoken. She seems wise beyond her years."

"Do you know if she's ever had any visions while awake?" the attorney said.

"Her mother didn't mention anything."

"As I'm sure you're aware, there have been a number of pet mutilations in the area recently. But it seems what happened at this little girl's house was particularly brutal."

The priest stared at his coffee without drinking. "Almost as if she were being singled out."

"Brian, you look like you could use something stronger."

"Well, I…"

The frail attorney got up and brought over a bottle of Irish whiskey and a glass.

"You'll have to pour," he said. "I don't trust these hands anymore."

The priest appraised the bottle. "Connemara Peated. I'm honored."

He poured himself a glass and took a sip. Sitting back, he closed his eyes and savored the taste.

"Does Sarah know what happened?" Harlan said.

"I don't think so. She stopped by my office after Elizabeth left and mentioned they were going to have coffee."

"I need to speak to her before they do. Will you excuse me a moment?"

"Of course."

When Harlan was finished, he put away his phone and sat next to the priest.

"Tell me about you," Fr. Brian said. "What do the doctors say?"

"Not much, I'm afraid." He indicated the oxygen concentrator. "A few more weeks perhaps. Mary sees to it I'm comfortable."

"I'd like to administer the Anointing of the Sick. Would that be all right?"

Harlan let out a weak chuckle that sounded more like a cough. "If you think it'll help."

Sarah and Elizabeth sat at a booth in the rear of the restaurant. Earlier, Sarah had promised Harlan on the phone that she would follow his instructions. Instead of coffee, they'd decided to have an early lunch. The server had already taken their orders. Watching her walk away made Sarah nostalgic for the days when Carter worked there.

"Something terrible happened at the house," Elizabeth said. "I still can't believe it."

After the server had brought their salads, Sarah said a silent blessing, prompting her companion to do the same. Sarah took a bite of food.

"Tell me about the old man's car," she said.

"Mia said it was the color of dirt. I remember seeing it —it was tan. She asked me if I'd noticed a bumper sticker. I hadn't. She told me it was a yellow smiley face."

Sarah dropped her fork. "Sorry, did you say 'smiley face'?"

"Yes. Have you seen the car?"

"Does Mia remember if one of the taillights was broken?"

"She didn't mention it."

Sarah's hands turned cold. And she had goosebumps. She rubbed both arms and took a sip of sparkling water.

"Sarah?"

"I *have* seen that car, although I've never met the owners. They're an elderly couple who live not too far from here."

"I'm finding it hard to believe that an old man and woman would be mixed up in an animal mutilation."

"Me, too," Sarah said. "Did you call the police when you discovered the remains?"

"A young officer came right over. He was awesome. He saved the last little puppy and took him to the vet for me. He even cleaned up the mess."

Sarah nodded. "Sounds like Tim Whatley."

"Yes! He was so nice. I still can't believe he'd go out of his way to do that."

"Tim's a great guy. Elizabeth, if you wouldn't mind, I'd like to take a look at the house."

"Why?"

Sarah scrunched her nose. "You mean, you haven't heard?"

Elizabeth stared at her realtor in amazement as she finished her story.

"Fr. Brian never mentioned anything about you being psychic."

"No, he wouldn't," Sarah said. "And it's not like I go around advertising. I mean, I'm in the real estate business, not fortune-telling."

"And you think you might—what's the word—*see* something?"

"I don't know. But it's possible I'll get a sense of who was responsible. You mentioned Mia's having a birthday party. I could come by then."

"Really?"

"One more present for Mia."

"Well, I'm sure she'd love to see you. But you don't need to bring anything."

When the server appeared with the check, Sarah handed her a credit card. "This one's on me," she said to Elizabeth.

"Thank you, Sarah. The party starts at one. Maybe you could come a little early, you know, before the other guests arrive?"

"No problem."

Outside, the women said their goodbyes. Sarah thought of something as her client walked away.

"Elizabeth?" The woman stopped. "I'd like to bring that friend of mine I mentioned, if it's okay."

"Carter?"

"Two for the price of one, baby."

"Absolutely. See you Saturday."

Sarah walked back inside and headed for the coffee bar. For a second, she thought she recognized Carter behind the espresso machines. But it was another girl with short dark hair.

"Doppio to go," she said.

She thought about what she and Carter might find at Elizabeth's house. And the old man. Why was it the little girl considered him to be the devil?

## Nineteen

Charlie watched the Waltons' house from inside a nondescript blue Chevy Malibu. He had been there over two hours, and his back hurt. He was parked a little ways down on the opposite side of the street. So far, no one had come in or gone out. Though he was happy to follow the Englishman's instructions, he would feel a lot better once the police arrived.

When he heard a door open and close, the investigator turned to find the thin, intense-looking next-door neighbor stepping outside with her trash. She wore a large wooden cross and had difficulty holding the bag as she made her way to the curb. She deposited it on the sidewalk. Before going back in, she looked at him.

His phone vibrated. He glanced at the number and answered.

"Charlie Beeks. Carl? Of course, I remember. No, still no word yet. They did? I see. Okay, thanks for getting back to me."

He wrote something down in his notebook. Ten minutes had passed when the Waltons' front door opened.

Charlie reached over to the passenger seat and grabbed his camera.

Focusing the telephoto lens, he took several pictures as the elderly woman who had frightened him so badly locked the door after her and, crab-like, came down the steps. Wearing an old dress, wool sweater, and socks, she carried a neatly wrapped present. The box was covered in solid purple paper and tied with a bright yellow ribbon.

He continued snapping photos as she made her way to her car. At first, she had trouble starting it. After two more tries, she gunned the engine, put the car in reverse, and backed out. She pulled away and disappeared over a rise in the road.

Charlie remained in his vehicle. In his experience, people sometimes returned within a few minutes because they had forgotten something. The last thing he wanted was to confront that unholy hag again. When he felt certain she was gone, he got out and stretched. Taking a quick look around, he walked across the street toward the house.

The front door was locked. Two cats appeared from the bushes, maowing at Charlie and rubbing themselves against his legs. Ignoring them, he tried looking inside through the front windows, but the heavy curtains made it impossible.

He trotted back down the stairs and walked around the side, where he found a basement hopper window. Ignoring the pain, he got down on one knee on the dry grass and peered inside. Everything lay in darkness. He slipped a hand into his jacket pocket and removed a small LED flashlight.

The powerful beam illuminated a long wooden table with a sewing machine at one end. Vaguely, he could just make out something in the back along the wall. It looked like a cot. Something lay on top of it. He shone the light up around the window. The latch was undone.

Wincing, he got up and searched the yard. He found a bucket of gardening tools next to a hose. Reaching in, he grabbed a trowel, then returned to the basement window.

Inserting the trowel, he wiggled it until the window loosened and he could grip it from the outside. He opened it a crack. A noxious smell hit him, instantly making him gag. He shut the window fast.

"What are you doing?"

His heart in his throat, he turned to find the scrawny next-door neighbor. Fingering her cross, she eyed him with suspicion. He got to his feet and showed her his identification.

"There's a dead body in there," he said. Her eyes widened. "When's the last time you saw Bud Walton alive?"

---

Lowering his right hand, the Englishman stepped away from the bloated corpse covered in blow flies. He had gotten nothing from Bud Walton—not a glimmer from beyond the veil. It frustrated him that someone so evil could continue to shield himself even after death. Perhaps the protection came from something even more sinister.

Lou and two paramedics were standing by. Everyone wore surgical masks. Before Alistair and the police chief left the basement, one of the EMTs helpfully squirted their hands with hand sanitizer. The Englishman turned to Lou.

"You must cremate the body as soon as possible," he said.

"Why?"

"Because it's evil."

Charlie waited outside, still holding his camera. Two police cruisers were parked along the street, as well as Lou's SUV, a van owned by a local locksmith, and the Englishman's Land Rover. The cops took statements from the neighbors. Someone interviewed Bethany Pruitt. The first to emerge from the house were Lou and Alistair. Charlie joined them.

"Chief," he said. "I got a call from the director of the boy's home. Bud Walton *was* there around the time James Stark disappeared. One of the employees was leaving work and remembered seeing his vehicle parked out on the main road."

Lou nodded. "So, the kid sneaked out and took off with the old man."

"Looks that way."

They moved aside as the EMTs came out next, maneuvering a gurney with a black body bag on it down the steps. Lou watched as they loaded the body into the awaiting ambulance.

"I couldn't find any signs of violence," he said. "It's possible he died from natural causes."

The Englishman took a last look at the body. "A bad heart."

"And how would you know that?"

"Educated guess. I only wish I was able to get more out of him."

Charlie laughed reflexively. "Are you saying you interviewed the deceased?"

Alistair ignored the question. "Chief, I gather you're not able to search the premises and collect evidence?"

"Not without a search warrant," Charlie said.

Lou nodded. "He's right. If in fact Mr. Walton died of natural causes, then no crime was committed."

"Shame," the Englishman said. "I suppose we'll have to find Mrs. Walton and continue the surveillance."

Charlie shook his head. "I don't know. Something tells me that's going to be tough."

"You think she might've fled?" Lou said.

"There's a good possibility she won't be back. Think about it. Why does a woman whose spouse died care more about delivering a present than laying her husband to rest?"

Alistair took his arm. "What present?"

Charlie scrolled through the pictures he had taken and handed over the camera. The Englishman studied the photo of the old woman carrying the purple and yellow box.

"Anyone we know having a party?" Alistair said.

---

Donnie and Debbie Fisk pulled Yoshi's Forerunner up to the fence and parked. New No Trespassing signs had been posted all the way down on both sides. Donnie climbed out and went around to the back of the vehicle to get the equipment while Debbie checked her backpack to make sure she had everything they would need, including extra battery packs.

The sky darkened as they approached the gate. Donnie positioned the bolt cutters and snipped off the padlock that secured the heavy chain. Tossing the lock and chain on the ground, he pushed the gate open.

He took a moment to admire the Dos Santos mansion. Picture-perfect clouds had gathered behind it, giving the house a forbidding appearance. He couldn't wait to get started. He hadn't done any kind of guerilla filmmaking since his student days at Orange Coast College.

"Let's hurry and get the camera set up for an establishing shot," he said.

Debbie did as he asked, expertly pulling apart the tripod legs and placing them securely on the ground. She mounted the camera, turned on the light, and waited for Donnie to attach a lapel mic to his shirt.

She stared at the house. A feeling of dread seeped under her skin. She found herself wishing they hadn't decided to go through with the plan. Maybe Gillian was right. There *was* something here—something threatening.

"Ready?" Donnie said, removing his glasses.

He faced the camera and raised the production slate he was holding. On it was written the name of the production, and the scene, shot, and take numbers. Below that was a bright digital clock display. He snapped the clapping stick closed, which started the clock. Then, he laid the slate on the ground and cleared his throat.

"And action," Debbie said.

Donnie rolled his shoulders, ran a hand through his hair, and smiled into the camera.

"So, we finally made it to the house, boys and girls. Now, as you'll recall, this place has quite a history. All kinds of naughty things went on behind these walls. But all that came to an end on Sunday, September 13th, 1925.

"That's when John Dos Santos was found dead by his housekeeper, Dolores Lopez. According to the physician who'd been called to the house, Dos Santos had cut his own throat with a straight razor. Let's go inside and have a look."

Donnie did two more takes, varying his monologue. When they were finished, they gathered everything and walked up to the front door. Debbie's legs ached, and she was cold. She imagined it was all in her head, since Yoshi had died here. Steeling herself, she followed her brother up the stairs.

The interior was bathed in shadow. Debbie set up the camera for a wide shot while Donnie did a quick tour. When he reached the cellar, the stench of rotting animal flesh drove him back into the kitchen. He decided to check out the second floor.

Standing at the top of the stairs, he examined the baling wire still hanging from the ceiling. His eyes drifted to the circle of dried blood on the floor. He read what was written on the wall. *Trick of the light.*

"Funny," he said.

He trotted back downstairs and found his sister taking light readings. He decided to check out the kitchen again and passed through a doorway from the dining room. Blinking, he thought he saw a woman disappearing into a back room. He removed his glasses and cleaned them on his shirt. When he put them back on, no one was there. His sister called to him from the other room.

"Hang on," he said. "I need to check something out."

"Be careful."

"When am I ever *not* careful?"

"Like every day?"

He followed the phantom to the back room and stood outside the door. Though he couldn't be sure, he thought he heard a tearing noise. It was faint and intermittent. When it stopped, he pushed the door open and looked inside without going in. It was a bedroom. Everything was dusty and the furniture ruined. A bare mattress lay on the bed frame.

"Cool, Dolores Lopez's room," he said. "Hey, Debbie?"

She didn't answer.

When he faced the kitchen, everything was clean and

sparkling, and the lights shone brightly. Panicked, he returned to the dining room, which was beautifully furnished, with fresh flowers on the table.

In the large foyer, two men wearing dark suits conversed quietly. One wore a homburg and the other a fedora. Outside, the sky was black.

"Am I dreaming?" Donnie said.

A third man, hatless and carrying a doctor's bag, trotted down the stairs and joined them. He had white hair and a beard and wore glasses. Donnie couldn't make out what the men were saying.

Frantic, he ran through the dining room and kitchen to the bedroom. The door was still open. Now, the room was clean and furnished. A woman in a coral chemise stood over the bed, hacking her bloody maid uniform to pieces with sewing scissors.

"I know what happened," he said.

She stopped cutting and looked past him at the doorway. A flicking noise made him jump.

He turned to see when, in a blur, something inevitable came at him.


When Debbie heard her brother's scream, she ran, knocking over the camera. She stood in the dining room, her heart thudding.

"Donnie? Okay, this better not be a…"

The door to the kitchen swung open slowly, the rusted hinges shrieking.

"Donnie?" Then, to herself, "Man up, Debbie."

She marched across the room to the doorway and gazed around at the kitchen. Then, she continued to the back room, where she found her brother.

He lay on his back in an ever-expanding pool of blood, with his gored neck as the source.

"Donnie?"

The back door slammed shut. Debbie looked up in time to see a man through the window as he ran toward the forest.

---

Tim Whatley was the first on the scene. When he arrived, Debbie Fisk was standing outside the house, covered in blood, her arms hanging limply at her sides. He jumped out of the police cruiser and ran past the open gate toward her.

"Debbie?"

When she didn't respond, he shook her by the shoulders. No reaction. He checked her over to make sure the blood wasn't hers. Satisfied, he ran back to his vehicle and popped open the trunk, where he found an unused patient blanket.

Using his teeth, he tore open the plastic and hurried back to the somnambulant woman, who stood shivering in silence. Gently, he draped the blanket over her shoulders. Then, he guided her to the backseat of the cruiser and secured her seatbelt.

"I'm just going to have a look inside," he said, taking out his weapon.

Staring at him with manic eyes, she grabbed his arm and squeezed it hard.

"No, don't go in there!" she said.

He pried her fingers loose. "I have to."

It took him only a few minutes to do a sweep. As he moved from room to room, the whispering—those evil, children's voices he had heard since the day he went to

Elizabeth Chernov's house—plagued him. Ignoring them, he continued his search.

The house was empty, except for Donnie Fisk's body. Tim knelt and checked for a pulse. Then, he went back outside. Another officer—Riley—had just pulled up.

Tim jogged over to his cruiser and explained the situation. He instructed Riley to wait for the ambulance. Debbie Fisk was in shock, and Tim wanted to get her medical attention asap. Checking on the woman one more time, Tim got behind the wheel and drove away.

Rain poured down out of swollen black clouds as they made their way down the hill toward the main road. Tim kept glancing at the rearview mirror to see if Debbie might have recovered. She stared straight ahead, frozen and unblinking.

Once he had reached asphalt, he radioed the dispatcher to let her know he was taking Debbie Fisk to Cottage Hospital. He promised to call the chief after she was admitted.

"Tim, what's going on?" Laurie said over the radio.

He glanced at Debbie. Almost in a whisper, he spoke into the mic.

"187," he said.

That was the code for murder.

———

Lou struggled to stay focused on the road as he drove through the rain toward Cottage Hospital. Why had Donnie and Debbie Fisk defied his order and trespassed? And now, though he'd done his best to get things into a manageable state, reporters from the *Dos Santos Weekly* were snooping around. He was confident neither Sarah or Carter had tipped them off. Still, they were a newspaper;

they had other sources. *You've got a real shitshow here,* Tiffany Gersh had said to him. Well put.

He pulled into the familiar drive and parked in an area reserved for medical professionals. Hurrying inside, he approached the desk in the lobby to find out where they were keeping Debbie Fisk. He jogged to the elevators and went up.

The charge nurse escorted him to the patient's room. There was no one in the other bed. Debbie lay on her side with her eyes closed. The nurse told him they had given her Trazodone to help her sleep.

"Do you think I can wake her?" Lou said.

"I wouldn't advise it, but you can try."

She left him in the doorway. For a time, he stood there, observing the patient. Her hair was washed, and she wore a hospital gown. From Tim's description, she had been covered in blood, presumably her brother's. Tim hadn't found the murder weapon.

For a second, Lou entertained the theory that it was Debbie who murdered her brother. But when he couldn't come up with a motive, he dismissed the thought.

One thing was clear. *Someone* had slit Donnie Fisk's throat and left him to bleed out. He surmised that Debbie must have discovered her brother and tried to save him. When she couldn't, she called 911 and, in shock by this time, waited outside for help to arrive.

Lou took a seat next to the bed. "Debbie?"

Groggy, she opened her eyes and tried focusing on the cop, who wore a neutral expression.

"What? Who…?"

"I need to ask you some questions. Then, you can go back to sleep."

"Donnie's idea to go back," she said. "I didn't want to."

227

"So, the plan was for the two of you to film the episode?"

"Yes. Used to do it." She yawned. "In college. You have to have the right…equipment."

"Can you tell me what you saw?"

"Nothing. Getting ready for a shot. Donnie disappeared into… into…the room."

"Which room?"

"In the back. Kitchen."

"Did you see who attacked him?"

"Man." She yawned again. "Running away. Woods…"

She closed her eyes. Lou realized he wouldn't get any more out of her. He'd come back tomorrow and ask her to make a formal statement. For now, he would make some notes based on the short interview.

It was almost five. He was scheduled to have dinner with Rachel. But he wanted to talk to Tim first. At the elevator, he pressed the down button. *A man running away into the woods.*

"Ghosts don't run," he said.

―――――――

Tim sat in front of the police chief's desk, a paper cup of espresso in his hands. He had never acquired a taste for fancy coffee but drank it to be polite. The police chief sat back in his chair, rubbing his eyes with the heels of his hands. Tim thought he might be angry with him.

"I know I should've waited for the ambulance," he said. "But Riley was there."

Checking his watch, Lou sat up straight. "You did the right thing. Debbie mentioned seeing a man fleeing the scene. Maybe tomorrow we can get a description."

"I wish I'd found the murder weapon."

"It might still turn up. Tiffany Gersh is up there right now. You shouldn't be so hard on yourself."

"Why did they do it, though?" Tim said. "Go up there, I mean."

Lou stood, startling the officer. "Do we have the camera equipment?"

"The guys accompanying Tiffany are supposed to bag and tag everything. I'm sure all that stuff will be here soon."

"Okay. Sorry to cut this short, but I'm meeting someone for dinner. Text me when they get back."

Tim wanted to tell his superior about the voices he had been hearing, but he was afraid. Before he knew it, the chief was gone.

---

Bethany Pruitt sat on top of her covers in bed, listening to the rain. A series of dull thuds accompanied it. The bible lay open on her lap.

Hesitating, she looked at the shadowy corner of her room where she had seen the dark apparition. As before, there was someone there. But this time it wasn't the man with the slicked-back hair.

A low, intense humming vibrated through the air, chilling her. A cold, clammy sweat beaded on her forehead. Bethany drew a breath and held it. From out of the shadows, *she* appeared.

Karen Walton.

At first, she was translucent. The old woman approached her, and Bethany could see through her to the hallway beyond. Now solid, Karen stood at the foot of the bed. A wave of foul, cold air passed over Bethany. She clutched her cross and began to pray.

229

"Listen to me very carefully," Karen said. "You want the nightmares to stop, don't you?"

Bethany nodded rapidly, her eyes tightly closed. The smell of sulfur filled the air. She could hardly breathe.

"I can help. But you must do exactly as I say."

"I promise," Bethany said.

"You were right. Sarah Greene is responsible for everything that's happened."

"I, I don't know anymore."

"Oh, but she is. You've always known. And you also know what must be done."

Bethany looked up, her eyes hopeful. "A sacrifice?"

"Yes, Bethany, a sacrifice." Knitting her brow, Karen clucked her tongue. "It is an unfortunate truth. Nothing good comes without a price. Wouldn't you agree?"

Unsure, Bethany nodded. Now, Karen's face was next to her, the piercing blue eyes glowing like fluorescent paint. As if by command, Bethany's bladder emptied.

"You will deliver Sarah Greene. To *him*."

Bethany looked toward the shadows and saw the dark man again, his eyes two red flames. The frightened woman tried to say something. But before she could, Karen used two hands to pull her mouth wide open—wider than physically possible.

Like a stag beetle, she crawled into Bethany's body, leaving nothing behind but polluted, sulfuric air. And the steady sound of the rain against the window.

## Twenty

Sarah waited uncomfortably in Lou's office while the mayor tore him a new one over the phone. She was quite familiar with Lou's temper and impressed at how well he withstood the shrill, relentless shellacking.

"No, I didn't authorize the filming," he said. "In fact, I —" He shot a disconsolate glance at Sarah. "Yes, I realize we now have three murders. We're doing everything we can to—"

While the mayor continued to rant, Lou balled his fist and banged it once on his desk. Then, into the phone, "Sorry, I dropped something."

The awkward, emasculating scene was painful to watch and went on for another two minutes. Sarah exchanged a sympathetic look with Carter, who sat next to her, equally uncomfortable.

"Okay, I will," Lou said. "And thank *you*, your honor."

Unlike his former outburst, he set the handset down and took a minute. Facing the women, he shook his head miserably.

"She's really pissed."

"I wasn't aware," Sarah said. "Are you okay?"

"Aside from the fact that we've become the murder capital of the world, I'm doing great."

"What's the mayor asking you to do?" Carter said.

"She wants me to bring in SBPD Homicide to help with the investigations."

Sarah made a face. "Don't tell me. Vic Womble."

"I don't like this any better than you. But it's gotten to the point where I need all the help I can get."

"There's one problem. Vic doesn't believe in the paranormal. He'll run this like a normal investigation and miss everything."

"What if he gets in the way?" Carter said.

Sarah nodded emphatically. "I think we're better off sticking with Charlie Beeks."

Lou toyed with his empty coffee cup. "I haven't mentioned him to the mayor. Charlie is ex-Homicide. I don't know, maybe I can sell it."

"Did you speak to Debbie Fisk again?" Sarah said.

"I took her statement this morning."

"How is she?" Carter said.

"Surprisingly well. She's pretty tough."

"Did she say why they went up there?"

"It seems they were contractually obligated to deliver both episodes. Donnie thought he could film what he needed at the house. Later, they planned to do an in-studio interview with some 'expert' to talk about John Dos Santos."

"Obviously, they can't deliver," Sarah said.

"Debbie told me there's a force majeure clause in their contract."

"What's that?" Carter said.

Sarah turned to her friend. "It states that the contract

can be broken due to an extraordinary event or circumstance beyond the control of either party."

"I'd say Donnie Fisk's death qualifies."

Lou looked at his notebook. "I was planning to charge Debbie with trespassing. But given the situation…"

"Lou, I'm so sorry this happened," Sarah said. "What do you need us to do?"

"Thought you'd never ask. I'm on thin ice. I'd like you to contact Debbie and see if the three of you can analyze the video they shot yesterday. Maybe it'll turn up some clues."

"As in supernatural clues?"

Carter raised her hand. "Won't she be busy with her brother's funeral arrangements?"

"I've asked our parents to take care of it," someone else said.

Sarah and Carter turned around to find Debbie Fisk leaning against the door jamb. Wearing jeans and a flannel shirt, she looked haggard. Her eyes were puffy. Her blonde hair wasn't combed, and she wore no makeup.

Carter got up and led the woman to her chair. Thanking her, Debbie took a seat.

"Debbie?" Lou said. "What are you doing here?"

"I want to find my brother's killer. I'll do whatever you say."

---

Sarah and Carter followed Debbie Fisk along the walkway past a lagoon dotted with waterfowl. Below, parents stood by while their eager children fed the ducks. Debbie unlocked her door and led them into a spacious suite. A laptop connected to a large monitor sat on the round conference table. Next to that were yellow legal pads and pens.

Wistfully, Carter gazed out the window. It was so peaceful here. She pictured herself dropping out of sight, switching off her phone, and holing up here for a month while ordering takeout.

"I didn't realize the Ramada was this nice," she said.

Debbie set down her camera equipment. "You guys want anything to drink?"

"Water, if you have it," Sarah said.

She was surprised Debbie was so together. The way she carried herself made her seem controlled—*purposeful*. Looking at her, you would never know she had been caught up in a horrible, violent act less than twenty-four hours earlier. The television personality handed her guests bottles of water from the refrigerator.

Debbie removed the memory card from the video camera and inserted it into an external reader attached to the laptop. She pulled up two more chairs and took a seat in the middle. Sarah and Carter sat on either side of her. Sarah noticed that, without makeup, Debbie had a sprinkle of freckles on her nose and cheeks, which made her seem more youthful.

Sarah and Carter waited as Debbie opened Final Cut Pro and imported the video she and Donnie had shot.

"We didn't even get through a whole card," the woman said. "Here. This is the first thing we did."

When Sarah saw Donnie Fisk wisecracking on the screen, she felt Debbie's loss. Setting aside her emotions, she reviewed the three takes, paying particular attention to the house. She looked closely at the windows but didn't see anything.

"How do you know John Dos Santos committed suicide?" she said to Debbie. Then, to Carter, "You never found anything like that in those old *Dos Santos Weekly* papers."

Debbie paused the video. "That's because they covered it up. By then, Thaddeus Pruitt was dead. The man who took his place did as he was told and published a story stating that John Dos Santos had died from heart failure."

"But how—"

"Donnie found the death certificate. Dos Santos cut his own throat with a straight razor." Debbie choked up. "My brother was really good at research."

"So, this rich guy is found dead in his bedroom by the housekeeper?" Carter said. She covered her mouth. "Oh my God."

"What is it?" Sarah said.

"I don't think it was suicide. Remember when I saw Dolores's ghost covered in blood? What if *she* killed him?"

"And Donnie?"

"Maybe that was her, too."

Debbie scoffed. "You're crazy."

Carter gave her the stink eye. "I forgot. You don't believe in ghosts."

"My brother was killed by a man. I saw him."

An uncomfortable silence fell over them.

"That still leaves us with John Dos Santos," Carter said. Then, to Sarah, "He died on September 13th, right?"

"Yes. And that's the date of Dolores's last journal entry."

"Wait a second," Debbie said. "There's a journal?"

"A friend lent it to us. We've been using it to try and figure out what happened."

"I want to see it."

Sarah shook her head. "Sorry, I don't have it anymore."

"You gave it back to Alistair?" Carter said.

"Joe was worried about me. He didn't want me having any more visions."

They spent the next half-hour viewing and re-viewing the rest of the shots. But there wasn't much there—just short clips of the foyer, parlor, and dining room.

"That's all there is," Debbie said.

Sarah stared at the screen in disappointment. "Do you have the footage you shot at the mausoleum? Maybe there's something there."

Carter's phone vibrated. When she saw who it was, she answered immediately. The conversation was short. She scooted her chair back and stood.

"I need to go to Montecito," she said. "Maybe you guys can continue without me."

"Okay," Sarah said. "I'd lend you my car but…"

Carter rolled her eyes. "I don't drive a stick."

Without looking, Debbie reached over and grabbed the keys to her rental car. "Take mine. It's the silver Prius, remember?"

"Thanks. I'll check in with you guys later."

After Carter left them, Debbie turned to Sarah. "What's in Montecito?"

"Some friends of ours," Sarah said, and left it at that.

---

When Carter arrived at Harlan's house, she found several cars in the driveway, including Lou's SUV. She rang the front doorbell, and Mary let her in.

"Library," the housekeeper said, and walked away.

Carter hurried over and opened the door. Inside, she found Alistair staring at the cold fireplace, wearing his black suit. Lou and Charlie sat on the sofa.

"John Dos Santos didn't die from heart failure," she said. "His throat was cut."

The Englishman motioned for her to take a seat.

She went on. "Donnie Fisk found the death certificate. It listed the manner of death as suicide."

Alistair studied her face. "But you don't agree."

Carter rubbed her bracelet. "I think Dolores might've murdered him."

Lou looked from one to the other. "What's the motive?"

"Desperation," the Englishman said.

He retrieved Dolores's journal from the desk and flipped through the pages.

"She was tortured by what happened to all those children. Sarah thought it odd that the last entry occurred on the same day Dos Santos died." He read aloud.

"'I have prayed and prayed for an answer. But nothing comes. I can no longer sleep, even when I am at home with my dearest Lelo. The evil that plagues this house will never stop. I know now what I must do. *Que El Señor me proteja.*'"

He reread the last line to himself. Then, aloud, "'May the Lord protect me.'"

The Englishman looked gravely at Carter and proffered the book. Shrinking away, she stared at him.

"I don't wanna see," she said.

"We have to be sure."

"Why don't *you* do it?"

He looked at his ring and straightened it. "Because she won't show me. Carter, please."

She turned to Lou and Charlie. They knew nothing of the world she lived in or the danger it presented. Yet they, too, wanted her to go down this road—she saw it in their eyes. She thought of her friend. Alistair had told her Sarah was at the center. And Carter had promised to protect her at all costs. Stifling a sob, she reached for the journal.

It was night. Carter was upstairs in the mansion. She stood in the shadows outside the doors to the master suite. Inside, a man shouted.

"What are you doing? GET OUT!"

Now, a muffled woman's voice.

"I'll do as I please."

The woman spoke more urgently.

The man said something else. Then, a dull thud.

The man laughed. "What are you going to do with that?"

But his laughter was cut short.

Steeling herself, Carter approached the doors. One of them banged open, and a young girl wearing a bandeau and knickers ran out and down the stairs. Carter went inside.

She moved past the sitting area into a large bedroom. Like the rest of the house, everything had been decorated in Spanish Revival.

A huge bed with intricately carved wooden posts stood in the center. On the nightstand was a pitcher of water, a glass and spoon, paper packets of white powder, and a needle and syringe.

A naked man lay dead in the middle of the bed, his throat slit. Dolores placed the razor in his left hand and closed his fingers around it. Her uniform was covered in blood.

Carter sat quietly, a hand on her forehead, as Alistair laid the journal on the desk. He poured a glass of brandy and brought it to her. Everyone remained silent while she drank.

"Now I know Dolores did it," she said. "I saw her put the razor in his hand."

Charlie looked at the others. "So, the housekeeper murdered him to save those children. And now he wants revenge?"

Lou shook his head. "And he's using others to get it."

"Yes," Alistair said. "Including our Mrs. Walton."

The Englishman retrieved a 4x5 photo from the desk and handed it to Lou. The police chief glanced at it, then showed it to Carter. She studied the elderly woman carrying the colorful present.

"I still don't see what all this has to do with Sarah," she said.

"There has to be a connection between Dos Santos and her."

"Do we know what happened to Dolores?" Charlie said. Carter shook her head.

Lou sat rubbing the back of his neck while the others stood. He was still no closer to solving the recent murders.

"What do I tell the mayor?" he said.

After the others had left, Alistair invited Carter to walk with him in the garden. The air was cold and dry. Birds chirped merrily in the trees.

"Sorry about earlier," she said.

"Don't be. You've got a right to be scared."

"So, do you always wear that suit?"

"Not whilst sleeping."

She laughed. "Well, it is pretty sharp. Can I ask? How did you become a Guardian?"

They found a bench and sat. Alistair looked out at the

garden. In a nearby tree, a robin hopped from branch to branch.

"I'd just graduated from university. Rather than look for a job, I decided to travel. Went to Australia and New Zealand, then Indonesia, and finally, Vietnam."

"Why so far?"

"I wanted to escape. I had a twin sister. She was in hospital at the time. I couldn't bear it. So, I left."

"Alistair, I'm so sorry."

"I loved Honor. She was the only one who laughed at my silly jokes."

"Can you tell me about her?"

"She loved peanut butter sandwiches with lavender tea. And Monty Python. And Emily Dickinson. When she fell ill, she... She was no longer my sister."

"What happened to her?"

"Brain tumor. Inoperable. I returned just before she died. I didn't recognize her. She hardly weighed five stone. She'd always loved travelling. Adored Italy.

"Anyway, after the funeral, I took her ashes and scattered them in the hills of Norcia."

Carter showed him her bracelet. "The monastery. I'll bet you visited the Monastero di San Benedetto in Monte. They made this."

He glanced at it. "A monk found me on my knees, weeping. I was in the middle of nowhere, feeling sorry for myself."

"Were you wearing the black suit?"

He side-eyed her. "That came later. I must've looked pathetic because he invited me to join the other monks for their midday meal."

"And the rest is history," she said. "Is that where the Guardians are based? Norcia?"

"No. But we have strong ties to the monks. St. Benedict and all that."

She touched his arm. "Thanks for sharing that with me. I was just thinking. Earlier, you said there must be a connection between Sarah and John Dos Santos. But what if we're wrong? What if it's between Sarah and *Dolores*?"

"You mean, they might be related?"

"Why not? Sarah believes Dolores was psychic, only she didn't realize it. And anyway, it might explain why Dos Santos wants to harm Sarah."

"But doesn't she have other family? He'd want to attack them, too."

"They don't live in Dos Santos. Also, he may not see them as a threat because they're not psychic."

He stood. "We need to find out. Can you research it?"

"As soon as I get home."

The Englishman laid a hand on her shoulder. "There's one thing. The closer we get to John Dos Santos and his secret…" Carter looked away.

"The more we put Sarah in danger," she said.

## Twenty-One

The doorbell at Casa Abrigo chimed, and Carter left the kitchen to answer it. When she swung the front door open, she found Sarah and Joe bearing dessert and red wine.

"Come on in."

"Something smells really good," Sarah said. "Don't tell me you've been taking cooking lessons."

"Nope. But I did plan the menu and let GrubHub deliver it.

"Nice," Joe said.

Seeing the kitchen again warmed Sarah's heart. Unlike the first time she'd visited the house before the renovation, it was truly a home now. The food had been laid out on the island, and places were set at the round oak veneer Italian table.

"Hope you like Indian," Carter said. "I thought we could serve ourselves."

Sarah took a whiff of the chicken tikka. "There's an Indian restaurant in Dos Santos?"

Joe smirked. "Said the clueless realtor."

Their plates full, they sat in white leather chairs. Joe waited for Sarah to say a blessing, then opened the wine.

"Oh," Carter said, fanning herself. "Did you try the samosas?"

After they had gotten through most of the meal while keeping the conversation light, Sarah set down her fork and smiled knowingly at Carter.

"So, I get the feeling this isn't just a casual dinner," she said. "What are you up to?"

Carter cleared her throat and took a large swallow of wine.

"I need to work on being more devious," she said. "Okay, here goes. Alistair asked me to do some research on Dolores Lopez, right? And—"

"Wait, is that why you sent me that random text, asking about my grandmother?"

"Lelo." Carter rubbed her bracelet. "Dolores was her mother."

Sarah blinked hard and looked at Joe. Then, to Carter, "Are you sure? I mean, *absolutely* sure?"

"Yes. It wasn't easy, but I was able to piece everything together using old newspapers and marriage records I found online."

Joe filled everyone's wine glass. "Not to be rude, but why am I here?"

"Because this concerns you, too. I mean, you are getting married."

Sarah scooted her chair back, and taking her glass, walked in a slow circle, looking at small details and straightening things here and there. When she faced them again, she had a look of determination on her face.

"The slender thread," she said.

. . .

They sat in the living room with coffee and slices of flourless chocolate cake. A sheaf of handwritten notes in her lap, Sarah sat next to Joe on the sofa as Carter paced in front of them like a basketball coach during the playoffs.

"I still can't believe it myself," the girl said. "I checked and rechecked everything. There's no mistake."

Sarah referred to the notes. "So, Dolores had an older sister, Rosa, who married John Dos Santos?"

"She died of the Spanish flu in 1918, just before he returned from the war."

"And in 1920, Dolores marries Nesto Lopez, who is later killed in a factory accident. Joe, she mentions the accident in her journal."

"They only had one child," Carter said. "Consuelo. Her nickname was Lelo. She was four when her father died."

"And eventually, Lelo marries some guy with the last name of Cruz."

Carter nodded. "Correct. Mateo Cruz. They were married in 1945, after the war ended. They also had one child, your father."

"Eddie never mentions his dad. I wonder what happened to him."

"They divorced in 1954. So, Eddie would've been—"

"Two."

"Right. I found a Mateo Cruz living in El Paso. I'm pretty sure that's him."

"Is he still alive?"

"No, he passed in 1998."

"This is too weird," Joe said, draining his coffee cup.

Sarah flipped through the pages. "Carter, when did my grandmother die?"

"1973. Your dad was twenty-one."

"He never liked bringing her up. A while back, I got

him to admit that she was psychic. He said she used her gift to help people."

"You think she might've been a ghost hunter, too?" Joe said.

"Definitely not. He said she would counsel friends and neighbors and people from church."

Carter took a seat next to her friend. "Remember when you said you thought Dolores might be psychic? What if she passed it down to Lelo, and then to you?"

"You mean, like a family curse?"

"Whatever you wanna call it. Earlier, you said something about a slender thread. What did you mean?"

"It was a clue Alyssa had given me," Sarah said. "I knew she meant a connection. But I never realized. It's a *bloodline*.

"That explains why John Dos Santos is so interested in me. Wow, I'm the great-granddaughter of a murderer."

No one said anything for a long time. Sarah got up.

"I need to talk to Eddie again. He had to know about Dolores and John Dos Santos."

"Are you going to mention about his grandmother being Lizzie Borden?" Joe said.

"Okay, that's not even funny. But, no. I want to see what he says." Then, to Carter, "Thank you for doing all this homework."

"Not a problem. Sorry I had to—"

"Forget it. In a way, I'm relieved to know why these things are happening. Want some help cleaning up?"

"No, you guys go on home," Carter said. "I plan to call Alistair later and tell him what I told you."

"I appreciate you letting me know first. Hey, don't forget. We have that birthday party tomorrow."

"Thanks for the reminder. I haven't even bought a present."

"Don't worry, I already bought two—one from each of us."

At the front door, everyone said their goodbyes. Sarah hugged Carter and kissed her cheek.

"Thanks again for dinner. How are you feeling about the painting?"

Carter turned around and admired it. A spotlight shone on it, making the ghost lurking in the window glow.

"I love it. Joe, thank you again for installing the light."

"Happy to do it."

After they had gone, Carter began cleaning up. Carrying cups and saucers, she stopped and looked at the painting. When all this was over, she *would* try to contact Frannie. Though she didn't expect them to resume their friendship, she could at least tell her how sorry she was. And maybe, if Carter was lucky, Frannie would do the same.

---

Joe pulled his truck into Sarah's driveway and waited for her to get out.

"You know what I miss most?" he said, looking at the front door.

"The incredible sex?"

He laughed. "Yeah, well." He kissed her hand. "Certainly that. And sitting with you on the sofa, sipping Talisker and listening to jazz."

"Me, too. We'll have that again soon, I promise."

"Sarah, I'm worried about this curse, or whatever you want to call it."

"It's not a curse."

"The point is, I nearly lost you twice. What if there's a third time?"

"Joe, I can't predict the future. No one can. But whatever evil is plaguing this town, we have to stop it. It's hard to explain, but I feel a duty to use this gift. I never asked for it. But God decided I should have it. My great-grandmother didn't know what it was, and she suffered horribly. Look what it made her do."

"When I was a kid, my sister and I attended Hebrew school," Joe said. "There's one quote that always stuck with me. 'A son shall not bear the iniquity of the father.' What your great-grandmother did in 1925 has nothing to do with you."

"I know."

"But I get it. It's one of the reasons I love you so much. You don't put yourself first. I'm scared, that's all."

"Me, too. But I've got Carter and Harlan, and Alistair now."

"And me."

"Especially you." She hugged and kissed him. "I adore you." She laughed. "I'd better go in before I do something stupid like inviting you in."

"Night, Sarah."

He kissed her and lingered in his truck as she walked to her front door. And that was when he decided. He, too, would pray. For Sarah, Carter, and everyone in Dos Santos.

---

Tim turned off Dos Santos Boulevard onto a familiar side street that led to the outskirts of town. Earlier, he had tried visiting Harlan but without success. He hadn't spoken to the lawyer since that business with the haunted mirror. And now, the old man was dying. The voices in the cop's head spoke to him constantly, telling him things—dark things. Harlan might have been able to help stop them. But it appeared Tim was on his own.

The streetlights were too bright, and he had to rub his eyes to focus. It didn't help that he hadn't slept well in days. Others might buy a bottle and hope to crash for a few dreamless hours. But Tim didn't drink, and he never took drugs—not even pain relievers.

He continued toward the wrong side of town, gritting his teeth against the constant drone of a demonic chorus that urged him to engage in behavior he knew was wrong. He fought these temptations every waking hour.

Though he hated this neighborhood, Tim patrolled it each night. This part of town was known informally as Squirrel Flats. Back in the day, the locals had dubbed it that because the main road used to be a major truck route. Each year, semis with tractor trailers ran over hundreds of the rodents who tried crossing the road.

Now, drug dealers and prostitutes used the dark, desolate street corners to ply their trades. Whenever they saw a police cruiser coming, they would scatter like cockroaches into the night. And that pleased the cop. One day, he would rid the streets of the filth altogether, using his gun as a winnowing fan.

A 7-Eleven was just coming up on the right. As usual, Tim would stop and use the restroom. He would buy a large black coffee to keep himself alert. Though he couldn't see them, he knew vagrants were lurking in the shadows. He'd deal with them later.

He was about to make his turn when a scantily dressed teenaged girl ran into the street, screaming and waving her arms at him. He pulled over and lowered his window, his right hand on his weapon.

"Thank God!" she said. "These guys tried to kidnap me and my friend!"

"When?"

"A few minutes ago. I got away, but they took her."

"Okay, get in."

She ran around to the passenger side and climbed into the front seat. When Tim saw her bare legs, he looked away.

He pulled into the 7-Eleven parking lot and stopped. It was hard for him to breathe, and he had to take a moment to pull himself together.

"Can you describe the kidnappers or the vehicle?" he said.

"They were these two weird dudes. Kind of gross-looking. One of them had dried blood down the front of his shirt."

Her top was too tight, and her black bra was showing.

"Hair color?"

"Dark, I guess. And their eyes. They were…not normal."

"What do you mean?" He inhaled her sweet perfume.

"They were black. Dude, like, *all black*."

"Okay, and the vehicle?"

"It was a white van with no windows. I-I didn't get a license number."

"Any markings on it?"

"Not that I remember. Wait, I feel like it might've been a rental. There was this sticker on the back with a company name and phone number."

"Do you know which way they went?" She pointed. "What's your name?"

"Kirsty."

"How old are you?"

Taken aback, she smiled with embarrassment. "Nineteen?"

"What are you doing out here?"

"I live in the apartments over there. My friend and I were just hanging out. I mean, we weren't—"

"Okay. Can you call 911? You can tell them anything else you remember."

"They took my phone."

"Use the one inside. I'm going to look for that van."

Tim waited for her to run into the store. He had an erection.

She hurried to the counter and spoke to the night manager. While she explained, she pointed at Tim's cruiser. The man leaned over and looked out. Reluctantly, he handed her a cordless phone.

Thinking about the girl, Tim felt ashamed. Willing himself to concentrate, he got on the radio and reported the incident, asking the dispatcher to put out an APB on the van. Then, he went in pursuit of the kidnappers.

He had been up and down practically every side street and hadn't spotted any vehicle fitting the description. Now, he headed for the railroad tracks. Another police cruiser came toward him, its light bar flashing. Riley. They parked side by side.

"Any sign of them?" Tim said.

"Nothin' so far."

"Okay, why don't you check by the old nursery. I'm going on up ahead."

Tim cruised the street that became a dirt road. He thought about Kirsty again—her smooth legs and plump, inviting breasts. He needed to focus. What had she said? *Dried blood down the front of his shirt.* When he realized where he was, he continued toward the Dos Santos mansion.

The house appeared stark and strangely beautiful in the yellow moonlight. A white van was parked outside the fence. He was about to go in when he remembered protocol and radioed for backup. All he could do was wait.

The voices in his head were clearer now. They urged him to do whatever he pleased with the girl. She wanted it —she wanted *him*. He tried ignoring them. It wasn't long before Officer Riley pulled up, followed by the police chief's SUV.

Lou climbed out, his gun drawn. He signaled for the other two cops to check the van. Somewhere, a barn owl hooted, its cry mournful. The police chief swept the property with his eyes. The other cops returned, gripping their weapons. Radio chatter punctuated the silence.

"We found cable ties, duct tape, and a medical bag with drugs and syringes," Tim said.

Lou walked up to the fence to check the gate. The lock had been cut. He undid the chain and walked into the yard. The others followed.

"Riley, you and I will go into the house. Tim, I want you to check the perimeter. There might be a cellar door. Be careful. When you're done, position yourself by the gate, in case they try escaping out the front."

Tim took off around the side as Lou and the other cop entered the house, weapons raised.

"Please, no," a girl said, her voice a faint echo.

The sound had come from the parlor. Lou glanced back at Riley. The cop snapped on his flashlight. Pointing his weapon with both hands, Lou made his way forward. The floor was covered in leaves and grime.

"Police!"

When Lou entered, he discovered a teenage girl lying on her side. She had on faded jeans shorts. Her white crop top had been ripped open. Whimpering, she covered herself with her hands.

Behind him, running footsteps. Then, a gunshot,

followed by another. Lou pivoted and stared at the open front door.

"Take care of her," he said to Riley.

Lou bolted outside, where he found Tim standing with his legs apart, gun raised. The body of a man lay motionless on the ground in front of him. Another gibbered as he tried crawling away, one leg bleeding badly. Two knives lay in the dirt.

Tim lowered his weapon. "They tried to attack me."

Putting away his gun, Lou stared at the two suspects, one of whom was most likely dead.

"Call it in," he said. "And handcuff that sorry sack of shit over there."

---

Lou stood outside the fence with the girl, who shivered in Riley's police bomber jacket. The EMTs rolled the gurney with the delirious wounded man toward one of the ambulances. The patient's pant leg had been cut off and his leg was bandaged. An IV was attached to his left arm just above the hand. After they had loaded him into the ambulance and closed the doors, Lou approached them.

"I assume you're taking him to Cottage. I'll follow you over so I can question him." The paramedics exchanged a worried look. "What?"

"I don't think you'll get much out of him, is all," the first one said.

"Why? Doesn't he speak English?"

"He doesn't speak anything. You know all that blood on his shirt?"

"Yeah?"

The EMT's eyes shifted. "Someone cut out his tongue."

Riley joined the police chief as the ambulance drove away.

"I need you to go to the hospital and ensure that guy stays handcuffed to the bed," Lou said. "Also, make sure they get his DNA."

"No problem, Chief."

"Where's Tim?"

"Last time I saw him, he was sitting in his cruiser."

Lou returned to the girl. "I'll give you a ride home. Wait in my SUV over there."

Nodding, she walked off. Lou checked Tim's cruiser, but he wasn't there. He continued on in the dark toward the tree line, where he found the cop looking at the stars.

"Tim?"

Tears streamed from his eyes. "The voices," he said. "They've stopped. Oh dear Lord, they stopped."

"What are you talking about?"

He wiped his nose with his sleeve. "It doesn't matter. Chief, I shot those guys because—"

Lou put a hand on his shoulder. "They had knives. You fired because they threatened you. That's what I want to see in the report. Got it?"

"Yeah. Yeah, I can do that."

"Go back to the station and write it up. Then, I want you to go home and get some rest."

Tim returned to his cruiser and drove off. Lou looked at the stars in the black sky. He trudged back to his SUV. Inside, the girl sat looking at the floor, her small shoulders shaking.

"It's okay," he said. "You're safe now."

Driving toward Squirrel Flats, he didn't ask her a lot of questions. He would wait until tomorrow. As they chatted, he learned that she lived with her mother, who was divorced and worked in town. The girl didn't have a job, and with no money, there was no prospect of school.

When they arrived at the apartment building, Lou pulled over and let her out. She began walking away. Then, she removed the jacket and laid it neatly on the passenger seat.

"Thank you," she said.

The girl hurried toward the building, where her friend was waiting for her. Crying, they hugged and went inside.

Lou headed back to his lonely condo on Church Street, thinking about the two men he and his officers had caught. He was happy they had saved the girl. With any luck, he'd be able to tie at least one of the murders to the suspects.

He thought about Tim. Under normal circumstances, he would've confiscated his weapon until the officer-involved shooting investigation. But these were not normal times.

Soon, the demolition team would tear down the cursed mansion. And on the day that happened, Lou would put on his dress shoes and dance on the remains.

## Twenty-Two

Sarah promised herself she wouldn't be angry with Eddie. She placed six bottles of Modelo in the refrigerator and threw away the carrier. Her father watched her in silence. Was his eye twitching?

"There," she said. "That should hold you for one or two days."

She opened a beer and handed it to him. Then, she removed her leather jacket and draped it over her chair. Taking a seat, she folded her hands and gave him one of her professional realtor smiles. He eyed her with suspicion.

"Aren't you having one?" he said. "I still don't see why you're asking all these questions. The past is the past. You can't change it, *mija*."

"No, I can't. But I can become smarter. Did Abuela ever talk about Dos Santos?"

"Not that I remember."

"But you must've known Dolores worked for John Dos Santos." She hadn't meant her tone to be accusatory. "Why didn't you tell me?"

"I didn't think you needed to know."

"Oh my God, Eddie. I *need* to know! I'm sorry." She got up. "Maybe I will have that beer."

He drank his in uncomfortable silence as she got herself one and took a seat.

"Tell me about Abuelo," she said.

"I don't remember him. And my mother never talked about him."

"You don't have any old photos?"

Avoiding eye contact, he picked at the label on his beer bottle. She was about to say something, but when she recognized his turmoil, she decided to remain silent. Then, he looked at her.

"Wait here," he said.

Sarah's father left the kitchen for a few minutes. When he returned, he was holding a brown leatherette photo album. On top was an old black-and-white photo with scalloped edges. He placed the things on the kitchen table.

"I almost burned these," he said. "If your sister hadn't caught me…"

She got up and hugged her father. He had been trying to protect her in the only way he knew how. She sat down and picked up the photo.

Sarah stood off to one side on the vast lawn in front of the Dos Santos mansion. It was daytime. The sky was clear, and there was a warm breeze carrying a sweet scent that she recognized as mountain lilac.

The photographer stood in front of Dolores and Lelo holding a large format rosewood camera with a leather bellows. When the little girl saw Sarah, she smiled at her.

"Sarah?" Eddie said. He was sitting next to her now.

She patted his hand. "I'm fine."

"The way you looked just now—your expression. It was like seeing my mother. I'm sorry I didn't tell you."

"It's okay."

She set aside the photo and opened the album. Turning the pages, Sarah felt herself moving through time.

She was transported to Santa Barbara in the late 1920s, continuing through the Great Depression, and on to WWII. The flood of living images came at her rapidly, making her dizzy.

When she arrived at a wedding photo, she placed her palm on the page.

Lelo and Mateo stood in the kitchen of a small bungalow. Sarah smelled the ocean through the open windows.

She stood in a corner, unseen, as her grandparents argued, alternating between Spanish and English. The tension grew.

They were fighting about Lelo's psychic ability. Mateo wanted a normal life with children and without ghosts. He begged his wife to stop.

Sarah removed her hand from the book, her head down. She knew now why her grandparents had divorced. Mateo had had enough. She wondered if the same fate awaited Joe and her.

"Why didn't you ever share this with Rachel and me?" she said.

Eddie took a long swallow of beer. "I thought if I put everything away, none of this would touch you or your sister. Then, Alyssa died, and you started having those dreams and visions. Just like my mother. It brought back all those memories."

He took Sarah's hand. "I begged God to spare you from what she went through. But I guess He has other plans."

"Do you have anything else of hers?"

"Some old letters. But there's nothing in there about Dos Santos."

"I'd like to read them sometime. Maybe when all this is over." She put on her jacket. "Thanks for showing me this."

He picked up the album. "Do you want to take it with you?"

"No. Promise me you'll let Rachel and Katy see it."

"I will."

"Can I have this photo, though?"

He handed it to her. Then, he kissed her cheek. "What are you going to do? About Dos Santos, I mean."

"I don't know," she said. "Nothing I do seems to help."

"There's always prayer."

"Yes. That is something I know how to do. I love you."

She hurried out of the house and got into her car. Soon, she would pick up Carter so they could attend Mia Chernov's birthday party. She thought again about the hundreds of images parading through her mind as she turned the pages of the photo album. This was something new. Maybe her powers were getting better—stronger.

"Let's hope they're good enough to defeat John Dos Santos," she said, and drove off.

———

Lou was standing with Franklin next to the body when Alistair Goolsby walked into the autopsy room. Seeing the

Englishman in the elegant black suit, Franklin nodded appreciatively.

"Finally," the ME said to his friend. "We're getting some class around here."

"Are you saying I don't have class?"

The Englishman approached the corpse. The blue sheet was folded down to the man's waist. The ME hadn't started the autopsy yet, so there was no Y-incision. The deceased looked to be around fifty. With numerous knife scars and dark hair flecked with gray. His nearly hairless arms and neck were covered in Satanic tattoos.

"Why didn't you ask Sarah to come?" Franklin said to Lou.

"She and Carter were unavailable. And I didn't want to wait. I appreciate you doing this, Alistair."

"Happy to help."

The Englishman stood there, waiting patiently. The police chief and the ME shared a confused look.

"Did you want us to wait over there?" Lou said.

"It might be better if you left the room." He gave them a tolerant smile. "If you don't mind."

"Sure, I guess."

When he heard the door close, Alistair positioned himself next to the body. He whispered a Hebrew prayer, and raising his hand, ordered the man lying in front of him to rise.

The table shook violently, as if from an earthquake, and chemical bottles on the shelves rattled against one other. One of them fell and shattered on the floor, releasing a powerful odor of isopropyl alcohol.

A luminous form emerged from the cadaver's chest, floated upward, and settled on the floor. The bewildered, naked man looked around the room. When he saw the Guardian's ring, he cowered.

"Who are you?" Alistair said.

Groaning, the man avoided the Englishman's eyes and shook his head violently. Alistair touched the man's lips, his fingers emitting a burst of blue sparks. The man came to attention and faced him.

"I said, who are you?"

"Nash."

"Just Nash?" The ghost blinked stupidly. "Where are you from?"

"Puyallup, Washington."

"Why did you kidnap the girl?"

"He wanted a sacrifice."

"Who?"

"You know."

"And James Stark? Was he a sacrifice, too?"

The ghost grinned at him with missing teeth, drool leaking from the corner of his mouth.

"They all are," he said.


When Lou and Franklin reentered the autopsy room, they found the Englishman sitting at a desk, calmly typing something into his phone.

"Well?" the police chief said, getting out his notebook. "Any luck?"

"He's called Nash. Sorry, that's the only name I could get out of him. Comes from the Pacific Northwest—Puyallup, I think he said."

He showed the men Google Maps on his phone. While Lou continued writing, Alistair rose and smoothed his pants.

"He admitted to kidnapping the girl. You should check his DNA against James Stark and Yoshi Kuroda."

"You think he killed them?"

"He and his friends."

The Englishman was about to leave when Franklin noticed his left hand. A long, bloody scratch ran the length of it all the way up to his shirt cuff.

"Let me clean that for you," the ME said. "We don't want it getting infected."

Franklin found cotton balls and Betadine and treated the wound as Lou finished up his notes.

The ME applied a bandage. "What happened?"

Alistair looked at his hand without much interest.

"He wasn't very keen on going back," he said, and walked out.

---

Sarah stood at Elizabeth Chernov's front door with Carter. Inside, children laughed. It sounded like they were playing a game.

"Do you think we should just walk in?" she said.

"Try the door."

It was unlocked. Sarah entered, delighted to find the foyer and living room decorated with colorful calaveras, musical instruments, and other Mexican-themed Day of the Dead items. Several small children raced past, laughing.

"Hello?" Sarah said.

Elizabeth came out of the kitchen, wiping her hands on her apron. "Sarah!"

"Elizabeth, this is Carter Wittgenstein."

After they'd finished introductions, the harried young mother reached for the gifts. "Let me take those."

"I'm sorry we couldn't get here sooner," Sarah said.

"Don't worry about it." Then, in a low voice, "You'll be okay to check out the backyard?"

"Sure. And don't worry, we'll keep it on the down-low."

"I'll put these with the other presents. Why don't you go outside. I'm afraid these little ones are everywhere."

"I love the decorations."

The woman laughed. "Oh, that. I thought for sure Mia would want something from *Frozen*. But she watched *Coco* at a friend's house the other day, and now she's addicted."

Sarah and Carter exchanged a knowing glance and followed the children's voices through the den to the backyard.

Carter noticed a picnic table decorated with a Día de los Muertos-themed tablecloth and crepe paper. Some of the children were using the playset. Others chased each other around the table. Though it was a happy scene, she sensed something dark. Something unwanted.

Then, Carter saw her—a poorly dressed woman of around thirty walking quickly toward a gate leading to the street. No one else seemed to pay any attention to her. Before exiting, she glanced back at Carter with eyes that were dead.

"I wonder where Mia is."

Startled, Carter turned to find Sarah standing next to her. They walked over to the dog's shelter, where they discovered the little girl standing inside by herself.

"Mia?" Sarah said. The child ran to hug her. "This is my friend, Carter."

"Hey, Mia. Happy birthday."

"Thank you, Carter. I was just saying hello to Flossie and her babies."

Thinking the same thing, the women exchanged a concerned look.

"Oh?" Carter said. "Are they here?"

"They're right over there."

She looked at where Mia was pointing and walked over. She stumbled on a gopher hole and, as she toppled forward, grabbed one of the redwood posts holding up the shelter.

Carter stood in front of the shelter against a harsh gray sky.

Two men and another woman—the one Carter had just seen in the backyard—attacked the golden retriever with hunting knives. The frightened animal howled in pain.

They'd made sure to do the puppies first so their mother could watch them die.

"Let's go, clumsy," Sarah said as her friend shrank away from the shelter.

"Sorry about that."

Composing herself, Carter looked at the little girl, who had her hands behind her back and wore a mysterious smile.

"Did you say hi to them?" Mia said.

Glancing at her friend, Sarah took the little girl's hand. Carter returned to the shelter.

"Let's go and find your friends," Sarah said. "Hey, I saw all those decorations. Wow."

"I love *Coco*."

"You know what? Me, too."

Carter spent another few minutes exploring the enclosure. Still thinking about the strange woman, she wandered into the house and continued on to the dining room. All of Mia's presents were arranged neatly on the table, including the ones Sarah had brought. She moved closer and stared.

There, toward the back, sat a box wrapped in purple paper and tied with a bright yellow ribbon. It was identical to the one she had seen in the photo of Karen Walton. As she stood there staring at it, Elizabeth walked past.

"Quite a haul, right?"

Carter forced a laugh. "I'll say. Do you happen to know who brought that one?"

Elizabeth came closer and looked at the purple present. "You know, I don't. Is there a card?"

She stepped past Carter and examined the box. A small, plain tag was taped to the top. It read simply, HAPPY BIRTHDAY, MIA.

"That's strange," she said. "It's not signed."

Carter looked around, and making sure no one else was listening, took the present.

"Elizabeth, we need to get this thing out of here."

"Why?"

"I'll tell you in a minute, but not here. Can you go find Sarah and meet me in the garage?"


Sarah and Elizabeth entered the garage through the kitchen. The light was already on. Carter stood over a work bench, holding a pair of scissors and staring at the open box. Sarah came closer and looked inside. The tissue paper was pulled apart, revealing a handmade doll.

"Oh my gosh, what a pretty doll," Elizabeth said, reaching for it.

Sarah grabbed her hand. "Don't touch it."

"Why? It's just a doll."

"No," Carter said. "It's not."

Elizabeth backed away. "I don't understand."

Sarah patted her hand. "It's okay. No harm done.

Carter and I are going to take this away now. Can you open the garage?"

"What about the rest of the presents?"

"I'm sure they're fine," Carter said.

Sarah smiled reassuringly. "Please wish Mia a happy birthday. Tell her something came up, and we had to leave."

"Okay. God, I just realized. Does that thing have anything to do with what happened to the dogs?"

Sarah hesitated before answering. Then, "Yes, but you and Mia are safe now."

Elizabeth laughed bitterly. "Fr. Brian asked me to pray the Rosary every day. With planning the party and everything, I haven't really been… That's it, I'm starting tonight."

She opened the garage door and waited as the two women left with the box. Carter had made sure to pack all of the paper and ribbon, as well as the scissors.

"God bless you both," Elizabeth said after they had gone.

---

A cold wind came up, blowing debris across Harlan's garden in Montecito. Sarah stood on a gravel path with Carter, watching intently as Alistair repeated what he had done with the cursed cat toy. The doll lay innocently inside the box.

Using his folding knife, he sliced its front open lengthwise. Avoiding the dark object inside, he touched the doll's head with two fingers. He prayed silently and raised his hand.

At first, nothing happened. Curious, he looked up at Carter. Obediently, she dropped to one knee next to him.

He positioned her right hand over the box and showed her how to splay her fingers like his. Together, they said the Hebrew prayer aloud.

This time, the doll and everything with it burst into blue flames and disintegrated into nothingness.

"Holy…" Carter said.

The Englishman sprinkled the ground with holy water, as well as his knife. Carter rose, and Sarah took her hand.

"There's something I don't understand," Sarah said to Alistair. "Why did it take both of you this time?"

"That was an unusually powerful spell. It's a good job you removed the doll before the girl could interact with it."

"What do you think Mrs. Walton's intent was?" Carter said.

The Englishman folded his knife and slipped it into his pocket. He started back toward the house.

"Alistair." He stopped and turned around. "What was she trying to do?"

"Kill her, of course," he said.

---

"Open the windows, will you?" Harlan said.

He lay in his bed with his eyes closed. His breathing was shallow. Alistair crossed the room and pulled back the curtains. After moving aside the sheers, he opened the windows all the way, allowing in fresh air and the sounds of birds. In the distance, a gardener raked one of the gravel paths, his wheelbarrow nearby.

The Englishman poured a glass of water and brought it over. He set it down on the nightstand and helped Harlan sit up. He had already told his fellow Guardian about Sarah's family history. The elderly attorney didn't react, and Alistair wondered if he'd known all along.

Harlan took a sip of water. "It's possible that if Sarah had not discovered the mirror, John Dos Santos would never have known about her."

"Or you."

"Or me. At the time, I wasn't aware that anyone in Dos Santos had that kind of ability."

The Englishman took a seat next to the bed. "Sarah told me that a woman called Bethany Pruitt had accused her of opening a door."

"In a way, she was right. Which is why I tried to thwart Sarah in the beginning."

"But her stubbornness won the day."

Harlan laughed weakly. "Yes. Which reminds me. How are things progressing with Carter?"

"She's incredibly talented—more than I realized."

"Is she ready, do you think?"

"Not sure. She's an excellent student. But she has trouble relying on her instincts. Sometimes, I think she's more comfortable around books."

"That's because she lacks confidence. You must find a way to instill it."

"How? You know how bad I am with people."

"Alistair, you have a great capacity for love. Honor knew that." The Englishman looked away. "Treat Carter as you would your sister. Watch over her. I promise you, she'll come around."

But he wasn't sure if he could. Was he ready to open that door again? Letting feelings in he had suppressed for years? If something happened to Carter, he couldn't bear it. He thought about his sister. What would she want him to do? Be *human*, of course.

"What about Mrs. Walton?" he said.

Harlan looked at him, unblinking. "You and Carter must find her. Sarah's life may depend on it."

## Twenty-Three

F r. Brian rang the bell and waited anxiously. When he had gotten the call, he hastily arranged for other priests to cover the morning Masses. Mary answered the door. He looked at her with concern. It was obvious she hadn't slept. Without words, she stepped back and allowed him to enter.

Carrying his black bag, he trotted up the stairs. She followed at a distance. The priest knocked once and entered the bedroom, where he found his longtime friend in the dying process. His skin was pallid, his breath faint.

"Have you given him anything?" Fr. Brian said to Mary.

"Morphine."

The lawyer's eyes were barely open as the priest opened his bag. He removed his purple stole, a small bottle of oil, holy water, and a black breviary. He kissed the stole and placed it over his shoulders, then sprinkled holy water on the patient and the bed. When he had done that, he leaned in and whispered.

"It's Brian. Would you like to make your Confession?"

Harlan nodded. The priest turned to Mary and asked her to leave. He began with the Sign of the Cross. Harlan did his best to tell his friend his sins. Then, exhausted, he went quiet. This time, Fr. Brian didn't ask him if he was sorry for what he had done.

"Please," the old lawyer said. "I want to receive Communion."

The last time Harlan had been to Confession, Fr. Brian had denied him absolution because he wasn't sorry for the deaths he had caused over the years. Never mind that the victims were evildoers. In the God of the New Testament's eyes, killing was wrong. When the priest didn't answer, Harlan looked away.

"You're right, of course. I might go to hell. But it won't be your fault."

The priest looked at his friend. Harlan had become so very thin, like a leaf fallen from a withered tree. He thought of John 20:23, and his heart ached. *Whose sins you forgive are forgiven them, and whose sins you retain are retained.*

Laughing bitterly, Fr. Brian shook his head. "You always were a crafty old bastard."

Harlan took his hand, knowing he had won.

"*Te absolvo,*" the priest said, making the Sign of the Cross over his friend.

Fr. Brian reached into his bag and took out a small, round, polished brass container. He opened it and removed a consecrated Host. With humility, Harlan put out his tongue. The priest laid the precious Host on it with care. Continuing to pray, he anointed Harlan's forehead and hands with the *oleum infirmorum*—oil of the sick.

. . .

Mary—and now Alistair and Charlie—waited outside in the hallway. She clutched her rosary. All of them prayed silently. The door opened, and the priest stepped out.

"You can go in if you want," he said.

The housekeeper averted her eyes. "Thank you, Father."

He made his way down the stairs slowly, stopping on the landing and looking out the tall window at the garden. The sun hadn't quite risen over the house yet, and the grounds were still in shadow. Choking back a sob, he walked down the rest of the way and left the house.

Mary stood next to the bed, holding her employer's hand. His breaths came short and rapid. He was near death. Helplessly, she looked at the others. When she turned back, Harlan was no longer breathing.

She pressed her ear to his heart and listened. Covering her mouth, she stepped back. Charlie took her hand, then put his arm around her and held her as she wept softly.

The Englishman came forward and, raising his right hand over the body, recited a psalm in Hebrew. When he had finished, he removed the ring from Harlan's right hand. He pulled out a blue velvet box from his jacket pocket and, with reverence, placed the ring inside.

"'Because I could not stop for Death,'" he said, "'he kindly stopped for me.'"

Surrounded by other parishioners, Sarah and Joe walked down the steps of Our Lady of Sorrows. It had been his idea to come with her to Mass, and she was elated. As they approached Joe's truck, Sarah got a call. She got out her phone and answered.

"Morning," she said as she climbed into the cab. *"What?"*

The phone fell into her lap as the voice on the other end continued speaking. Joe heard Carter's voice faintly, asking for Sarah.

"What happened?" he said.

His fiancée looked at him. A single tear fell from her eye. "It's Harlan. He passed away this morning."

The news hit Joe like a body blow, but not because he felt anything for the elderly attorney. He hardly knew him. No, it was Sarah. He was afraid for her. He reached for the phone.

"Carter? It's Joe. No, she's here. We're in Santa Barbara." He glanced at Sarah. "I don't think that's a good idea."

"What is it?" Sarah said.

"Alistair wants you to meet him at the house. I don't think you should."

She wiped away her tears. "I have to." She took the phone from him. "Carter? I'll be there."

They drove most of the way in silence. Though Joe was furious, he tried not to show it. He had never been to Montecito before. Despite her grief, Sarah guided him to their destination.

They passed through the gates and headed up the driveway. He pulled up next to Carter's MINI Cooper.

"Want me to wait out here?" he said.

"No. Why don't you head back. I'll catch a ride with Carter."

"You can still get out of this."

"I can't." She leaned across the seat and kissed him. "I love you."

The front door opened, and Mary appeared. Sarah got out of the truck and walked toward her. When they were inside, she hugged the grieving housekeeper.

"Mary, I am so sorry. Was Harlan able to see a priest before…?"

"Fr. Brian came right away." She sighed. "Everyone's in the library."

Steeling herself, Sarah followed her. When they went in, she found Charlie and Carter sitting on the sofa. Alistair stood next to the fireplace, which was lit. She recalled Harlan telling her that the fragrant wood came from the yew tree, imported from Sardinia. As soon as Sarah sat, Carter hugged her.

The Englishman stood there alone, deep in thought. The uncomfortable silence went on for more than a minute.

"Alistair?" Mary said.

Seeing the others looking at him, he reddened. "Sorry. There's still so much to do. I'd hoped Harlan would be with us. I know he wanted to."

"What about the funeral arrangements?" Sarah said.

Mary leaned over. "Those were made weeks ago."

"And where will he be buried?"

"He won't," the Englishman said. "We plan to cremate the body and scatter the ashes."

"It's the only way," Mary said, wringing her hands.

There was a knock at the door. A moment later, Elsa appeared. Mary rose.

"I hope everyone can stay for breakfast," she said, and left the room with the maid.


Food had been set up on the buffet. There were fresh bagels, lox, and various flavors of cream cheese, as well as fresh fruit. Everyone else was getting food. Though she wasn't hungry, Sarah decided to fix herself a plate.

When everyone was seated, Mary led them in a blessing. As they ate, the mood lightened. Mary told the guests the story of how she had come to work for Harlan. Charlie revealed how he'd been hired, and Sarah finished with her first meeting with Harlan, after which she had formed an admittedly unflattering picture of the attorney.

"Turns out, he was a sweetheart," Sarah said. "And he cared so much about people."

"Indeed," Alistair said. "And on that note, I'd like to talk about what remains to be done in Dos Santos. Charlie, can you—"

"Can't we take a minute!" Sarah said. The room was still. "Harlan—a man we all cared for and respected—is *dead*. Can we at least say a prayer?"

Mary stood. "Sarah's right. I'd like us to say a 'Hail Mary.'"

Everyone lowered their eyes as Mary led them in the prayer. When they were finished, she took her seat.

"Thank you," Sarah said.

Charlie glanced at Alistair, unsure what to do. The Englishman nodded, and Mary excused herself. The investigator wiped his mouth with his napkin and swallowed some coffee.

"Okay," he said, setting his notebook on the table. "A couple of nights ago, two men abducted a girl and brought her to the Dos Santos mansion. We believe they were going to kill her there."

"Are they in custody?" Carter said.

"One of them is. The other is dead. Lou told me he likes them for the Yoshi Kuroda murder and, possibly, James Stark. He's ordered DNA tests."

"Do you think anyone else is involved?" Sarah said.

"Unknown. Now, we're still looking for Karen Walton, but so far, nothing's turned up. Carter, you finding that cursed present was lucky."

Charlie and Alistair exchanged a look. "Alistair is of the opinion that, whatever Mrs. Walton's agenda is, she's not finished."

"Which is why we have to find her," the Englishman said.

Sarah nodded to her friend. "What can Carter and I do to help?"

"I'm planning a visit to the mausoleum, and I'm taking Carter with me."

The girl put her hand on Sarah's. "We realize you can't go there because of what happened."

"There must be something I can do."

"There is," Alistair said. "I'd appreciate it if you could continue your research. And if you're up to it, I'd like you to take back your great-grandmother's journal. Perhaps it will lead you to the truth about John Dos Santos."

"Okay, I will," Sarah said. "But I may need to get drunk first."

---

Carter pulled into Sarah's driveway and parked. Sarah got out and started toward her front door. She stopped and walked up to the driver-side window.

"Forget something?" Carter said.

"I hate to ask, but can you stick around while I look at the journal?"

"Of course."

Sarah opened the front door, setting off the alarm. She walked across the foyer to the panel and disabled it.

"When did you get an alarm system?" Carter said.

"Right after I found that cursed object."

Sarah walked into the living room and set her purse on the Italian coffee table. She zipped it open and stared at the black book inside.

"Maybe we should have a drink first," she said.

Carter stared at the book. "Great idea."

Sarah marched into the kitchen and returned with an ice-cold bottle of Orvieto, two glasses, and a tea towel. She set everything down on the table. Using the towel, she took out the journal. She poured the wine. Exchanging a nervous glance, they clinked glasses and, sitting on the sofa, tried the Orvieto.

"Don't you think it's a little strange," Sarah said, "that a doctor had the journal in his possession?"

"Now that you mention it. He must've been the family doctor."

"But why would *he* have the book and not Dolores?"

Carter took a huge swallow of wine. She tried reaching for the book, but her friend grabbed her hand.

"I have an idea," Sarah said. "What would happen if we held it at the same time?"

"You mean, like, going back there together? Would that even work?"

"There's one way to find out."

"I'm not sure Alistair would approve of this."

"Do you always do what that Englishman says?"

Carter gave her the stink eye. Their mouths set, they nodded and placed their hands over the journal, their fingers hovering just above it.

"On three," Sarah said. "One...two...*three*."

Sarah and Carter found themselves in the parlor of the Dos Santos mansion, standing next to a wall.

"Holy shit," Carter said. "We totally did it."

It was night, and the house was filled with well-dressed men and women who appeared to be celebrating with drinks and appetizers as Paul Whiteman's recording of "Somebody Loves Me" played on a Victrola. The front door was open. The breeze coming in was warm and carried with it the scent of mountain lilac.

They inched their way along the wall when a well-dressed young man brushed an older woman as he passed.

"I beg your pardon," he said.

He turned and looked at Sarah and Carter. They held their breath. Seeing nothing, he continued on.

"I could smell his sweat," Carter said.

"You mean the scented talcum powder didn't do its job?"

When they entered the dining room, Sarah found her great-grandmother speaking in low tones with a man she didn't recognize. He had longish white hair, a trim beard, and round black glasses. After a moment, Dolores entered the kitchen through a side door. The man waited for a time, then followed.

"Should we go after them?" Carter said.

"You go ahead. I'm going to take a look upstairs."

Alone now, Carter passed through the dining room to the kitchen and continued on to the back room, where she found the door slightly open. Through the crack, she saw Dolores and the white-haired man standing near the bed.

"I don't know if I can," the housekeeper said.

"You must. You're the only one."

"But if I fail, he'll—"

He took her hands in his. "You won't. We can no longer abide this. He must be stopped."

"But—"

"And what about your nightmares? Eliza tells me you've suffered horribly these past months."

"Yes. And now my daughter has the affliction."

"Don't you see? He's evil."


By the time Sarah reached the stairs, it was dark. Somehow, hours had passed. Outside, a fierce wind tore through the trees. Branches scratched the windows like monstrous claws tearing at the house. Clinging to the banister, she made her way up.

On the second floor, she continued past closed doors toward the master suite. A bone-chilling carnal moaning sounded through the door.

"Stop, you're hurting me!" a girl said.

"I'm just getting started."

Afraid for the girl, Sarah went inside. From the sitting room, she saw John Dos Santos naked under the sheets. He was incredibly thin, and his face was gaunt. On the nightstand lay drug paraphernalia.

A young girl wearing a bandeau and knickers stood next to the bed, shaking. He had her hand and tried dragging her back into bed. Sarah moved to the doorway.

John turned and faced Sarah with hatred in his eyes. "What are you doing? GET OUT!"

Startled, she looked behind her and saw Dolores coming toward him. She pulled the girl's hand free, and the child backed away.

"This has to stop," Dolores said.

John glared at her and, folding his arms, looked away. "I'll do as I please."

"Enough, John. You must stop. These are innocent children."

"I'm here to take away their innocence."

Sarah hadn't seen the girl slipping into the bathroom. When she returned, she had something in her hand.

She grabbed Dolores by the arm and swung her around violently. The housekeeper fell backward, hitting her head against the dresser.

The girl approached the bed. Sarah saw what was in her hand. It was a straight razor. John looked at the girl and laughed.

"What are you going to do with that?" He guffawed in her face, his eyes taunting and vicious.

Enraged, she brought her hand down in one quick motion and sliced his neck open. Surprised, he grabbed himself and tried to stop the blood squirting through his fingers.

On her feet now, Dolores gently took the razor away from the girl.

"Leave now," she said.

The girl ran from the room and down the stairs as John lay in his bed, delirious. When his hand dropped from his neck, a pulsing bright red stream coated his sheets.

Eventually, the blood slowed to a trickle. Then, his eyes flew open. They were black.

"I curse you all." His voice was like knives tearing at the sky.

Reaching his trembling hand toward her, he died, slumped over the side of the bed.

With difficulty, Dolores lifted him up and placed him on his back. Her face, hands, and uniform were covered in blood. With quiet deliberation, she positioned the razor in his left hand and closed his fingers around it.

Shaken, she walked past Sarah into the sitting room where a black Bakelite rotary dial telephone sat on a low table. She picked up the receiver and made a call.

"He's dead," she said, and hung up.

Sarah felt herself being pulled upward, away from the scene. Below, Dolores wiped down the phone with her apron, then left the master suite and headed down the stairs.

Soon, everything shrank to a pinpoint and was gone.

Sarah and Carter sat next to each other, both stunned. The journal lay on the table in front of them.

"It was the girl," Sarah said. "My great-grandmother didn't kill him."

Her hand jittery, Carter refilled their glasses and took a huge swallow of wine. "She was planning to, though."

"What?"

"With that man we saw. The one with the beard. He was trying to convince her."

Sarah clicked her fingernails on her glass. "So, when she went upstairs, she *was* going to kill him. But the girl got to him first."

"I just wish I knew who that guy was," Carter said. "He mentioned someone named Eliza."

"*Eliza.*" Sarah set down her glass and, using the tea towel, opened the journal and read the first entry.

I am keeping this journal at the recommendation of my dear friend Eliza Warrington.

"I think Eliza was married to that guy," Sarah said.

"So, *three* people planned this?"

"I don't know. Today's Sunday—the library's closed. I'm going there tomorrow when they open."

Carter sighed dramatically. "Meanwhile, I'll be in the ninth circle of hell with Alistair."

"The mausoleum?"

"Yeah." The girl poured herself more wine.

"Are you going to be okay to drive home?" Sarah said, eyeing her.

"No."

"Okay, it's after two. Why don't you hang out here. Then later, I'll cook. Might as well make a night of it."

"You know, ever since I met you, my drinking has gone up into the triple digits."

"You're welcome."

"Anyway, I should be sober enough later to run over to The Cracked Pot for some dessert."

"See, this is why I keep you around."

"So, it's not my scintillating personality?"

"That, too."

## Twenty-Four

Tiffany Gersh was late. Hurrying down the hallway at police headquarters, she had to maneuver between two officers heading her way. She found the conference room and walked in. Lou Fiore and Charlie Beeks were already seated, drinking coffee and chatting.

"Sorry, guys," she said, and placed her worn black nylon messenger bag on the conference table.

"Want an espresso, Tiff?" Lou said.

"No, thanks. And what did I tell you about calling me 'Tiff?'"

He side-eyed Charlie. "I forget."

She reached in and pulled out a sheaf of papers. Then, she laid out three reports—one for each of them. Pressing her lips together, she blew stray strands of hair from her face and slid into a chair.

"Okay, your hunch was right, Lou," she said. "The DNA from those guys you found at the Dos Santos mansion matches samples we took from the clothing of Yoshi Kuroda."

"And James Stark?"

"Him, too. I'm no lawyer, but I think you have enough here to get a conviction."

Charlie scanned the report. "And we think there were probably others, right?"

The police chief nodded. "I'm holding several people for questioning but they're refusing to cooperate. Tiffany, as a precaution, I got their DNA, too."

Lou reached over and grabbed five evidence bags, each containing a cotton swab. He handed them to the CSI technician. Then, he drained his coffee and stood.

"With Charlie's help, I think I've got a pretty good picture. Outsiders have been coming into Dos Santos, committing crimes and, in a few cases, murder.

"I also think they're the ones responsible for all these animal mutilations. I'm pretty sure they've been using that old tunnel to come into town undetected."

The investigator looked at his notes. "That's what Harlan and Alistair think."

"Tiffany, you proved that the soil taken from Leon Vogel is a match for what you found on James Stark. That tells me these freaks have been coming into Dos Santos for decades. But the violence has escalated only recently."

The technician gathered the rest of her things and, getting to her feet, addressed both men.

"I'm pretty much in agreement with you. But there's still one thing we haven't been able to answer."

"What's that?" Lou said.

"*Why* are they coming here?"

Lou glanced at Charlie and swallowed. "I'd tell you what I think, but then, you'd stop calling me up for dates."

"Does this have anything to do with Sarah Greene?"

"It has everything to do with her."

"Look, boys, I deal in science." She sighed. "And the

awful things people do to each other sometimes. Are you saying there's a paranormal angle to what's going on?"

"I never thought I'd hear myself admit it. But yes, I do."

Tiffany looked at Charlie, her hands on her waist. "What about you?"

"You're looking at an ex-Homicide cop. Believe me when I tell you, there's no other explanation."

"Either you two are in serious need of therapy—or *I* am. Tell you what. I'll stick to what I'm good at. Evidence. See ya."

A minute later, Charlie got up to leave and stopped at the door. "Maybe we *are* crazy."

"Crazy and scared," Lou said.

---

Sarah sat at a table at the public library, the familiar pile of history books in front of her. Though she was still grieving over Harlan, she had important work to do. She'd gone through most of the books the last time she was here and was unable to find even a single photograph of John Dos Santos, much less anything about his past. And all those letters she had borrowed from Bethany Pruitt were no help either.

She flipped through a coffee table book she'd skipped the last time. It covered the history of Dos Santos from its founding through just before WWII. She was mainly interested in 1925.

Turning the pages, Sarah was disappointed she hadn't experienced the moving through time effect she'd felt when looking at her grandmother's photo album. She wondered if she could coax her mind into bringing to life the history she saw on the pages before her.

She considered a full-page black-and-white photo of the downtown area circa 1920. It looked as if it had been taken at a corner on Dos Santos Boulevard. People in fine clothes, some in motion and blurred, paraded up and down both sides of the street. The sidewalks looked new. Black Ford Model T cars passed by lazily in both directions.

Closing her eyes, she pressed two fingers against the page while trying to clear her mind. She slowed her breathing. An erratic ball of light sputtered behind her eyes, then fizzled. *You can do this, Sarah.*

She decided to focus on a woman walking near the camera. She wore a stylish below-knee length drop-waist dress that had a loose, straight fit. She had short bobbed hair and a cloche hat. She was among a group of other similarly dressed women.

This time, when Sarah closed her eyes, she heard the woman laugh, with the sounds of the street as her accompaniment. Excited, she opened her eyes.

The photograph came to life with voices, cars honking, and someone in a window playing the accordion. The animated scene lasted for no more than a few seconds, then the picture froze.

"Wow," she said. "Can't wait to tell Carter."

She continued through the book until she arrived at a photo entitled "Founders Day Picnic, 1925." Around twenty people stood in two rows, smiling into the camera. Everyone was dressed up, including the children. A Rolls-Royce Silver Ghost was parked nearby. Sarah scanned people's faces with her fingers, then stopped.

"It's her." She closed her eyes.

. . .

Sarah found herself standing next to the photographer as he prepared to take the portrait. The air was filled with talking, laughing, and music from a nearby bandshell. The smell of grilling hot dogs reminded her she was hungry.

The photographer gestured to a child. "A little closer, dear. Thank you."

She was the girl Sarah had seen in the mansion, standing proudly in the front row. She wore the same blue silk dress, and there were matching ribbons in her hair.

Behind her on a riser stood the woman who had taken the girl upstairs that night at the mansion. Sarah recognized the distinctive silver filigree comb. And there was the white-haired man with the beard and glasses. Some of the other men she recognized from the parlor at the mansion. Her gaze traveled to the center of the group.

*There.* It was John Dos Santos, wearing an expensive gray suit with wide lapels. His long black hair was combed straight back, and his eyes were hooded. He wore no hat.

His cheeks sunken, he looked at Sarah instead of the camera. She felt herself being drawn to him.

Before she knew it, she was standing directly in front of him. All of the other sounds faded away, replaced by a keening that gave her a blinding headache.

"Your time is almost here, Sarah Greene," he said.

Back in the library, Sarah stared at the photograph. As her headache subsided, she studied the caption and identified the young girl as Cassie Morton. The woman behind her was Florence Rill. The man with the beard was Dr. Paul Warrington, and next to him, his wife, Eliza.

Sarah got out her phone and took a picture. She studied the page again, her eyes lingering on the bearded doctor. Then, she took out her phone and searched her contacts. When she located Debbie Fisk, she texted her.

> Hey it's sarah. Name of the doctor who signed death
> cert donnie found?

> Sure hang on… paul warrington.

> Thx. Talk soon. :)

Carter had said the doctor and Dolores were working together. That was why he'd recorded the manner of death as suicide, to protect the girl. And he took the journal, probably to keep it from falling into the wrong hands and implicating Dolores—and himself.

Sarah opened her laptop and did a Google search for Cassie Morton. After getting sidetracked by contemporary women with that name, she refined her search and got a hit. The link took her to a *Dos Santos Weekly* front-page article dated November 2, 1925.

## YOUNG LADY MURDERED; WOMAN ARRESTED
### Cassie Morton Stabbed Multiple Times and Left to Die.

A fourteen-year-old girl was found dead in Dos Santos Park by a young married couple walking their dog. The incident occurred just after sunset. Police were called to the scene immediately. Although details of the tragedy are lacking, it is evident that well-known local socialite Florence Rill killed the girl.

The couple, who do not wish to be identified, claimed

they heard screams and saw Miss Rill fleeing the scene. When police officers arrived at her home to question her, they discovered bloody clothing but no murder weapon.

Cassie Morton was an orphan who had lived with Miss Rill for several months. Police are unable to determine a motive at this time.

"Did they kill you because of what you did?" Sarah said.

She needed Carter. Sarah tried calling her without success. She let out a groan, which caught the attention of the other patrons. Casting her eyes down, she gathered up her belongings and left the library.

Outside, she left Carter a lengthy voicemail, detailing everything she had discovered.

---

Alistair parked the Land Rover just outside the cemetery gates. Carter climbed out of the passenger side. Her hands were freezing, and there was a coppery taste in her mouth. Nervous all the way over, she must have bitten the inside of her cheek.

The Englishman hadn't said very much on the trip over, and Carter was unclear on what exactly they were looking for. But whatever it was, she knew it centered around the sarcophagus.

He removed his black leather gloves and walked toward the rear of the cemetery, as if unaware that someone was with him. For every one of his strides, she had to take two and did her best to keep up.

When they arrived at the mausoleum's entrance, Alistair stopped and looked at the sky. It was early afternoon now, and white, fluffy clouds rolled across an endless expanse of bright blue.

"Wait here," he said. "Just going to have a gander."

He walked away and disappeared around the side of the building. She looked across the cemetery. The trees seemed closer together than usual. But how was that possible?

"What're ya doin'?" someone said.

She let out a squeak and wheeled around to find the groundskeeper she had seen the last time she was here.

"We're just checking out the, the mausoleum."

"Thought all that TV nonsense was over and done with."

"No, we still have to…"

Alistair appeared and stood next to Carter. He addressed the caretaker.

"We won't be long," he said. "The police know we're here, if you'd care to contact them."

"Ain't got time to be callin' people," he said, and stomped off.

"A little techy, don't you think?" Alistair said.

The groundskeeper called to them over his shoulder. "And don't leave that door open like the last time."

The Englishman went after him. "Hey, wait! Was someone else here recently?"

"A woman. Never seen 'er before. Said she was a friend o' the family. Friend, my ass."

"Can you describe her?"

"Old, white hair, kinda mean lookin' now that I think of it." He waggled his fingers. "She got these crazy eyes, ya know?"

"When did this happen?"

"Oh, two or three nights ago mebbe. Can't remember."

"Did you happen to see her car?" Carter said.

"Oh, that was a real beauty. Seen better days, though. '66 Buick Skylark GS. Love that car. Well, I got rakin' to do."

"Karen Walton," Carter said to Alistair.

"Yes. But why was she here?"

"Can I ask what exactly we're doing?"

"Haven't I told you?"

"Not really."

"Oh." Then, pasting on a goofy smile, "My bad."

She laughed. "You do realize no one says that anymore, right?"

Feeling more confident, she pushed the door open, and they walked inside. Rays of light from the high windows cut through the floating dust motes. Everything was still.

Deliberately, Alistair crossed the room, heading for the iron door that led to the crypt. He stumbled over one of the stones.

"Careful," he said, pointing, as Carter followed.

He pushed the heavy iron door open and looked inside. Carter got out her phone and switched on the light. While Alistair circled the sarcophagus, she shone the beam at the walls.

For a second, she thought she caught a glimpse of someone standing in the shadows. When she looked again, no one was there.

"This place is the heart of the evil that's been plaguing this town," the Englishman said.

"Not the mansion?"

"No. There are other spirits there, but this is where John Dos Santos lives."

The iron door scraped, the grating noise making Carter jump. When she looked at it, the door was exactly as they had left it.

Alistair tried moving the lid of the sarcophagus, but it was frozen in place. He crouched a little and examined the seam.

"Just like the last time," Carter said. "When the *Dubious* crew was here."

"We need to get at those bones. If we can burn them, we might be able to stop what's been happening. Can you give me a hand?"

He and Carter tried pushing the lid together, but it was no use. It was as if it was welded to the rest of the structure.

"I don't get it," Carter said. "Did they cement it shut?"

"No. They used a spell."

Her mouth fell open. "You've got to be shitting me."

He arched his eyebrows at her, then focused on the lid. "Could you step back a bit?"

Carter scooted out of the way as the Guardian leaned over the sarcophagus and laid his hands on it. Closing his eyes, he said something in Hebrew that she didn't recognize. He made his right hand into a fist and pressed the ring against the lid.

In seconds, the room began to shake, filling the air with dust that got into their eyes and noses. Voices wailed, as if awakened from an eternal sleep. Wisps of white smoke came out of the walls and whirled around them, the luminous tips becoming fingers that gripped the lid, trying to keep it in place.

Now, cracks appeared in the stone, blossoming out from around Alistair's ring. Blinding light shone through them. Then a whoosh, followed by silence. The white tendrils were gone.

Coughing and wiping her eyes, Carter stood close to the Englishman.

"Right," he said.

When he gave the signal, they pushed the lid sideways. This time, it slid away easily.

"I don't think I can help you lift it off," she said. "It's too heavy."

"That's all right. I just need to see inside."

They moved it a little more. Borrowing her phone, he shone the light at the interior of the sarcophagus.

"Damn," he said. "Empty."

---

The sunset over the ocean was breathtaking. Sarah and Joe followed the host to their table on the terrace. She had always wanted to have dinner at the Bella Vista Restaurant at the Four Seasons, but somehow they'd never gotten around to it when they were married.

The host pulled out her chair at a table next to the railing, and Sarah took a seat. The host handed each of them a menu and let them know a server would be with them shortly.

"Sure it's not too cold?" Joe said, looking up at the patio heater.

"It's perfect."

She had bought a Katie May glisten dress for the occasion and wore a Veronica Beard black jacket she'd found on sale around Christmas. Dressed all in black, she felt slightly wicked.

"You look stunning," he said. "It's taking every ounce of willpower I have not to leap over the table."

"Control yourself, Joseph."

She smiled demurely as she perused the menu, acutely aware of her own urges. Soon, a server took their drink orders. When their wine came, Joe raised his glass in a toast.

Sarah's watch vibrated. She ignored it. When it went off again, she glanced at the number. It was Carter. They had already exchanged texts about meeting tomorrow. She'd call her friend later.

"Do you need to get that?" Joe said.

"Nope."

"Okay. Here's to my ex-wife becoming my wife. And no backing out."

"No need to worry about that. This time, it's forever."

They clinked glasses and tried their wine. Joe set his down and twirled his fork.

"I'm really pleased you agreed to come," he said.

"Why wouldn't I?"

"I did bring another woman here that one time."

"Things change. And besides, we weren't together anymore. Sorry I got mad at you."

Sarah had decided on the pear and beet salad, followed by the Sumac honey glazed duck breast. This felt like old times. Looking out at the water, she realized she'd never been happier. If it turned out that they didn't have children, she would make the most of their relationship. They would enjoy growing old together.

"So, how'd it go at the library?" he said.

"Very strange. I found a little more information on John Dos Santos. Oh, and I've discovered a new talent. Making photographs come to life."

He dropped his fork. "Sorry, but it sounded like you said—"

"If I concentrate, I can put myself *in* the picture. It's like I'm there."

"You're scaring me."

"And I've also learned to control my visions whenever I touch certain objects. You remember that journal?"

"The one you had to handle with potholders?"

"I don't need to do that anymore. I can turn the visions on and off now."

"Does Carter know about this?"

"I plan on letting her know when I see her."

She decided not to tell her fiancé about what John Dos Santos had said to her. Joe was just getting back to his old self after his brush with that cursed object.

"Don't forget," she said. "We're seeing Fr. Brian tomorrow around nine."

"I'll be there."

"I think he might have some good news about our marriage."

"Want me to pick you up?"

"No, I'll meet you there. I have to see Alistair after. Joe?" He looked up. "Thank you. For this, I mean."

He took her hand and rubbed the engagement ring with his thumb. "I love you, Sarah."

"I love you more," she said.

---

Joe left Sarah at her front door with a passionate kiss to remember him by. She practically floated into the house, where she found her discerning cat waiting for her.

"Hey, you," she said, and set the alarm for the night.

Maowing, Gary followed her into her bedroom. A little drunk, she tried removing her shoes and tipped back onto the bed. Laughing, she laid her phone on the nightstand to charge. She picked up the photo of Dolores and Lelo. The little girl's beaming face made her smile.

Her phone vibrated. When she looked at it, "No Caller ID" displayed. She let it ring through. In a few seconds, the number rang again. On the third call, Sarah picked up, expecting to hear a recorded telemarketer message.

"Sarah?" It was Carter.

"Hellooo," she said, giggling as she slid out of her dress.

"Something's happened."

Plopping onto the bed, Sarah became serious. "Carter, what's wrong? You sound—"

"I need your help."

"What?" She looked at her watch. It was after ten. "Where are you?"

"At Bethany Pruitt's house."

"What happened? Can you—"

"I can't explain right now. Can you just get over here?"

"Okay, okay. Um, I really shouldn't drive. I'll book an Uber and meet you there."

"Hurry."

The Uber driver pulled up to Bethany's house. Sarah thanked him and got out. She'd changed into jeans and her leather jacket. It had gotten cold, and the wind blowing through the trees reminded her it was still winter. On the way over, Sarah kept wondering why Carter hadn't used her own phone to call. Dead battery?

The house was dark, and Carter's MINI Cooper was nowhere in sight.

"Did she get dropped off here, too?"

She hesitated at the gate and looked over at the Waltons' house. Also dark. Somewhere, a dog howled. Though she didn't want to be here, the memory of how frightened her friend had sounded made her decide to go through with it. She walked up to the front door and rang the bell.

"Sarah, is that you?" Carter said through the door.

"Is everything okay in there?"

When the door opened, Sarah found Bethany Pruitt staring at her with distracted eyes. There was something hypnotically dangerous about them. *She's not blinking.*

"What?" Sarah said. "But I thought…"

An ear-splitting noise tore into her brain, making her legs wobble. She felt someone grab her hand and pull her inside.

Shadows on the walls moved like ghosts, and she thought she heard Bethany say something about John Dos Santos. But she couldn't make out the words because the forlorn dog was still howling.

Before Sarah could scream, a blackness fell over her eyes like a smothering blanket, and she crumpled to the floor, unconscious.

———

Elizabeth Chernov climbed out of bed the moment she heard her daughter scream. When she got to the little girl's room, she found Mia sitting up in bed, holding herself and shivering.

"Mommy, something happened to Sarah!"

Her mother sat on the bed and held her daughter. "Shh. It's just another nightmare. Sarah is fine, honey."

"No, she's not. The mean lady took her."

She helped Mia scoot under the covers. Then, she kissed her on the forehead.

"I don't like these dreams," Mia said, practically in tears.

"I'm going to stay with you until you fall asleep, okay?"

"Okay."

"Now, I want you to say the 'Angel of God' prayer I taught you."

They recited it together. By the time they had finished, the little girl was fast asleep.

Elizabeth sat in the rocker she'd used often when her daughter was a baby. And, silently, she said a different prayer. She begged God to take away Mia's nightmares so that she might live a happy, normal life.

## Twenty-Five

Impatient, Joe shifted in his chair as Fr. Brian answered a few emails. When he looked at his watch again, he saw that it was nearly nine-twenty. Sarah would never consider being late for an appointment with the priest, especially now that it looked as if they would be able to get married without complications.

"I don't get it," he said.

Fr. Brian looked at him over his reading glasses. "Why don't you try calling her again?"

Joe pulled out his phone and dialed, then disconnected.

"It went to straight to voicemail. I'm worried, Father. What if she had an accident?"

"Let's try not to imagine the worst. There may be a logical explanation. In any case, we'll need to reschedule."

Sighing, Joe got up. "Sounds good. I'll tell Sarah the good news. She'll be thrilled."

Outside, Joe returned to his truck. There was a heaviness to his gait, as if he were walking on the bottom of the ocean. *Is this real?* He started the engine and, before pulling out, called Rachel at the office.

"Hey, Joe," she said. "I thought you and Sarah were in that big meeting."

"You mean, she's not there?"

"No. Isn't she with you?"

"Rache, I've got to go."

"Joe, what's going on? Where's Sarah?"

"I don't know, but I'm going to find out. I'll keep you posted."

He remembered Sarah telling him she had an appointment at Harlan Covington's house. Backing out, he headed for Montecito.

When he entered the community, he tried remembering how to get to the lawyer's house, since he never had an address. Fortunately, he found a few familiar landmarks and found his way.

At the gate, he identified himself and drove in. Carter's MINI Cooper was parked in front of the house. He jumped out and ran to the door. An attractive older woman answered, wearing black.

"Mary, is it?"

"Yes. We were expecting Sarah. Are you Joe?"

"Yeah. I need to speak to Carter. Is she in there? Oh um. My condolences."

"Thank you, Joe."

She led him to the library and, knocking once, opened the door. Carter was inside with the Englishman and another older man.

"Sorry to disturb you," Mary said.

Carter stared at him. "Joe, what are you doing here?"

"It's about Sarah." He came in and stood in the middle of the room. "I can't find her."

Concerned, Alistair approached him. "When was the last time you saw her?"

"Last night. We had dinner together. Then, I dropped her at her house."

"Curious," the Englishman said. Then, to Carter, "And you haven't spoken to her?"

"She left me a voicemail yesterday, and we exchanged a few texts. I know she was planning to be here."

The investigator got to his feet and put his hand out to Joe. "We haven't formally met. I'm Charlie Beeks."

"Oh yeah. You and Sarah went to Seattle that one time."

"That was quite a trip. I ended up with a few bruised ribs. Nothing to do with your fiancée, of course. Have you seen her car?"

"No, I haven't."

"Well, she could've been in an accident, I suppose. Have you tried the hospitals?"

"I'm going to her house now to see if her car is there."

"Keep us informed, will you?" Alistair said, devoid of any shred of empathy.

Joe bristled. "Sure. Sorry to have interrupted you."

"Let's crack on," the Englishman said.

He was about to ask Carter a question when she got up and followed Joe out.

"I just need a minute," she said.


Joe and Carter stood next to his truck. Sensing his frustration, she touched his arm. He pointed at the house.

"I really don't like that guy," he said.

"Alistair? Yeah, he's an acquired taste. Listen, it's gonna be okay."

"I hope so. It's just that, with all the craziness lately, I'm worried that something happened to her."

"Let's think positive." On an impulse, she kissed his cheek.

"Thanks, Carter. You're a really good friend to her. I hope you know that."

His truck disappeared down the long driveway. Carter felt pangs of guilt for not sharing what she believed—that, most likely, something *had* happened to her friend. After everything she'd done to protect Sarah, her worst nightmare may have come true. And it had John Dos Santos written all over it.

Charlie came out of the house and headed for his rental car.

"What's going on?" she said.

"Alistair suggested I meet with Lou."

"Let me get my purse. I'll follow you over there."

He placed a hand on her arm. "He's asked that you stay here with him."

Vexed, she shot a glance at the house. Then, muttering something about control freaks, she headed back inside.

---

When Joe arrived at the police station, Tim was waiting for him at the desk.

"I'll take you back," the officer said.

Joe followed him through the security door and down a long hallway to a conference room. Lou Fiore was there with Charlie Beeks. Tim closed the door and joined them.

"Hello again," the investigator said.

Lou flipped through his notebook. "Have a seat, Joe. I checked with our dispatcher, and also SBPD, highway patrol, and the sheriff's department. No one reported an accident involving Sarah's car."

"I just came from her house. Her car's not there. Lou, I haven't gotten back to Rachel."

The police chief looked at his notebook. "I've already spoken to her."

"So, what's the plan?"

Lou glanced at Charlie. "We're going up to the mansion again. I asked another officer to do a quick check. It's still locked up tight. But I want to see for myself."

"We should probably take another look at that tunnel you found," Charlie said. "And also Karen Walton's house."

"Good idea. I'll send someone over to her house right now."

"What about the mausoleum?" Tim said.

Lou nodded. "Riley's already been there. He didn't find anything."

Joe looked around the room. "I can't sit around doing nothing. I want to come with you guys."

"Sure," Lou said. "I think we should stay together, though. We've arrested a couple more of those crazy-eyed drifters. There might be more out there."

Before walking outside, they had decided to use two vehicles—Lou's SUV and Joe's truck. Distracted, Joe backed out of the parking lot when another vehicle cruised past him, missing him by inches.

"Careful," Charlie said.

Joe took a deep breath, checked his mirrors, and continued backing out.

"It's like a nightmare that won't end," he said.

"And it all started with that mirror Sarah found?"

"Yeah. Things escalated from there. She almost died, you know. Then, there was the women's shelter. And now…"

"We'll find her, Joe. In my experience, it's best to focus on working the case."

They rode the rest of the way in silence. Joe had been so excited to tell Sarah they could be married right away. They'd already agreed they didn't want a big ceremony—not like the last time. They would have a Mass, followed by a small reception at Sarah's house.

Joe had mentioned visiting his family in New York after the honeymoon. His father had been doing much better since the stroke. When he told his mother the news over the phone, she wept with happiness.

But there was a very real chance none of those things would ever come to pass. He didn't want to think that way, but it was evident that some great evil had befallen the town. And, like a vortex, Sarah—the woman he wanted to spend the rest of his life with—had been swallowed up.

When he came over the rise and saw the mansion, Joe felt sick. Though in reality it was just an old house, there was a malevolence about it that was palpable. Lou and Tim were waiting for them at the gate. Joe and Charlie joined them.

The police chief unlocked the gate and walked in, with the others following. Immediately, Tim headed around the side of the house.

"Riley radioed in to let me know he found nothing at the Walton house," Lou said to Charlie.

"It was worth a shot."

At the front steps, Joe turned sharply, looking off toward the trees.

"What is it?" the police chief said.

"Haven't you noticed? There were birds singing a minute ago. Now they've stopped."

The men looked at one another warily and continued into the house. Tim rejoined them.

"There's a cellar door around the side," he said. "It's still locked."

Lou took out his gun. "I'm going to find the entrance and go down there. You and Charlie check upstairs."

Tim and the investigator got out their weapons and headed for the stairs. Joe followed Lou through the dining room into the kitchen, where they found a door. Joe pulled on it. It was stuck.

Lou put his gun away, and together, they yanked the knob. It flew open, releasing a stench that gagged them. His weapon in one hand and a flashlight in the other, Lou descended the wooden stairs first.

"Sarah?" Joe said.

Silence greeted them as they reached the bottom, where all the animal carcasses lay. Stacks of crates were scattered randomly across the floor. Lou shone his beam at the walls. Joe walked past him and, using the light on his phone, ran his hand along one of the crates.

On the wall behind the stacks were shelves filled with mason jars. Assuming they were canned fruit and vegetables, Joe was about to turn back when he thought he saw someone staring at him from one of the shelves. Shining his light, he gasped.

"Lou, come here," he said.

When the police chief had joined him, Joe moved his hand, directing the flashlight beam at a particular jar.

"What is that?"

The color draining from his face, Joe stared at him. "It's an eye."

The men pushed the crates aside. Lou squeezed past and played the flashlight beam over the shelves, starting at the top. There were dozens and dozens of jars, each containing human eyes and tongues, floating lazily in a clear liquid.

"Mother of God," Lou said.

Joe sat in his truck on the phone, doing his best to calm Rachel, while the others stood outside the gate. When Tiffany Gersh's vehicle arrived, Lou went to meet her. Everyone exchanged a quick greeting as Joe joined them. She and her partner entered the house with their equipment.

"Tim, stay with them until they're finished," Lou said. "I'll leave you the SUV." Then, to the others, "Let's check out the tunnel."

Following the police chief's directions, Joe made his way along a fire road toward Cold Spring Tunnel. Lou sat up front, and Charlie was in the backseat of the extended cab.

"How's Rachel?" Lou said.

"She's in pretty bad shape. I told her to close up the office and go home."

Out of frustration, he gripped the wheel harder. The mansion had been another dead end, and still no Sarah. He was aware that time was short. Every second that passed increased the possibility they wouldn't find her alive. If that happened, he wasn't sure he could go on.

---

At Cold Spring Tunnel, the men found the gate chained up, just as the police had left it. Lou unlocked it, and they walked in. This time, Joe brought a flashlight.

"How many of those jars did you find?" Charlie said.

Lou followed his beam through the darkness. He had barely heard the question.

"Maybe a hundred," he said.

"I'm just thinking about the bodies Sarah and Carter found in Washington. Twenty kids."

"Did you hear something?" Joe said.

They stopped and listened. At first, there was nothing. Then, the sound of shuffling footsteps. Lou raised his weapon.

"Charlie, stay with him."

Instinct taking over, the investigator waved Joe toward the wall and, raising his gun, kept vigil as Lou headed off into the darkness.

"This is the police," Lou said. "Identify yourself."

Silence, followed by more footsteps. Lou tensed as shadows formed in front of him. There were two figures—both men. Thirties, maybe. Bedraggled. Their eyes were black as onyx.

"Freeze," Lou said. "Hands in the air."

Ignoring his instructions, they kept coming. Snarling, they rushed him.

Lou fired twice, the deafening sound reverberating throughout the tunnel. They dropped mid-stride, both shot in the chest.

Charlie and Joe came out of the darkness and stared at the bodies. Putting away his weapon, Lou knelt and tried to find a pulse. Both had taken a bullet in the heart.

"I need to call this in," he said.

When Joe arrived at Eddie's house, Rachel was waiting outside the front door, her arms folded tight in front of her. She was shaking, and her eyes were red from crying. As he walked up to her, she embraced him and wept against his shoulder.

"What's happened to her?" she said, hardly able to get the words out.

"Let's go inside."

She took his hand and led him to the kitchen, where Eddie and Katy sat in grave silence.

"Thanks for coming," Eddie said. "Want a beer?"

"No, nothing, thanks."

Joe cupped Katy's chin and stroked her hair. He took a seat and folded his hands on the table.

"We've checked all the likely places, and still nothing. Lou said he'd conduct a door-to-door search, if he had to."

"Have they tried tracing her phone?" Eddie said.

"Lou's working on it. I haven't heard anything."

Eddie ran a trembling hand through his hair. "Why would someone take my daughter?"

"We don't know for sure if they did."

"What other explanation is there?"

Joe had never seen Eddie upset, and he worried it might trigger a heart attack. While in pre-med at UCSB, he had read a paper on takotsubo cardiomyopathy, or stress heart attack. Japanese doctors were the first to describe the condition. With his drinking and bad diet, Eddie was a prime candidate. When Joe answered him, he tried keeping his voice even.

"The police are doing everything they can. They've brought in extra officers from Santa Barbara."

"Have you eaten?" Rachel said, redirecting the conversation.

"Thanks, Rachel. I'm not hungry. Look, I wish I had better news."

"What about Carter?" Eddie said. "Can she help?"

"She and that English guy are doing their own investigation, along with Charlie. I'm hoping to hear something soon."

Eddie pounded his fist on the table. "I told her not to get involved. She won't listen!"

"Aunt Sarah was trying to do the right thing," Katy said, her eyes defiant.

"Do the right thing, and this is what happens."

"I don't want to have this conversation right now," Rachel said, and left the room.

Getting to his feet, Joe touched Eddie's shoulder. "I'm going back to Sarah's, in case she returns. I'll call you if I hear anything."

Eddie patted his hand. "Thanks, Joe."

Katy walked with Joe to the front door and hugged him.

"Are you okay?" he said.

"I'm going to pray a novena. And I've asked my friends to do the same."

"Good idea. See you, kid."

"Joe?"

He was already down the steps. "Yeah?"

"Please find my aunt."

"I will. Night, Katy."

Insensate, he made his way home, wondering how exactly he would find Sarah. And if when he did, whether she would be alive.

## Twenty-Six

The doorbell woke Joe. Groggy, he sat up, remembering he had fallen asleep in Sarah's guest bedroom. Gary was curled up next to him, and when he reached for his phone, the cat looked at him with squishy eyes. He glanced at the time. 5:15 a.m. The doorbell rang again, this time more insistently. For a fleeting moment, he thought it might be Sarah.

Still dressed, he swung his legs over and stood. Running a hand through his short hair, he went to answer the door. When he opened it, Lou was standing there, carrying a white plastic bag.

"You look like shit," the cop said.

"Come in. Want coffee?"

Joe led Lou into the kitchen and pointed vaguely to a bar stool as he got a coffee filter from the cupboard.

"Joe, we found her car," Lou said.

"Where?"

"It was parked in Santa Barbara on State Street. A parking attendant called it in."

While the coffee brewed, Joe collapsed on a seat next to him and rubbed his eyes.

"Sorry, I didn't get much sleep. What was her car doing in Santa Barbara?"

"That's the big question. Her purse and phone were inside, as well as her Apple watch."

Lou laid the bag on the counter and removed the electronic devices. Both were lightly dusted with fluorescent fingerprint powder.

"I don't believe she was ever there, Joe. But someone wanted us to think that. We're dusting the car for prints.

"I was able to get Sarah's phone records. She received a call from a blocked number at 10:13 on what I'm assuming was the night of her disappearance."

The coffeemaker beeped, and Joe poured them each a cup. "That was right after I dropped her off."

Lou took a swig and wiped his mouth. "How did she seem when you left her? Was she planning to meet anyone?"

"She said she was going straight to bed. To be honest, she'd had a little too much to drink. Trust me, she was very content."

Joe refilled their cups as the police chief started pacing.

"Okay," Lou said. "So, she's probably getting ready for bed—a little tipsy, granted. And she gets a call. Whoever this person is, the number is blocked."

"Which means Sarah didn't know them."

"And yet, they convince her to drop everything and meet them someplace."

"What would be so important, she had to go out in the middle of the night?" Joe said. "The only ones I can think of who she'd do that for are her family and Carter. And me."

"Would she have driven, do you think?"

"Absolutely not. Sarah was hardcore about not drinking and driving."

"Right. So, what? She books an Uber or Lyft?"

"We both use Uber."

"Great. I'll get in touch with them and find out who picked her up and where they took her."

"How long will that take?"

"Depends on whether they're dicks about it and make me get a subpoena."

"I'm so stupid," Joe said. "Hang on."

He ran into Sarah's bedroom, retrieved her laptop, and returned to the kitchen, where he opened it on the counter.

"Uber should've emailed her a receipt for the trip." Joe tried logging in several times without success. "Dammit! Thought I knew her password."

Lou grabbed the phone. "Let's try this. What's her passcode?"

"I don't know that either."

"Well, these things are pretty hard to crack," Lou said. "I'm better off working with Uber directly."

"Okay. Let me know what you find out. I'm going home to shower and change. Then, I'll see Carter."

Lou grabbed Joe's arm and squeezed it. "Try to stay positive. This is a good break for us."

The police chief swallowed the rest of his coffee. He left his friend and walked out the front door.

"Yeah, a good break," Joe said, unable to keep himself from imagining the worst.

---

Sarah lay motionless on a cot, feeling herself partly in this world and the realm of the dead. Weak rays of light fell on her from a faraway window. The place she was in was cold and damp and smelled of earth.

The wool blanket covering her made her itch. She tried moving her hand to scratch her face but could not lift it. Though she was frightened, her pulse was steady. Her eyelids made two slits from which she could barely perceive things around her. She sensed someone nearby.

Bethany Pruitt stood over her with impassive eyes that betrayed no mercy. Sarah wondered why she'd done this, then remembered what the woman had said about a sacrifice.

Was this what she'd been talking about? Was she planning to kill Sarah in some misguided attempt to avert the evil that had descended on Dos Santos? She wanted to plead with the old woman—tell her that this wasn't the way. That Bethany needed help. But Sarah couldn't speak.

She tried recalling what exactly the deranged woman had done to her to incapacitate her. Had she given her a drug? But it was no use; she couldn't remember. She didn't *feel* drugged. Rather, she felt as if she were floating in a void, in and out of consciousness.

But there was something in the void—something Sarah didn't want to face. Somehow, though, she knew she would have to. It was why Bethany had brought her here. She thought of Cassie Morton, remembering what the newspaper had said about the young girl's death. *Stabbed multiple times and left to die.* Had Cassie been a sacrifice?

Tears welled, blinding Sarah. And she was filled with anger. Rage at the person who had taken her. And an acute disappointment at herself for putting her own life in danger when she could have taken Carter's advice and run away.

She thought of her father and Rachel. And she pictured her beautiful niece, Katy, who she would never see grow up. All because Sarah had chosen to do the right thing.

Bethany moved closer, positioning herself so her prisoner could see her better. And that's when Sarah realized the woman wasn't wearing the wooden cross. And her eyes. They were blue and piercing—not at all like Bethany's. *Who was this woman?*

"Your time is almost here, Sarah Greene," Bethany said in a voice that was unrecognizable.

Those were the same words John Dos Santos had said to her in the library.

*I curse you,* she thought. *I curse you all to hell.*

---

Carter opened her front door, and seeing Joe, she pulled him close and held onto him. They stood that way for a while, Joe patting her back and speaking words of comfort.

"I should've made her go away," she said, sniveling.

He caught a tear with his thumb, making her smile in spite of herself.

"Let's go inside."

Nodding, she led him to the kitchen. He took a seat at the small table. She grabbed a paper towel and blew her nose, then threw it away and washed her hands.

"Can I get you anything?"

Though it was only nine-thirty, he was tempted to ask for a beer.

"I thought maybe we could grab something to eat," he said.

She regarded herself. Barefoot. Dressed in a Lululemon black jogger and white tank top. She ran her fingers through her uncombed hair.

"I don't know if I can go out right now."

"I get it. Look, why don't you take a shower and get dressed. You'll feel better. If you have any eggs, I can make us some food."

"Are you sure?"

"I need to keep busy. Go on, I got this."

"Okay," she said, and trotted up the stairs.

Joe opened cabinets, looking for a pan. He smiled as he recognized Sarah's method of organizing cookware. In a few minutes, he heard the shower. He found eggs, cheese, and a bag of frozen peppers. Pouring a little olive oil into the pan, he got started.

Freshly showered and wearing clean clothes, Carter realized she did feel better as she hurried down the stairs. She had on jeans and an Oxford shirt. She hadn't bothered drying her hair.

"Something smells good," she said, walking into the kitchen.

Joe had set two places at the table and was pouring the coffee. She took a seat and placed her napkin on her lap. He set down a cheese and veggie omelet with toast made from crusty bread. Then, he served himself.

"I appreciate you doing this," she said. "Sorry I'm such a mess. How are *you* doing?"

"Trying to hold on." He took a bite of his omelet. "I have some encouraging news."

After he told her what he and Lou had discussed, she put down her fork.

"But who would she have gone to see?" she said.

"I've been racking my brain. But I keep coming up with either you or someone in her family."

"And you said the number was blocked?"

"That's another thing. If it was a person she knew, wouldn't they have called her from a recognizable number? Hey, have Alistair and Charlie had any luck?"

"I don't know. I'm supposed to see them later."

Joe felt his phone vibrate and pulled it out of his pocket. When he saw the number, he answered.

"Hello? Fr. Brian? Okay, I'll be right there." He disconnected and looked at Carter. "There's some little girl in his office. Says she knows where Sarah is."

"Little girl?" Carter blanched. *"Mia."*

---

Joe and Carter got out of his truck and hurried into the parish office, where they found the child playing with blocks. Mrs. Ivy was at the computer, occasionally glancing over at her guest.

"You can go in," she said to them.

When Joe entered, he saw a woman around his age sitting in front of Fr. Brian's desk. The priest looked up and greeted Carter and him.

"Carter, I think you know Elizabeth Chernov. Elizabeth, this is Sarah's fiancé, Joe. Let's move over to the sofa."

When everyone was comfortable, the priest closed his office door and pulled up a chair, facing them.

"It seems Elizabeth's daughter has been suffering from nightmares."

"What has this got to do with Sarah?" Joe said.

"I'm getting to that. Elizabeth, why don't you tell Joe and Carter what you said to me."

Her cheeks flushing, the woman cleared her throat. "Look, I know this is probably going to sound crazy. I came to talk to Fr. Brian about the nightmares. When I mentioned Sarah, he told me she's missing?"

"That's right, but—"

"Two nights ago, Mia had another bad dream. She

said she saw Sarah. And someone else. A woman she called 'the mean lady.'"

Carter turned to her. "Did she describe her?"

"No, but she saw her again last night. She was so scared, I brought her here."

Carter shot a glance at Joe. "Do you think it would be all right if we asked Mia about the woman?"

Elizabeth looked at the priest, who smiled encouragingly.

"I think it will be okay, Elizabeth," he said.

He opened the door and asked the little girl to join her mother. Setting down a block, she got up, and skipping in, went immediately to her mother.

"You remember Carter, don't you?" Elizabeth said. "And this is her friend Joe." Shyly, the girl twisted back and forth. "They want to ask you about Sarah."

"What do they want to know?"

Carter reached out her arms. Giggling, Mia hopped onto her lap.

"Your dress is so pretty," Carter said.

"Thank you."

"Do you remember what the mean lady looks like? Does she have white hair?"

"Mm-mm."

"What color is it?"

"Mixed."

Carter looked at Elizabeth.

"I think she means gray," the child's mother said.

Carter addressed Mia again. "When you say she's mean, can you tell me what makes you think that?"

"Um…her eyes."

"What color are they?"

"Blue. But not the normal kind of blue."

Impatient, Joe knelt in front of the child. "Mia, can you tell us where Sarah is right now?"

The girl made a face. "It's cold in there. And she's sleeping."

"Yes, but *where?*"

She looked at Carter and, in a whisper, said, "I'm not supposed to tell."

Frustrated, Joe turned her toward him. "Mia, where is Sarah?"

Fr. Brian took Joe's arm, urging him to stand. "I think that's enough."

Though disappointed, the last thing Joe wanted was to scare the little girl. Nodding, he took a seat on the sofa. The priest leaned over, his hands on his thighs, and looked into the little girl's innocent eyes.

"Thank you, Mia. You've been very helpful."

"You're welcome."

Everyone was on their feet now. Elizabeth was about to walk her daughter out when Mia turned to Joe.

"Sarah doesn't like the dream she's having," she said.

When they were gone, Carter looked sharply at Fr. Brian. "You do know that girl is psychic, right?"

The priest glanced at Joe. "I suspected as much."

"Have you told her mother?"

"I think she knows."

"You need to prepare her, Father. Or Mia could suffer, thinking something's wrong with her."

"Yes, you're right," he said. "Her father is due home in a few days. I'll have a talk with both parents." Then, to Joe, "Sorry we couldn't find out more."

"We learned a lot," Carter said. "If Mia did see Sarah, that means she's alive."

In the parking lot, Joe had just started the engine when his phone vibrated.

"Hello, Lou?" he said.

"I think we found her. I'm heading over there now."

After the brief conversation, Lou texted Joe the address. He did his best not to break any speed limits as he headed back to Dos Santos.

"I know that address," Carter said as they got onto the freeway. "It's Bethany Pruitt's house."

"The crazy woman who's been harassing us?"

"*She's* got Sarah. Oh God."

Carter remembered what the unhinged woman had said about the town needing a sacrifice. But with Joe already keyed up behind the wheel, she didn't dare upset him any further. Instead, she said a prayer that the police would make it in time and that Sarah would be alive and safe.

## Twenty-Seven

Lou turned onto Bethany Pruitt's street and parked at an angle. Four police cruisers were already there, blocking traffic in both directions. Tim and the other officers waited in the yard for the police chief. Unholstering his weapon, he jogged toward them.

"Tim, see if you can find a back way in."

The police chief waved two officers forward. Gun raised, he approached the front door as the others moved to either side. Taking a breath, he pounded on the door with his fist.

"Bethany Pruitt, this is the police!"

Inside, a woman let out a small cry. He tried the door; it was unlocked. As he pushed it open, he saw a woman of around seventy standing in the foyer, clutching a curved utility knife in one hand. She looked at him with frightened eyes, unsure what was happening.

"Bethany Pruitt?" he said. "Ma'am, drop the knife. I said, *drop the knife*."

She didn't comply. Instead, she cocked her head like a

curious puppy until the small bones in her neck cracked, unnerving all of them.

"Where is Sarah Greene?"

Her face relaxed into a mask of cold, soulless conviction. Her piercing blue eyes bore into Lou, filling him with a dread he had no ability to comprehend. For a split second, he forgot where he was.

"You're too late," the woman said in an amplified voice that didn't sound human. "*He* has her now."

Sweat pouring into his eyes, Lou inched closer to grab the knife.

"Stop!" She raised the weapon. Looking past him, she smiled wanly.

"Lou, what's happening?" Joe said behind him.

"Stay back, Joe!"

"Yes," the woman said, her voice like velvety poison. "We wouldn't want to get blood all over Carter's pretty shirt."

Feeling the strength leave his legs, Lou licked his lips. Something unnamed urged him to shoot her. He resisted.

"Where is Sarah?"

"I'm bored," she said, pouting. "You can have the old bitch."

She raised the knife to rip her own throat open. Tim moved in from behind and jammed a stun gun into her neck. For several nerve-shattering seconds, she spasmed like an electrified rag doll.

Letting go an animal-like howl, she arched her back as a column of yellow smoke issued from her wide-open mouth. Dissipating, it left the reek of sulfur in the air.

Bethany released the blade and, slipping into unconsciousness, collapsed on the floor.

"What in hell…?" Lou said.

Everyone stood staring at the still body. Recovering himself, Lou turned to Tim.

"Cuff her," he said. Then, to the other officers, "I want you to scour every inch of this place until we locate Sarah Greene."

Joe and Carter stayed close to Lou as he strode into the kitchen. Farther away, footsteps pounded as the other officers checked the bedrooms.

Lou found a door leading to a basement. He gestured for Joe and Carter to stand back, then tried the knob. It was unlocked. He flung the door open, revealing wooden stairs.

"Sarah?" he said.

He was greeted with silence as he made his way down in the dim light of the cloying enclosure. Joe and Carter followed nervously. Across the room, stood an old washer and dryer. When he got to the bottom, Lou saw her.

"Oh dear God," Joe said.

He pushed past the police chief to the cot where Sarah lay. Kneeling on the cold cement, he pulled back the blanket to find her hand. Lou and Carter hovered on either side of Joe while he felt for a pulse. After a few seconds, he let out an anguished sigh.

"She's alive."

"Oh thank God," Carter said, covering her mouth.

Tim appeared at the top of the stairs. When Lou saw him, he said, "We need an ambulance!"

Riley helped the handcuffed Bethany Pruitt into the back of his cruiser while a paramedic loaded the gurney carrying Sarah into the ambulance.

Joe embraced Lou. "Thank you so much."

"Keep me posted on her condition."

"I will. Can you call Rachel and let her know?"

"Of course."

As Joe walked off, Carter gave the police chief a hug.

He looked back at the house. "I don't get it. Why would Bethany Pruitt want to harm Sarah?"

"You saw," she said. "That wasn't Bethany. I'm worried this isn't over. Sorry, I have to go."

She hurried off to join Joe.

"Not over," Lou said to no one. "God in heaven."

---

Joe approached the nurses' station with Carter. The charge nurse led them to Sarah's room. He found his fiancée unconscious. An IV ran into her left arm, and a pulse oximeter was clipped to the middle finger of her right hand.

"Has the doctor been in yet?" he said.

The nurse checked the chart. "No. I'll see if he's here."

Joe sat beside the bed, with Carter standing behind him, her hand on his shoulder. In a few minutes, a man in his fifties and wearing a medical lab coat walked in. Joe got up to greet him.

"I'm Dr. Shein, the neurologist," he said. "Are you Sarah's husband?"

"Fiancé. Joe Greene. And this is our friend Carter Wittgenstein."

While the men spoke, Carter used the opportunity to sit. As she reached for Sarah's hand, a massive iron wall rose from the floor, separating Sarah and her.

Carter scooted away and looked at the others, who were still speaking as if nothing had happened. When she turned toward the bed, everything appeared normal.

The doctor read the chart and, confused, looked at Joe. "The patient's name is Greene also?"

"It's a long story."

"There doesn't appear to be anything physically wrong with Sarah. We did a blood test and didn't find the presence of any drugs. Does your fiancée drink?"

"Not excessively."

"Why can't she wake up?" Carter said.

Dr. Shein put down the chart and moved next to the bed. He peeled back an eyelid and, using a penlight, examined Sarah's pupil. Straightening, he clapped his hands loudly next to her ear.

"SARAH!" he said.

Taking her left hand, he used his thumbnail to press the nail bed of her index finger. She didn't react to the pain.

"Something is causing her to remain unconscious, but we don't know what it is yet. I'm going to order a CT scan."

"She had one recently," Joe said. "When she was in here the last time."

"Good. I can use that for comparison. Can I ask why she was admitted?"

"She had a seizure that resulted in a minor brain injury."

"That is interesting. Is she prone to seizures?"

"No. In fact, I don't think she's ever had one before."

"I'm also going to order an EEG."

Sarah listened as Joe continued his conversation with the doctor. She wanted to tell them she could hear everything going on around her. But she was drifting somewhere far off, and try as she might, she couldn't find her way back.

After the doctor left, she felt Joe squeeze her hand and

kiss her. She sensed Carter coming near. Why was her friend afraid to touch her? Carter and Joe continued speaking as if Sarah wasn't there. In her mind, she screamed in frustration.

Now, Sarah was alone, and a darkness descended over her. Somewhere in the murky distance, the sound of machine gun fire and screaming men's voices broke the silence.

She felt herself being drawn to a place she didn't want to go—the faraway place filled with violence and death. But she had no choice. She was no longer in control. Someone else had taken over. Someone who, in her soul, she feared.

Sarah walked on duckboards in a trench. Soldiers carrying weapons ran past her—some *through* her—their faces covered in grime.

She climbed a short wooden ladder and peered out at the smoke-filled horizon, past the barbed wire of No Man's Land. Hundreds of bodies lay in the low mist of a gray, forbidding landscape.

Somewhere in the distance, the figures of two women appeared. The first wore a long white dress. Slowly, as if unsure, they made their way toward Sarah over the uneven ground, past huge craters filled with rainwater.

They seemed unaware that the soldiers behind them, shouting in German, were firing weapons. Was it possible? Were she and those other women truly on a battlefield?

Then, the women vanished. Sarah was alone again. As she descended the ladder, a profound feeling of loss overcame her. Yet something compelled her to continue to her ultimate destination.

Bethany lay in bed, handcuffed to the railing. Lou had arranged for her to be driven to a hospital in Goleta. He didn't want her anywhere near Sarah, especially after what he'd witnessed at the old woman's house. Something from hell had come out of her—he *saw* it.

He sat next to the bed, his notebook on his lap, and wondered how to proceed. The suspect was frail and didn't appear to be a threat to anyone. Though sympathetic to her situation, he knew he had to conduct the interview as he would for any other crime.

"Bethany, do you understand that you're going to be charged with false imprisonment? That's punishable in both criminal and civil court. I asked you this before. Do you have a lawyer?"

She stared at him, as if he were out of his mind. "I didn't do it. It wasn't me."

"Are you saying you didn't lure Sarah Greene to your house, then restrain her in your basement?"

"She *made* me do it."

"Who, Sarah?"

"No, *her*. Karen Walton."

"Your next-door neighbor forced you to imprison Sarah? Did she threaten you physically?"

Bethany's voice became an urgent whisper as she twisted the blanket with her free hand.

"She got inside me."

She grabbed Lou's hand, making him drop his pen. His first instinct was to pull free.

"You have to believe me. It was her. *She* did it all."

Lou retrieved his pen and stood. The old woman whimpered, probing her chest for a cross that wasn't there.

"I must tell you," he said, "I'm seeking a court-ordered

psych evaluation." Then, more to himself, "It might help your case."

She didn't seem to hear him, though, and continued pulling at the blanket, muttering what sounded like a prayer. Sighing, he put away his notebook.

"Sarah is in mortal danger," she said.

Lou stopped in the doorway. "Why do you say that?"

"I don't think anyone can save her."

When she looked at him, her eyes were wild with fear. He realized this was not the woman he first encountered when he arrived at her house.

Bethany Pruitt was a victim, too.

---

Rachel sat next to the hospital bed, holding Sarah's hand.

"Sarah? Honey, I'm here." She turned to Eddie and Katy. "I wonder if she can hear me."

"I think so," Eddie said, his arm around his grand-daughter.

The charge nurse appeared in the doorway. "You're Sarah's family, right?"

"I'm her father," Eddie said.

"I'll let the doctor know you're here."

A few minutes went by, then Dr. Shein entered. After introductions, he laid the file folder he was carrying on the overbed table and flipped it open as the family members gathered around.

"There are several common causes for someone to be in a coma," he said. "Brain injury, stroke, infection. In some cases, we find evidence of a toxin.

"In Sarah's case, none of those things are present. Unfortunately, until we can determine an actual cause, we're treating this as a non-traumatic coma of unknown origin."

"Is her brain activity normal?" Rachel said.

"Great question. The EEG measures basic brain waves —alpha, beta, theta, and delta. There are other more complex waves, of course. We look at these patterns to help us spot any abnormalities."

He pointed to a series of colored brain diagrams. "To be frank, I've never seen brain activity like this. It's almost as if Sarah has left herself and is focusing all her attention on something else."

"That's because she's psychic," Katy said. "Right, Mom?"

Groaning, Eddie shot his granddaughter a baleful look.

"What?" she said. "Everyone knows she is."

Nonplussed, Dr. Shein looked at Eddie. "Your daughter is a medium?"

"She doesn't call herself that," Rachel said. "It's more of a, of a special talent for…"

"She sees ghosts," Eddie said, tamping down his anger.

The doctor nodded, as if a patient had just revealed that there were fairies in the room.

"I see. Well, whatever this is, she's busy doing something important right now."

"Why do you say that?" Rachel said.

"Because she's concentrating very hard. Look at these beta and gamma waves."

Eddie put on his reading glasses and perused the chart. "Is there a way we can snap her out of it?"

"You mean, like ECT? No. That would be extremely dangerous. We're going to continue monitoring her to see if her condition improves. That's all I can tell you, I'm afraid. I'll be in touch."

After the doctor left, Rachel kissed her sister on the cheek. "We'll be back tomorrow."

"Bye, Aunt Sarah," Katy said.

Eddie squeezed his eldest daughter's hand and walked out without saying anything.

---

Sarah found the familiar dugout and lingered in the doorway. Outside, the sounds of gunfire and exploding shells continued.

The young man she had seen the last time she was here lay unconscious on a cot while being treated for a severe chest wound. A pile of bloody bandages lay on the floor.

Hunched over the soldier, a medic who couldn't have been more than twenty poured carbolic acid onto the affected area. He proceeded to cut away tissue too damaged to be repaired. Then, using bullet forceps, he dug out the shrapnel.

A nearby explosion knocked him to the ground as dirt fell from the ceiling. The medic checked to see if the wound had been contaminated. Sterilizing his hands and instrument, he continued. When he had finished, he soaked fresh bandages in carbolic acid and wrapped them around the patient's chest.

An American officer appeared next to Sarah, watching the medic as he placed a blanket on the patient.

"Well?" he said.

The medic stood and saluted, which the officer returned.

"Sir, I don't think he'll make it through the night."

"What about the rest of his squad?"

"All dead, sir."

"I see. Do your best, soldier. And let me know if Cpl. Dos Santos wakes up. He's a helluva fighter, that one."

Sarah was alone now with John Dos Santos as he slept. It was night, and the drop in temperature made her shiver. The fighting had subsided. Intermittently, the sky turned white hot as flares descended from parachutes over No Man's Land.

How was it possible John had survived this? She remembered something Harlan had told her once. That John Dos Santos had been a good man. *Something happened to him over there. He came back different.* Had this been John's plan all along? To bring her here and show her what had transpired all those years ago?

Wanting no part of his origin story, she prayed she could leave this place. She pressed her St. Michael medal between her finger and thumb and closed her eyes.

"Please, God," she said. "I want to go home."

## Twenty-Eight

Lou held his tongue as the mayor railed at him over the phone.

"Your Honor, I understand. We've got officers on the streets. Yes, and I've called in assistance from SBPD. What? No, I don't know why the violence has escalated."

Tim rushed in and was about to say something when Lou held up a warning hand.

"No, we're advising people to stay indoors. I'll— The National Guard? No, that's not necessary. Okay. I'll be in touch."

Lou put the handset down and sank into his chair. His armpits were drenched, and his tongue felt fuzzy. Idly, he wondered if he had a fever.

"Sorry, Chief," Tim said. "I thought you should know. Bethany Pruitt is dead."

"How?"

"She had a fatal stroke. One of the orderlies discovered her this morning. They tried reviving her, but it was too late."

Sadly, the police chief shook his head. "What she did wasn't her fault. Something possessed her. Literally."

He rubbed his eyes and glanced at the dregs at the bottom of his coffee cup. Then, he got up and, checking his weapon, grabbed his jacket and walked out.

"Let's go," he said.

Tim followed him. "Where to?"

"Back on the streets. We've got random acts of violence, looting, destruction of property, and people claiming they've seen the devil. Just another friggin' day in paradise."

They were halfway down the hallway by now.

"What do you think's causing it?" Tim said.

"I don't know. But it started after we found Sarah. It's like…" He stopped short.

"Chief?"

Lou looked at the cop intently. "Like somebody gave the order."


Lou drove his SUV toward downtown, then turned onto Dos Santos Boulevard. Strangely, there were no cars in the street.

The manager of The Cracked Pot stood outside the restaurant with several servers, staring at his shattered window. Far off, the voice of someone identifying themselves as the police advised everyone to move indoors.

Somewhere, a woman screamed. Accelerating, Lou drove further on until he saw an SBPD cruiser parked in the middle of the street, the driver-side door open. He stopped abruptly.

Grabbing their weapons, he and Tim got out. A woman lay injured on the asphalt, her head bleeding. A gunshot caught the police chief's attention.

"Help her," he said.

He ran off to find the source of the gunfire. As he approached an alley, he found a group of derelicts standing in a circle. They hadn't seen him.

Pressing himself against the wall, he grabbed his radio and requested backup. A minute passed. Then, Tim appeared.

"She'll be okay," the officer said. "Someone called 911."

"Okay. We've got six adult males in the alley. There may be an officer down."

They checked their weapons. Lou signaled for them to go in.

"Police!" he said. "Hands in the air." No reaction. Then, to himself, "Screw this."

He fired a warning shot at a dumpster at the end of the alley. The grubby-looking men's faces were expressionless. He and Tim moved in and, using their guns, waved them back toward a brick wall.

An SBPD officer lay unconscious on the ground. He was bleeding from the abdomen, his weapon still in his hand.

Lou patted down the suspects and found a bloody hunting knife. Tim checked the officer's vital signs. A black SBPD prisoner transport van screeched to a stop on the street. Tim waved in the other officers.

In a few minutes, they had handcuffed the suspects and placed them inside the van. Two EMTs rolled a gurney through and lifted the wounded police officer onto it.

"Okay, Tim," Lou said. "We've got a long day ahead of us."

Carter came into the library at Harlan Covington's house, out of breath. She felt as if she had been running ever since she got the call. Alistair and Charlie sat in the Chesterfield chairs, waiting for her. Both looked grim.

"Sorry I'm late," she said. "It's like a war zone out there. Someone attacked me as I left my house."

Concerned, Charlie stood. "Are you okay?"

"I think so." She stared at the floor.

Unlike the investigator, Alistair watched her as if observing a physics experiment.

"What did you do?" the Englishman said.

"I…" She sank onto the sofa and folded her hands. "I used my bracelet."

"The person who assaulted you was a demoniac?"

"Yes."

Alistair stood. "They've been called."

"By John Dos Santos?" Carter said.

"I'm sure of it. They're creating fear and confusion."

"To what end?" the investigator said.

"Despair."

The Englishman poured himself a whiskey. He raised his glass to the others as an offering. Charlie and Carter declined.

"I've been to see Sarah," he said, taking a sip.

Carter looked at him. "When?"

"This morning. I tried breaking through to speak to her and was met with a wall."

"That's exactly what happened to me. I went last night and tried again."

"And were you successful?"

Carter sighed miserably. "Nothing was clear. I was only able to get glimpses. But I feel like she's somewhere far away, in another time."

"She is."

"I don't understand," Charlie said. "Where exactly is Sarah?"

Alistair finished his drink. "France 1918."

Carter looked at him, astonished. "That would mean she's…"

"In the middle of a war. The Battle of Valenciennes, to be precise."

"How can you possibly know that?" Charlie said.

"Because that was where John Dos Santos was wounded."

Carter got to her feet and, her hand shaking, managed to pour herself a glass of whiskey.

"So, he brought her there," she said.

"And he doesn't intend to let her go."

"There must be a way to rescue her."

"Therein lies the problem," the Englishman said. Then, to Charlie, "Would you excuse us?"

"Of course."

The investigator left the room and closed the door. Alistair escorted Carter to a chair by the fire.

"Your hands are cold," he said with kindness. "I'm afraid neither you or I have the power to reach Sarah."

She finished her drink in one gulp and coughed. "I haven't really tried, though. Maybe if I concentrated…"

"It won't help," he said. "We have to find John Dos Santos's body and destroy it. Then, the violence in the town will stop. And Sarah will be released."

"But we checked the sarcophagus. There's nothing in there. *No body*."

"It has to be in that building."

"What if it isn't?"

He looked into his glass, then finished his drink. "Then she'll remain in a persistent vegetative state. Until she dies."

"No, there must be another way to…"

He extended his index finger and lifted her chin. She found it almost impossible to see him through her tears.

"I know this is a bitter truth," he said. "But we must remain resolute."

"But if the body isn't in the sarcophagus…?"

He rose and, grabbing the whiskey bottle, refilled their glasses.

"I've been thinking a lot about what that cemetery worker said. Why would Karen Walton go there?"

"I don't know," she said. "To get something?"

"In a way, yes. I think she went there to receive her instructions."

"Wait, that would mean…" Carter looked into Alistair's calm eyes. "Oh, shit. His body *is* there."

―――――

Joe sat motionless in the hard plastic chair, holding Sarah's hand. Intermittently, her eyelids fluttered, as if she were dreaming. A nurse entered and touched his shoulder. Stretching, he looked up at her.

"You've been here a long time. Why don't you take a break? We can look after her."

"Maybe later. I'd like to stay, if that's okay."

"I'll check back in a while." She stopped at the door and smiled. "She's lucky to have you."

He squeezed Sarah's hand, praying she would open her eyes.

―――――

Sarah stood next to John's army cot. Occasionally, he coughed himself into partial consciousness, then fell back into a dark, troubled sleep.

On a small table nearby, she found a black Bible and a rosary, among other things. She reached for a packet of correspondence tied up with a ribbon. She loosened it and drew out the letter that was on top. It was written by her great-grandmother.

My dearest brother-in-law,

I hope you are well. You must be surprised to hear from me and not my sister. It took me a long time to compose this letter, and even longer to send it. The news I bring is not good.

Your beloved wife Rosa passed away three days ago. As you know, she and I volunteered to help care for patients suffering from influenza. Though I remained healthy, my poor sister succumbed to the sickness and never recovered.

She was such a brave girl, John. You would have been proud of her. Her cheerfulness helped many who were suffering. I pray with all my heart that this news will not discourage you. Everyone here wants you home. We pray for you every day.

With all my love,

Dolores

A tear fell from Sarah's eye onto the page, obliterating some of the words. When she turned to John, he was staring at her, his breath a death rattle. He tried speaking to her, but his voice was faint. She knelt and, taking his hand, moved her ear close to his mouth.

"There is nothing left," he said, his voice thin.

Backing away, she looked at him sharply. "That's not true. You can still have a life. You can do good."

His breathing was labored and wheezy. "I've spent my life…doing good. And for what? So I could die in this godforsaken place?"

"Rosa would have wanted you to have faith."

"Why is it," a voice said behind Sarah, "you Catholics always preach about faith when you barely live it yourselves?"

Getting to her feet, she turned to find the officer who had been in the dugout earlier. Only now, his eyes were black as he leered at her.

"Surprised?" he said, and glanced at the patient.

"Who are you?"

"Let's just say I report to the big guy." When she glanced upward, he laughed. "No, not Him."

"What do you want with John?"

"Many things."

"What do you want with me?"

"You? I wanted you to die. That's why I sent Peter Moody. Then Laurel Diamanté. But you're a spunky little thing, aren't you?" He rolled his eyes. "And anyway, that bore of a Guardian Harlan Covington was protecting you."

"You mean, he spoiled your plans?"

"Hmm. It was partly my fault. Okay, it was *all* my fault. It's what happens when you send in the clowns."

Sarah regarded the demon standing before her. His eyes were normal. He no longer wore the uniform of a United States Army officer. Now, he was dressed in an expensive bespoke black wool suit. Picking off an invisible thread from his lapel, he admired himself.

"I have to say, that Englishman is quite the dresser."

Then, in a flawless British accent, "And he's *mad* about Carter."

Sarah laughed. "I don't think so."

She looked past the intruder at the trench outside. The fighting had stopped.

"Are you saying you *can't* kill me?"

"Oh, I could," he said. "But I'm not allowed."

"So, there *are* limits to your powers. Interesting. Now who's the clown?"

Suddenly enormous, he glowered at her, his skin lizard-like and his eyes a flaming red. When he spoke, his voice boomed, shaking the ground.

"DO NOT MOCK ME!"

Frightened, she tried making herself small against the wall. From here, she had a view of the demon in front of her and John on her side. Clearing his throat, the unholy angel, who appeared human again, calmed himself.

"Is that what you really look like?" she said.

"A bit. You wouldn't like seeing my true appearance." He made a pouty mouth. "Your poor little eyes would cook like eggs on a griddle. Anyway."

He slapped his hands together. "Big John, you're up."

With weak, rheumy eyes, the young soldier stared at the demon and reached out a trembling hand.

"John and I have come to an agreement," the demon said.

Though he was speaking to Sarah, he was looking at his victim.

"He knows he's dying. Got that baseball-sized hole in his chest. And he also knows his wife is dead." He shook his head. "Doing good for others, then dying in the process. That's gotta hurt."

Sarah stared at John, understanding everything. *Some-*

*thing happened to him over there. He came back different.* Dropping to her knees, she grasped his hand.

"John, please in God's name, don't despair! He's not worth your soul!"

John wavered, looking from Sarah to the demon, then back to her.

"There is nothing left," he said with finality.

He closed his eyes and stopped breathing. She continued to hold his hand. Then, as if resuscitated by some invisible force, he opened his eyes again and stared at her craftily.

"I'm so pleased you got to see this," the demon said to her. "It'll give you a chance to think long and hard about what might've been."

"What are you talking about?"

"Killing you didn't quite work out the way I'd hoped. So, I've decided to make you my prisoner." Then, in a stage whisper, "That *is* allowed."

She took in the room, desperately trying to think of a way to get past the creature.

"John will be transferred to a hospital. Then, he'll be sent home, and... You know the rest.

"As for you, Sarah Greene, you will remain here. You'll see the seasons change. There'll be another war, of course. Eventually, you'll notice the forests and wetlands. There's even an abbey. I'm told it's quite beautiful.

"Yes, this is your home now. Until your physical body withers and dies. Poor Joe. I suppose they could still have the wedding ceremony. Honeymoon might be a bit tricky."

Enraged, she leapt to her feet and beat his face and chest with her fists. He remained stoic and unaffected. Her hands running down his clothes, she collapsed to the floor, sobbing inconsolably.

*"Why?"* she said.

"Oh my goodness. They said you were bright. Thought you would have figured it out. You have a choice to make. Can you guess what it is?"

He looked at her coquettishly, his hands folded comfortably in front of him. Slowly, she got to her feet and, wiping her eyes, came to within a breath's distance of his face.

"You can go to hell," she said.

Joe woke with a start. Sarah's hands gripped the blankets. Her head moved slightly, and she moaned. He leaned over and lifted an eyelid. The pupil was dilated, and her eye moved back and forth rapidly.

Her St. Michael medal had slid to one side. Reaching around her neck to retrieve it, he jerked his hand away. The medal was blazing hot.

He went into the bathroom and got a washcloth. Then, he lifted the sacramental and placed it in the center of her chest. Incredibly, the glowing metal didn't burn Sarah's skin.

The nurse who had come in earlier returned. "Everything okay?"

When she saw Sarah's back arching violently, she left to get a doctor. In a moment, a young resident entered with her and approached the patient.

"What's going on?" he said as he scanned the chart.

Joe got to his feet. "She's fighting."

The doctor looked up, annoyed. "But isn't she comatose?"

Joe grabbed his arm. "She's fighting for her life."

With the nurse taking notes, the doctor examined Sarah as if her fiancé weren't there. Exasperated, Joe stormed out.

．　．　．

Joe found an empty family visiting room at the end of the hallway and went inside. There, he made a call.

"Carter? Yeah, I'm still at the hospital. It's about Sarah. No, she's not awake…exactly. I think she's in trouble. Whatever you and Alistair can do. I can't…"

He took a minute and, clearing his throat, spoke softly into the phone.

"Please," he said. "I can't lose her."

## Twenty-Nine

A sharp wind had arisen, bringing dark clouds and lightning. With precision, Alistair navigated the Land Rover around the trash cans and burning refuse that littered the street.

Approaching the Waltons' house, he spotted them standing in the front yard. A grimy band of men and women of various ages. There were at least twenty. They stood in a half-circle, guarding the front door.

Carter looked past the Guardian. When she saw them, she thought of the monsters who had attacked Sarah and her at the women's shelter. And the jeering one she'd killed. Her palms sweated and blood pounded in her ears.

The vehicle came to a stop a little ways off. Rubbing her St. Benedict bracelet, she recited the St. Michael prayer to herself.

"I don't know if I can do this," she said, her voice cracking.

"Remember your training. And also remember, Sarah is counting on you."

"The show must go on? That's a low blow."

"Let's send this lot back where it came from."

Before she could debate any further, he got out of the car and walked deliberately toward the house. In his black suit, he seemed out of place in the modest neighborhood. He looked like an actor who had gotten lost and needed directions to the set.

"Alistair, wait!" Carter said.

She climbed out and, catching up to him, tugged his sleeve.

"Tell me I can do this."

"You can. You have great power." He tilted his head toward the demoniacs waiting for them. "They're the ones who should be frightened."

"You mean, frightened of *this*."

She showed him the bracelet. He said nothing.

When they reached the gate, the demoniacs faced them as one, their eyes like black glass. Some snarled. Others opened their mouths, revealing rotting teeth, and let out animal noises that, incredibly, sounded authentic. Cows lowing and pigs squealing.

Carter closed her eyes and thought of Sarah, trapped in a netherworld. Her anger rising, she looked at the Guardian.

"I'm ready," she said.

He opened the gate. She took a deep, calming breath and exhaled. Then, she entered. As soon as she set foot inside, a wave of hate-filled energy rained down on her. The angry sky seemed to complement the foulness of the creatures standing there. They lowered their heads menacingly and stared at her with hooded eyes.

Undeterred, she marched forward and, extending her right arm, she spoke the fatal words.

*"T'h tzrch lmvt."*

Nothing happened. Her heart lurching, Carter looked back at the Guardian with desperate eyes.

"Have faith in yourself," he said.

She faced the demoniacs. They inched toward her, convinced she was weak. She touched the bracelet and, closing her eyes, steeled herself. Then, she repeated the words, this time with authority.

A bolt of lightning ripped through the clouds and, with a deafening crack, struck the ground between the demoniacs and Carter. A pulsing blue light rose from the earth like a wall, becoming a deadly shroud that descended on the evildoers.

Struggling to free themselves, they ignited in a holocaust of blue fire that consumed them instantly, even swallowing their agonizing shrieks and animal howls.

Carter kept her arm in the air until the last of the demoniacs had turned to ash. As the flames died down, thunder shook the neighborhood, and rain began to pour down.

The Guardian walked up to her and, laying a hand on her shoulder, took in what was left.

"I did it," she said.

"Well done, you."


Alistair descended the stairs to the basement. The cadaverous odor from the cot where Bud Walton's decaying body had lain hung in the air. Carter covered her nose and mouth with her hand as she followed the Guardian down.

He stood in the middle of the floor and took in the room. The wooden table with the sewing machine and bits of fabric stood in front of him. Pieces of ribbon and cloth littered the ground. Standing next to him, Carter studied her surroundings. Her companion seemed to be focused on something she was unable to see.

"Is someone here?" she said.

He reached for her slender hand, their fingers intertwining. At first, Carter saw nothing different. Then, the air visibly rippled like water running down glass, and she saw them.

Children—hundreds of them—hollow-eyed and mournful.

"Oh dear God," she said. "Were they all killed here?"

"Some were murdered in other states. Washington, Oregon, and Nevada."

"The Waltons?"

"For decades, they directed the killing for the glory of the evil one."

"Is this what it's like for you all the time? Seeing so many dead, I mean."

"It's my job," he said. Then, to the children, "Show me."

In unison, they pointed up and to the left. The wall fell away, revealing the inside of the mausoleum.

Karen Walton passed through the iron door and approached the sarcophagus, which no longer stood in the center of the room. Now, it was off to the side and at an angle. In front of it was a rectangular opening in the ground. As the old woman descended, the image faded into nothingness, and only the basement wall was visible.

The Guardian raised his right hand and showered the children with a beneficent white light. Glowing themselves, they ascended, one after the next, until they were gone.

Alistair directed his hand at the ground. As he prayed, the veins in his temples throbbing, the earth juddered. From out of the ground, a small girl with blonde hair and yellow ribbons ascended, joining the others.

Releasing the Guardian's hand, Carter knelt at the spot where the girl had appeared and picked at a yellow ribbon stuck in the ground. Using two hands, she began clearing away the dirt, exposing more of the ribbon.

Searching the room, Alistair found a spade and used it to dig. After a few minutes, he stopped. Carter stared into the hole. The ribbon was tied around wisps of long, blonde hair. Clearing away more of the dirt, she discovered a child's skull.

"She died just before Sarah arrived in Dos Santos," the Guardian said.

"I remember her telling me she'd tried to help Lou find a missing girl. Is this her?"

"Yes. Let's go. I'll call the police chief on the way and let him know."

When they reached the stairs, Carter stopped and looked at him intently.

"Those things you showed me," she said. "Will I see them, too?"

"Up to you. Do you want to?"

Looking away, she thought about the question. Instead of answering him, she started up the stairs.

---

When Carter walked into the hospital room with Alistair, she found Joe standing at the window, looking out and sipping coffee.

"Hey," she said.

He hugged her and greeted the Englishman with a nod.

She looked at Sarah, who was still. "Have you been here all day?"

"I don't want to leave her."

Alistair crossed to the bed. He was about to touch Sarah's hand when Joe stopped him.

"It's okay," Carter said. "He's trying to communicate with her."

Unsure, Joe backed off. "I still don't know what's going on."

"We can't explain everything just now," she said. "It's like, she's in a dream and can't wake up."

"How long will she…?"

Carter looked at Alistair holding Sarah's hand. "I don't know."

The Englishman stepped away from the bed. "Same. Can't break through."

Carter moved closer. "Want me to try?"

"Not yet," he said. Then, to Joe, "I need your help."

"Me? Why?"

"There's something we have to do. For Sarah."

Joe looked at Carter, uncomprehending. Then, he said to the Englishman, "What do you need?"

"We must return to Dos Santos."

"But what about Sarah?"

"Carter will stay with her. I promise you, she won't leave her side."

Joe shook his head. "So, now?"

"Yes, now."

Looking around the room, Joe felt for his keys. He went to his fiancée and kissed her cheek tenderly.

"Be back soon, my love," he said.

Overcome with emotion, Carter wiped her eyes and took a seat next to Sarah as the men left the room without speaking.

The rain continued to pour as the light faded from the sky. Squinting through the windshield, Joe pulled his truck up to the entrance of Resurrection Cemetery. Instead of parking on the street, he drove past the gates. Using a road that veered to the side, he continued toward the mausoleum. When he had reached his destination, he turned the truck around and backed up to the entrance.

He and Alistair climbed out of the truck. Joe pulled the tailgate open and handed a pickaxe, shovel, and a flashlight to the Englishman. Then, he grabbed a red plastic five-gallon gas can and another flashlight. He was about to walk in when Alistair blocked his way.

"Wait here a moment," he said.

Alistair set the tools and flashlight down and entered the mausoleum. Inside, he was greeted by seven men with greasy hair and dirty faces. The Guardian walked forward and faced the men.

This time when he raised his hand, there was no blue fire. Their chests glowing, the dark creatures began burning from the inside, erupting in flames and screaming hellishly. Soon, there was nothing left but the ash carried away by the wind.

"What in hell was that?" Joe said as the Englishman rejoined him.

"Just tidying up a bit."

Alistair picked up the tools and flashlight and reentered the mausoleum, with Joe following.

"There's something in here that opens a chamber below ground," the Englishman said.

"You mean, like a switch?"

"Or a release of some kind."

Using their flashlights, they examined the interior. Taking his time, Joe ran his hand over the wall up high and all the way to the floor. Catching on, Alistair entered the crypt room and did the same. After some time, the Englishman returned.

"Anything?" he said.

Joe moved the flashlight beam over the floor. "Something's different."

He picked up the shovel and dragged the blade noisily on the floor. Then, he dropped it and, laying the flashlight on the ground, knelt and worked his hands over the tiles.

"When I was here with that film crew, there was this one tile," Joe said. "Everyone kept tripping over it. They're all smooth now."

"I remember."

The Englishman dropped to one knee and joined Joe in probing the tiles.

"I think it's this one," Joe said. "Hand me the pickaxe."

Joe used the blade to pry a tile loose. Alistair reached over, and grabbing a corner, he lifted it off the floor, exposing an iron handle lying flush to the ground. He lifted it straight up and turned it clockwise.

A loud clacking in the next room got their attention. Joe ran in as the sarcophagus slid away from its base at a forty-five-degree angle.

The Englishman joined him and, handing Joe one of the flashlights, approached the opening and peered inside, where stone steps led into darkness.

"Get the petrol," he said.

Alistair and Joe stood in the middle of a chamber made completely of stone. As the twin flashlight beams danced across the floor, rats scurried away to find the darkness.

In the center of the floor on a stone pedestal stood a coffin made of rosewood with brass fittings that were still shiny. Alistair walked up to it and lifted the lid. Inside, he found a man's bones draped in rotting clothing.

"Gotcha," the Englishman said.

"I don't understand. Why do we have to burn the bones?"

"You've heard of saints' relics, yes? Why do you suppose people are always so keen to touch them?"

"I don't know. Because they believe in—"

"Because they contain a great healing power. Like those relics, these bones possess an *evil* power. And it's this force that prevents Sarah from awakening. We have to destroy them."

Joe removed the cap from the red can and began liberally pouring gasoline on the body when someone stepped out of the wall and faced the men.

It was Sarah.

She was radiant, her hair flowing, wearing the nightgown she had on in the hospital. Joe dropped the can and staggered back as she opened her arms to him.

"Don't do it, Joe. Please? I'll be stuck in this nightmare forever. And we can never be together."

He looked desperately at the Englishman, who regarded the apparition without emotion.

"What do I do?" he said. "What if she doesn't ever wake up. I can't just let her—"

Alistair's expression didn't change. "Tell me about Sarah."

Joe looked at the apparition again. At the eyes that were pleading and the fingers desperate to touch him.

"Joe," she said. "All that matters is that we're together."

He turned to the Englishman. "No. Sarah wouldn't want that. She'd sacrifice herself if it meant she could save others."

Furious now, Joe faced the apparition. "You're not Sarah."

He righted the gas can and continued dousing the body.

"NO!"

The anguished voice shook the room. The vision of Sarah decayed into a huge, grotesque beast with leathery skin and red eyes. With a deafening shriek, it vanished.

The Englishman put a sympathetic hand on Joe's shoulder. Joe emptied the can and, stepping away, took out a box of wooden matches from his jacket pocket. He lit one and stared at the flame.

"This better work," he said.

He tossed the match into the coffin. Soon, an all-consuming fire engulfed the body, sending billows of black smoke drifting across the chamber. Choking, the men gathered up everything and staggered up the stairs.

Outside, a torrential rain poured as Alistair spoke into his phone.

"Now," he said, and disconnected.

After packing up their equipment, the men left the cemetery.

---

Alyssa led Carter across No Man's Land as intermittent gunfire from well-placed machine gun nests erupted out of the grayness of the landscape.

Wearing her white dress and gold crucifix, the spirit gripped Carter's hand. Together, they made their way over the battle-scarred terrain at twilight toward the Allied side.

Now, Carter understood the place where Sarah was—a horrific dreamscape of war and death—and she prayed fervently she and her friend would make it home safely.

The women crossed the battlefield past hundreds of

dead bodies and craters full of rainwater. When they had made it halfway, the gunfire ceased.

A German soldier in his late teens climbed out of the trench, staring dumbstruck as the women moved away.

While he stood marveling at the ghostly apparition, another soldier raised his rifle and fired a shot. The first soldier turned and yelled at him.

*"Lass sie in Ruhe!"* he said. *"Sie sind Engel."*

In silence, they and the rest of the German soldiers observed the women disappearing into the low mist that clung heavily to the ruined land.

Carter had heard the young soldier and, recalling her high school German, translated the words in her head as she and Alyssa continued toward the Allied trenches.

*Leave them alone. They are angels.*

Descending a ladder, they stood on the duckboards. Carter stared at the rough walls of the trench fashioned from wood slats and sandbags.

Soldiers wearing Brodie helmets and carrying weapons moved past, hardly speaking. Alyssa guided Carter along the winding path until they reached a dugout toward the end. She touched Carter's shoulder and vanished.

Sarah sat on an empty cot, her eyes closed and her hands clasping her St. Michael medal. She was praying. As her friend approached her, she looked up.

"You came," Sarah said.

"What, you thought I wouldn't?"

The women embraced and wept with happiness. Carter placed her hands on Sarah's face and looked into her eyes.

"I'll always be here for you."

"How touching," a voice from behind said to them.

Pivoting, Carter saw an ordinary-looking man dressed as an Army officer of the period, his hands on his waist, appraising them. Sarah drew Carter back and faced the demon.

"You have no power over me," she said. "Or her."

"Perhaps. But I have time."

In an instant, he was next to Carter, his hot breath on her face.

"I could be wrong," he said. "But I don't think you have what it takes, Carter Wittgenstein."

"I was strong enough to make it here."

"If I were you, I wouldn't push my luck."

Looking around the dugout, he found a chair next to the small table. He sat and, producing a bottle and glass out of the air, poured himself a drink. He offered one to the women. They made no move to accept. Shrugging, he drained the glass and set it down.

"Go back to your precious life, Sarah Greene," he said. "Marry Joe. Have children, if you can. But remember, we are as old as Time, and we are patient."

He flicked his index finger at her.

Sarah flew away at an extraordinary velocity, traveling through a vortex of light and shadow.

The wall of souls that had plagued her since she was a teenager was no longer visible. Instead, a vast field filled with people—many in torment—waited in an infinite void for her to help them. And she knew she would.

When Sarah opened her eyes, Carter was holding her hand. It was night. The hospital room was silent.

"Okay," Sarah said. "Did that really happen?"

"Yep. It was Alyssa who brought me to you."

"Alyssa? What about John Dos Santos?"

"He's where he belongs," a familiar voice said. "In hell."

When Sarah looked up, she saw Joe standing in the doorway.

"Joe…"

Carter rose so he could be close to his fiancée. They embraced for a long time, saying nothing. Joe turned to Carter and took her hand.

"I don't know what you did, but thank you."

She smiled. "Hey, it's my job."

Sarah looked at the doorway, expecting the Englishman to walk through any moment, wearing his black suit.

"Where's Alistair?" she said.

---

Alistair Goolsby steered the Land Rover over the muddy road through the abandoned nursery in Squirrel Flats. The rain had become a drizzle, and the moon shone faintly through the heavy clouds that promised another storm.

When he reached the dirt clearing in the center of the property, he discovered Karen Walton's Buick hidden behind a row of tall potted trees.

He stopped and, leaving his black leather gloves on the seat, got out. Making his way over the wet ground, he headed for the driver's side.

Drenched in dark blood, she sat motionless in the front seat, her frozen hands gripping the steering wheel. Her eyes were gouged out and her throat was slit. A pair of sewing scissors lay next to her on the seat.

The Guardian stepped away and, raising both hands,

recited the beginning of Psalm 3 in Hebrew. Then, he spoke the rest in English.

"'Rise, O Lord! Deliver me, O my God! For You slap all my enemies in the face; You break the teeth of the wicked. Deliverance is the Lord's; Your blessing be upon Your people! Selah.'"

All of a sudden, the ground swelled. The earth behind the vehicle split open and continued to pull apart until a massive hole appeared. Miles deep, fire licked up from it.

As the ground shook, the Buick containing the cursed remains of Karen Walton rolled backward into the pit and was swallowed up. Then, the hole closed, becoming an undisturbed dirt clearing.

The Guardian recited a final Hebrew prayer, returned to the Land Rover, and drove away into the night.

## Thirty

Rachel clicked the SUBMIT button and sat back, waiting for the results. When "100%" appeared on the screen, followed by "Congratulations!," she pumped her fists in the air and whooped.

"Excuse me?" someone said.

Rachel turned around and found Elizabeth Chernov and her daughter standing in the doorway. The little girl grinned at the over-excited lady. Her cheeks flushed, Rachel got up.

"I'm practicing for the real estate exam."

"Looks like you did pretty well."

"Didn't miss any this time. Elizabeth, right?"

"Yeah. Sorry, I was looking for Sarah."

"She's out right now. Um, bunch of stuff to do for the wedding."

"Oh, right."

Elizabeth took a seat in front of the desk and placed Mia on her lap.

"I wanted to let Sarah know that we've decided to sell

the house. My husband got a promotion, and we're moving to Connecticut."

"Really? I hear it's quite beautiful there. I'll let Sarah know when she returns, and we can get the paperwork going."

Elizabeth and Mia were leaving Rachel's office when Sarah walked in through the back door, wearing designer jeans, a Fendi T-shirt, and a new black leather jacket.

"Elizabeth?" she said.

"Sarah." She laughed. "Oh my gosh, you look amazing!"

"Thank you."

Sarah knelt and gave the little girl a big hug, making her giggle. Mia whispered in her ear.

"I prayed for you," she said.

Sarah kissed her. "Thank you."

Elizabeth turned to Rachel. "Would it be okay if Mia stayed with you for a few minutes while I talk to Sarah?"

"Not a problem." She began opening desk drawers. "I've got a box of LEGOs in here somewhere."

Elizabeth took a seat in Sarah's office. Sarah closed the door and, leaning on the edge of her desk, listened attentively as Elizabeth explained about the move.

"I couldn't be happier for you," Sarah said. "And don't worry about the house. I'm sure it'll sell quickly."

Elizabeth made a face. "Even after…what happened?"

"It won't be a problem. Trust your realtor."

"So, any wedding jitters?"

"No. It's a sure thing this time."

"There's something I wanted to talk to you about. It has to do with what happened."

"Mia isn't in any danger now," Sarah said, anticipating her question.

"I know. Fr. Brian came over the other night to talk to

my husband and me about my daughter. I'm still trying to get my head around it."

"She's a special child."

Elizabeth looked up at Sarah, her eyes glistening. "She sees things that… They frighten her."

"I know."

"Because you see them, too?"

"Yes. And so does Carter."

"I never really thought about people who could… I mean, as Catholics, we're not supposed believe in those kinds of things, are we?"

"Elizabeth, I feel like there's a question you want to ask."

"I just want to know—I need to be sure—that my daughter will be okay."

Sarah embraced the woman. "Yes. But you must continue to pray. And don't ever let *anyone* tell Mia there's something wrong with her. There isn't. She has a gift—a gift that God gave her."

Sarah opened a desk drawer. "I'm glad you stopped by. I have something for Mia."

When they walked into Rachel's office, Sarah and Elizabeth found the little girl building a tower of LEGO blocks. Everyone said goodbye. Before they left, Sarah knelt and hugged Mia. She handed her a white jewelry box.

"I want you to have this."

Excited, the little girl opened the box and found a St. Michael medal on a gold chain.

"Whoa."

Sarah looked up at the girl mother. "It's been blessed."

She removed the medal from the box and fastened it around Mia's neck, then flipped her hair over the chain.

"What do you say?" Elizabeth said.

The girl hugged Sarah. "Thank you."

"Do you know the St. Michael prayer?"

"Mommy is teaching it to me."

"Good. I want you to say it every night."

"Okay. I love you, Sarah."

"And I love you."

Her arm around her sister, Sarah watched as Elizabeth and her daughter walked out. At the door, Mia turned and gave her a heartbreaking little wave.

"You're a real softie, you know that?" Rachel said.

"At your service."

---

In the living room at Casa Abrigo, Lou stood in front of the painting, trying to decide whether he liked it. Frank Sinatra's "You Brought a New Kind of Love to Me" played over hidden speakers. The music sounded especially good to him. Wearing a blazer and a pair of nice pants, he studied the girl sitting at the desk, then the ghost girl behind her looking through the window.

Rachel appeared at his side and laughed when she realized he was humming along tunelessly to the song. She had on a new dress and heels. He looked at her admiringly as she handed him a glass of red wine. Then, he pulled at his collar and took a huge, nervous swallow. Leaning over, he whispered in her ear.

"I love you." Taken aback, she stared at him. "Is something wrong?"

"No, I just..." Her cheeks reddening, she kissed him.

When someone passed them, he turned around and pretended to appraise the painting. She slipped her hand into his.

"I can't get over how much that girl looks like Carter," he said.

"There's a story behind it. Tell you later."

She walked away to talk to Eddie and Katy. Holding a beer, her father gazed at his surroundings, a little overwhelmed.

When Lou turned around, he saw Charlie Beeks walking toward him. Mary Mallery was with him.

"Some do, huh?" Lou said.

The investigator nodded. "I'll say. It was nice of Carter to put this on."

"So, all quiet out there?" Mary said.

Lou scanned the room and noticed Tim, who was chatting with Elizabeth Chernov and her husband. Sipping a soft drink, he seemed happy and relaxed.

"We haven't heard a peep in days," Lou said. "I don't think any of my officers have even given out a traffic citation."

"Well, that's good news."

"Charlie, I wanted to thank you again for all your help."

"I was glad to do it," the investigator said. "I only wish Harlan was around to celebrate with us." Then, to Mary, "Want something to drink?"

"White wine, please."

When Charlie had gone off, Lou sidled up to Mary and lowered his voice.

"Are you and he…?"

She blushed. "We're just friends."

"So, where's Alistair?"

"By now, Italy," Mary said. "Scattering Harlan's ashes somewhere. Norcia, I think he said."

"I never got a chance to thank him. Do you think we'll ever see him again?"

"I hope not. Because that would mean…"

"Oh, right. Good point."


Sarah and Joe sat in the kitchen with Carter. Everyone was dressed up. Sarah took her friend's hand.

"It means so much to us that you organized this," Sarah said. "Thank you."

"I'm just glad we could finally do it."

"It's a wonderful party," Joe said.

"So, now that you have a wedding date, have you guys thought about where to go on your honeymoon?"

"We were thinking of Italy," Sarah said.

"That's such a coincidence because— Sorry, go on."

"I thought we might go to Florence first. Then Rome. Then London for a few days."

Carter sipped her wine, a little distracted. "Sounds like a great trip."

"What about you?" Sarah said. "Did you ever decide whether to look up your friend?"

"Frannie? Actually, I have. I'm going to Sausalito to stay with my parents for a few days. I also plan to see Frannie."

"I'm so happy for you, Carter."

"She was shocked to hear from me. We were both crying on the phone. When I told her about the painting, she practically fainted."

Rachel walked into the kitchen and headed straight for Joe.

"Sorry to interrupt," she said. "Eddie's feeling a little left out. He could really use another man to, you know, talk about beer or jockstraps or something."

Laughing, Joe got up. "On it."

When they'd left, Carter scooted her chair closer to Sarah.

"I need to tell you something," she said. "I wasn't sure how to do it. After Sausalito, I'm going abroad for a bit."

"Vacation?"

"Not exactly. I'm meeting Alistair in Italy."

Sarah narrowed her eyes. "Okay, I always thought you… Never mind."

"What?" Carter said. Then, as it came to her, "No, it's nothing like that. *Ew!* He's taking me to meet someone. A teacher. Of Guardians."

Sarah felt around for her glass and took a large swallow of wine as Carter looked at her intently. She remembered the very last words Harlan had said to her. *You must let her go.* And she tried not to cry.

"I didn't even know you were… Is this what you want?"

"It's something I'm destined for," Carter said.

Sarah put a hand over her mouth. "I just realized. When we were in that horrible place, the demon told you something. He said—"

"He said he didn't think I had what it takes."

"Is that what he was talking about?"

"Yes. Do you remember that night outside the women's shelter?"

"How could I forget? Surrounded by demoniacs."

"When I killed that one, something in me changed. It's hard to explain. It was like a door opening."

"Just because a door opens doesn't mean we have to walk through it," Sarah said.

"But don't you see? Since then, I've gotten stronger. I would never have been able to save you if Alistair hadn't—"

"*Alistair?* Is he the one who convinced you to do this?"

"No. But he supported me—he believes in me. The choice was always mine."

As if her friend were slipping away, Sarah held Carter's hand between hers.

"Will you ever come back to Dos Santos?" she said. "Because I don't think I can do what I have to without you."

"I'm not going away forever. I promised I would always be here for you. And I will. But I need to do this. Can you understand?"

Sarah nodded without saying anything. Carter got up and refilled both their glasses.

"Now, come on," she said. "This is supposed to be a party."

*Psst. Before you go…*

## HOW ABOUT A FREE BOOK?

Sign up for the author newsletter to learn about special offers and new releases. Oh yeah, and you'll get a free book in the bargain.

Learn more at stevenramirez.com/newsletter-caya.

# About the Author

Steven Ramirez is the award-winning author of the supernatural suspense series SARAH GREENE MYSTERIES. A former screenwriter, he also wrote the acclaimed horror thriller series TELL ME WHEN I'M DEAD. Steven lives in Los Angeles.

## AUTHOR WEBSITE
stevenramirez.com

facebook.com/byStevenRamirez

instagram.com/byStevenRamirez

twitter.com/byStevenRamirez

goodreads.com/byStevenRamirez

bookbub.com/authors/steven-ramirez

Made in the USA
Las Vegas, NV
07 May 2021